HER
PLEASURE

NIOBIA BRYANT

HER PLEASURE

www.kensingtonbooks.com

DAFINA BOOKS are published by

Kensington Publishing Corp.
119 West 40th Street
New York, NY 10018

All Kensington titles, imprints, and distributed lines are available at special quantity discounts for bulk purchases for sales promotion, premiums, fund-raising, and educational or institutional use.

Special book excerpts or customized printings can also be created to fit specific needs. For details, write or phone the office of the Kensington Sales Manager: Kensington Publishing Corp., 119 West 40th Street, New York, NY 10018. Attn. Sales Department. Phone: 1-800-221-2647.

The Dafina logo is a trademark of Kensington Publishing Corp.

ISBN-13: 978-1-4967-3069-5
ISBN-10: 1-4967-3069-0
First Trade Paperback Printing: July 2021

ISBN-13: 978-1-4967-3071-8 (e-book)
ISBN-10: 1-4967-3071-2 (e-book)
First Electronic Edition: July 2021

10 9 8 7 6 5 4 3 2 1

Printed in the United States of America

For my cousin, Farrah Yolanda Moultrie,
who I know is in heaven dancing with my Mama.
Gone too soon. We all miss you so very much, LoLo.
Nothing will *ever* be the same. Nothing.

11/7/1977 – 9/13/2019

The Prelude

2016

"*B*reaking news. There has been an arrest in the recent shooting
of Georgia Coletti. Just moments ago, Eric Hall, Sr., a prominent
New Jersey businessman and philanthropist was arrested and charged
with the attempted murder of Coletti. What has been revealed about
the shooting is Coletti was not his intended target. His true aim was
for Jessa Bell, whom you may remember rose to infamy after writing
a bestselling book about her lover—who was also the husband of one
of her best friends—stalking and then attempting to kill her before
taking his own life. Here's the first twist: that man was Eric Hall,
Jr. We can only speculate on what motives the father had for trying
to take the life of Jessa Bell, but someone close to the matter says that
Bell and Hall, Sr. were contentious over his attempts to take custody
of the daughter she bore for his son. But there's another twist. Jessa
Bell, after claiming to be reformed, went on to open a business—
Mistress, INC—where she helped spouses catch their cheating husbands. It was at the midtown Manhattan offices of her business that
Eric Hall, Sr attempted to take her life, but instead his deadly aim
landed on Georgia Coletti . . . the long-lost daughter of Jessa Bell
from when she just a teen. Yes, another shocker. Thankfully,*

Coletti has awakened from her coma and is in stable condition as she recovers with both adoptive parents and her birth mother at her side. Eric Hall, Sr. has been denied bail. We reached out to Jessa Bell and her publicist for a comment on the arrest, but they declined to offer one. We will continue to report as this multilayered story— believe it or not—continues to develop. This is Maria Vargas report- ing for WCBL."

Silence reigned as the three women—friends—sipped on fruit-infused seltzer as they sat before the seventy-inch tele- vision of the stylish media room. A commercial for a national auto insurance company filled the sizable room with a com- ically upbeat jingle.

"Well...I'm glad Jessa's daughter is okay."

Jaime Pine shared a look with Aria Livewell before she eyed their friend, Renee Thorne, over the rim of her crystal wine glasses.

Fuck them all.

"What?" Renee said at her disdainful expression. "Geor- gia had nothing to do with that mess Jessa Bell brought on our lives. She didn't torment us—*her friends*—with a stupid message mocking which of our husbands were cheating on us with her and then write a book and go on tour bragging about the shit."

Jaime took a deep sip of her drink, wishing it had the calming effect of wine instead. "And then try to sue me twice for half the estate of my sorry-ass husband for the baby she had with him," she muttered, hating that a former friend still evoked anger at the very thought of her duplicity.

"She's lucky they found out who shot at her because any of us coulda tried to take the trick out," Aria said, settling her drink in the cup holder of her leather recliner before she splayed both hands on her belly, rounded with her second child with her husband, Dr. Kingston Livewell.

Jaime felt pensive as she remembered the night a few weeks ago that an inebriated Jessa Bell had returned to the

Richmond Hills subdivision and wreaked havoc in their lives once more. Spilling secrets and delighting in their pain because they rebuked the olive branch she extended by revealing to Renee that her second husband was cheating on her.

Weaponizing the secrets of her ex-friends against them.

Mocking Aria for the financial troubles she and her husband were facing as his second medical practice struggled to thrive.

Exposing that Renee was cheating on her husband with her first husband—and first love—Jackson, who was raising an outside child with the woman with whom he cheated on Renee in the first place.

Also, revealing to Renee, a devoted mother, that her daughter, Kieran, was using pills to get high while her son, Aaron, was contemplating gender reassignment surgery. Things no mother wants to hear from a vengeful shrew and not directly from her children who were away in college.

Jaime released a short but heavy breath at Jessa Bell taking pure delight in informing her that she had lain with Jaime's ex-boyfriend, Graham Walker. That hurt. Still hurt. *How could he?* Somehow, they had worked their way from her paying him for sex to falling in love.

Silly of me falling for a former manwhore that I used to pay for sex.

Her grip tightened on the glass as she imagined his tall and sculptured body atop Jessa's, as she mocked her.

"To hell with Jessa Bell," Jaime said, letting her anger and hurt fuel her. "Eric, Sr. should've had better fucking aim."

Chapter 1

Five years later

Time heals.

For that, Jaime was grateful. And happy. Maybe for the first time.

Thank God.

She took a sip of her rum punch as she looked out at the idyllic turquoise waters of the Grand Anse Beach in Grenada. The West Indies island, northwest of Trinidad and Tobago, with its white sand, warm climate, and scenic views was the perfect backdrop for the luxury boutique all-inclusive beach resort. As she moved to lean her bikini-clad body in the open doorway of the beachside suite, she smiled at her two friends in the distance on chaise lounges, soaking up the sun and enjoying beachside room service from beautiful Grenadians with skin bronzed by melanin and the Caribbean sun. They had only been on the island a few hours and already the drinks were plentiful and the food divine—she was instantly addicted to crab backs, the island's creamy version of stuffed crab shells. The amenities of the Black-owned boutique beach resort were specially crafted to make you feel pampered, have fun, and explore. The island was brimming with history and culture. The music. The vibes. Beauty and light.

I love it here.

And I love him for sending me and my friends here.

Allowing herself another sip of the sweet concoction made with dark rum that was native to the country, Jaime smiled into her drink as her belly warmed at the thought of him. Her man. Her lover. Her love. Not her everything. Not her completion. They came together as two whole beings looking to add value to each other's lives. That real shit. Grown folk shit.

For the first time, she loved and was loved back without complications. No drama or suspicions. No games. It was all good.

So damn good.

Jaime bit her bottom lip and closed her eyes with a little grunt as she remembered the heated hours they shared in his king-sized bed last night before she and her friends boarded his private jet for their week-long girl's trip.

Shit, I almost overslept this morning.

Memories of his head buried between her thick brown thighs led her to fan her warm neck with a little sigh.

Life was damn good.

The past—the last ten years or better—was more of a footnote in her life and not the sum of it. For that she was glad. Now she could think back on her marriage, destroyed by a lack of love, respect, good sex, and trust, without a wild range of emotions. The anger had faded—at herself for not knowing she was worthy of more, at her mother for teaching her that her husband should be her everything as if a god, and at the men in her life for exploiting her weaknesses.

No more.

That silly message Jessa Bell sent was meant to taunt and torment, but it ended up being Jaime's salvation. That day had led to a reckoning and in time she hadn't cared which husband was guilty when faced with the truth hidden by her seemingly perfect marriage to Eric Hall, Junior.

Perfect bullshit.

For her the marriage was over regardless—his possible guilt as the lover to one of her best friends was irrelevant. She hadn't even maintained her own fidelity. Just once. But once was enough. Especially with the one she chose to give her the pleasure her husband was ill-equipped—psychologically and physically—to do. So, by the end of that day, she packed a bag and moved out.

And then the real fun began.

Needing a diversion from that small but indelible chapter of her life during her post-Eric days, Jaime pushed off the door frame to turn and walk inside the den with the ends of her sheer pastel cover-up slightly floating in the air behind her. The décor of off-white with splashes of beachy colors was calming, but it was her cell phone on which she was focused. Setting the crystal goblet on the Sedona redwood sofa table, she dug her device out of her monogrammed designer tote.

"Jaime!"

She turned with her phone in hand as Aria came to a stop in the wide entryway with the stone terrace and beach as her backdrop. "What's taking you so long?" she asked, pushing her rose-gold aviator shades atop her massive afro shaped curls.

Jaime slightly shook her head in wonder that Aria's slim-thick body in a tiger print bikini had carried two children—a ten-year-old and a six-year-old. Unlike her, Jaime had not. And unlike her, Jaime wasn't altogether sure she wanted children.

The mark her mother, Virginia Osten-Pine, left on her life—with all her rules of being a proper lady and wife based on societal pressures, religious zeal, and the judgments of others—had led Jaime into a marriage severely lacking in warmth, love, and respect while pretending otherwise. The abuse wasn't physical, but allowing a man to not only make her feel less than in private and then standing at her side while she smiled and pretended otherwise in public was abuse all its own. It was a highly functioning lie and less than she—or anyone—deserved.

She hadn't known how it felt to live her truth in those days.

For the first time in years, she longed for a cigarette and licked her lips to help curb the urge.

"Nothing," Jaime finally answered her, still holding her phone as she shifted her temporary waist-length braids behind her back before grabbing her drink and crossing the space to step out into the Grenadian heat.

"*This* is paradise," Aria said, replacing her shades before she spread her arms wide and tilted her head back as they crossed the terrace and walked under the brief shade of a towering palm tree.

"Yes, it is," Jaime agreed as a cooling wind caressed her body.

"I needed this," Aria sighed.

Jaime eyed her, knowing her friend spoke the truth. Of the three marriages tested by the silly message of a vixen, Aria and Kingston's had survived. Not even the serious financial woes of Kingston opening a second medical practice six years ago had shaken their foundation irrevocably. As far as she knew things were better. But she could only know what she was told.

She opened her mouth to ask if all was well on the home front but paused, wanting to be sure the question was from true concern and not just curiosity. Daily she checked to make sure the selfishness and pettiness of her past were gone. In the past, she used to be so miserable she took joy in others' pain and plight to feel better about her own mess. "Everything okay?" she asked.

Aria's pause was noticeable.

Jaime assumed she too was assessing whether shadows of the old Jaime lingered.

"Just some work stuff," Aria said, sounding vague.

Jaime forced herself to release the annoyance that rose at the thought of her friend still not trusting her after so many years. *I left the stain, and I must allow time for it to fade.*

Aria used to be a freelance writer who had snagged interviews with celebrities for top African-American magazines, but after her debut fiction novel failed to thrive—no matter how brilliantly written—her option for another book was not picked up and the couple's money troubles led to her taking on work as an editor of a successful magazine that transitioned to a digital-only platform. So many times, she had admitted that her desire to write was fading in response to the duties of her full-time job.

"Well appreciate the break from it all...even my godchildren," Jaime said with a smile.

Aria slightly nodded her head in agreement. "You owe your guy one helluva blowie," she said with a wink just as they reached Renee lounging on a citron chaise lounge with her eyes closed as she luxuriated in the sun that was deepening her already caramel complexion to golden and made her ultrashort hair glow like a halo.

"Swallow and all," Renee agreed, briefly opening one eye to look up at them.

"Cum up and then clean up," Aria added with her signature brash and bold style.

The old Jaime would have blushed in shock and embarrassment. Felt disrespected even.

She's long gone.

"Done and done," Jaime admitted as she removed her

sheer wrap and lay it over the back of the orange lounge chair. She removed her gold metallic slides and dug her toes into the heated white sand for a few moments before claiming her seat and crossing her ankles.

"Don't make me miss Kingston," Aria said with a little moan as she stretched her form across the middle chaise.

"And both of you stop rubbing your men in my lonely face," Renee said. "My shower head does not match up."

Aria gave her a consoling pout. "It's consistent as fuck though," she offered.

Renee smiled broadly. "There's that. For its purposes, it *never* disappoints."

Jaime glanced over at her, ever amazed that although Renee was older than them by almost a decade, she didn't look it except for the flashes of silver in her close-shaven hair. Although she wore a more modest one piece and had a slight pudge in the middle, she was still a stunner. She knew if her friend wanted to claim a man—whether as a lover or more—finding one was no issue. After two failed marriages where her heart was broken by infidelity, Jaime could understand Renee's reluctance to try love again.

Been there. Done that.

"I understand protecting your heart, but *other* body parts?" Jaime asked.

"Let that thing live before it dies, girl," Aria added, picking up her glass of rum punch from the clear serving table beside each lounge.

Jaime chuckled as she looked up and down the length of the beach. The stretch of it near the resort was more private but still, people lounged nearby relishing the clear turquoise waters with blue skies and emerald green hills in the distance. "And what better place than heaven on earth," she said as she eyed a tall, muscled man walking out of the water. "Look at what God has created."

The women all eyed him. This stranger with skin as dark as blackberries that glistened from the sun and water dripping down every hard contour of his body barely covered by white trunks that came to his muscled thighs. The wet material clung to his inches, leaving no doubt he was built to please.

"Well amen to that," Renee sighed with a slight bite of her bottom lip.

"Let him bless you," Aria said.

Jaime picked up her phone and let them enjoy the show. She had enough dick in her life.

Good dick, too.

She took a few selfies and posted them to Instagram just as her notification for a new email sounded off. Hoping it wasn't one of her staff at her interior design firm interrupting her vacation, she opened it.

A new Google alert.

"Let me see if this cougar can catch some tender meat," Renee said.

"I know that's right," Aria cheered her on. "Walk to the water and I'll see if he's looking."

"Jezebel," Jaime muttered, feeling her entire body tense as she opened and read the news story.

"What's wrong?" Aria asked her.

Jaime forced her body to relax as she rotated her shoulders and glanced over at Renee pausing in her walk to stretch her Amazon-like figure. "Jessa," she muttered, trying not to clench her teeth at the very thought of the woman they'd foolishly thought was a friend.

"Oh, *that* Jezebel," Aria sighed. "What that bitch up to these days?"

"Falling on her feet once again," Jaime said. "She just married Horatio Montgomery."

"The businessman?" Aria asked.

"The millionaire businessman," Jaime amended. "That evil cat has nine lives. Maybe ninety-nine."

"And how, may I ask, do you know about this?" Aria asked, reaching to take Jaime's phone from her hand to read through the news story. "I thought you deleted the google alert on her name."

Jaime released a heavy breath. "It hasn't gone off in five or six years," she said, by way of avoiding answering the question.

"And now we have info that offers absolutely nothing to our lives," Aria said handing the device back. "Delete it, Jaime. Let's move on from Jessa. Let's never speak her name again. Let's pretend she doesn't even exist."

"For so long my life has been entwined with hers," Jaime explained. "And in the past every time I thought we were done with her, the bitch would pop back up out of the blue. I wanted to stay ready."

"*Fuck* her," Aria stressed. "Fuck her life. Fuck her soul. Fuck every bit of that bitch from her red bottoms to the tips of her red fingernails. Fuuuuuck her."

Jaime smiled. It was hard not to. Aria's funny was constant.

"Fuck her," Jaime agreed as she deleted the Google alert. "No more Jessa."

Aria raised her glass of rum punch. "Absolutely no more," she said.

Jaime lifted her glass as well to toast to that.

They fell silent and looked on as Renee entered the water and then swam to emerge in the direct line of vision of the chocolate angel. She had his attention as she glanced at him before walking over to them with water dripping down her body.

"Got 'em?" Renee asked them as she stretched some more for good measure.

"Got 'em," Aria confirmed.

Renee glanced back over her shoulder and gave him a smile at finding his eyes on her. Smooth as hell, she picked up a towel and began to slowly dry the wetness from her body, keeping his attention.

"A brother that fine has to have a woman," Aria said.

Behind the cover of her shades, Jaime shifted her gaze to Renee whose hunger for him—or maybe any man—was clear. "Other people's dick is off the menu," she reminded her, thinking of the mess her friend got herself into years ago when she cheated on her husband with her ex-husband who was newly married to his pregnant side chick. Some *Maury* and *Jerry Springer* blended kind of a mess.

"Excuse me, Ms. Pine."

All three women looked up at the uniformed woman now standing beside Jaime's lounger. She was the concierge assigned to their suite and her smile was bright with her white teeth against her caramel complexion and crimson red lips. "I knocked on the door but when I didn't get an answer, I decided to try the beach," she said with her island accent. "I figured you might be limin' on the beach."

"Liming?" Jaime asked.

"Relaxin'," the woman explained of the island lingo.

Jaime eyed the wooden name tag pinned to the white polo shirt she wore with white shorts. "How can I help you, Charmaine?" she asked.

"I have a message for you," she said before extending her arm and handing over a thick manila envelope.

"Thank you," Jaime said, already knowing that it could only be from one person.

The woman gave them one last charming smile before she left them.

"Open the door," she read to herself.

Wait? What?

She sat up and swiveled on the chair to look past the serene patio shrouded by tropical flowers and potted plants to the inside of the spacious suite at the intricately carved wooden front doors. *Was he on the other side?*

Her heart raced as she rose and pressed her bare feet into the depths of the hot sand as she quickly ate up the distance.

"Jaime, what's wrong?" Renee called behind her.

She ran across the beach with ease to grab both of the bronzed handles to turn and fling the doors wide open. "Oh," she said in a breath, moving quickly from disappointment to surprise at the four strangers standing there.

Another note was pressed into her hand. She opened it quickly. "Friends to cherish you. A chef to nourish you. A mixologist to relax you. A musician to serenade you. A massage to spoil you," she read in a whisper. "My love? All for you."

This man. This man. This man.

Jaime's heart continued to pound as she clutched the note, pressing her thumb against his bold and slashing initial while she watched them all unpack their supplies. The chef and bartender claimed the kitchen. The masseuse and guitarist set up on the patio.

Jaime walked back to the beach, finding only Aria. "We have a pampering suite set up inside," she said, proud of yet another treat from her man. "Where's Renee?"

Aria began gathering her things. "Clearing out the cobwebs," she said, looking past Jaime's shoulder.

She glanced back and then her mouth dropped to see Renee and her chocolate angel frolicking in the water together. Her eyes widened when he pulled her body close to pick up against his as she wrapped her arms and legs around him. "That happened quickly," she drawled, walking back to the villa.

"Horny is as horny does, girl," Aria said.

Bzzzzzz. Bzzzzzz. Bzzzzzz.

Jaime smiled as she picked up her phone and the screen was filled with the face of the man she loved. She answered the FaceTime call as she moved away from Aria for privacy. "Hey you," she said.

"I had a break in between meetings and thought I'd check on you," he said, his voice deep and delicious.

She held the phone up away from her face and then panned it up and down her body as she posed for him, pausing at the spots he loved the best. "Just getting some sun," she said.

"Damn. That's one hell of a bathing suit, Jaime," he said.

"When browning, the more skin exposed the better," she advised him.

"And making me wish I was there," he said, his voice swelling with his desire as his brown eyes seemed to darken in color.

"To do what?" she asked, turning as she eyed a couple walking up behind her hand in hand.

"Make us cum," he countered.

As she flooded with warmth, Jaime gave him a look that was more playful than scolding. "Don't let being horny get you in trouble while I'm away," she said, tapping a coffin-shaped glossy nail against the screen.

"You never have to worry about that," he assured with a serious expression.

And she knew his words were real.

Since she met Luc Sinclair a little over a year ago, he had been nothing but a man of his word...

His eyes were on Jaime as she moved about the condo. She could feel it even when her eyes weren't on him. It made her nervous. All of her cool and polished demeanor was shattering under his gaze. With a steadying breath, Jaime turned to face him. "It's a beautiful space, but I believe with my help it will be stunning. A real showcase," she said.

Luc leaned against the wall with his arms crossed over his chest in a navy V-neck sweater and denims with his feet bare. "I entertain a lot," he said. "In this world, the show of success breeds more success."

"True," Jaime agreed. "And I am the woman for the job."

"I believe you are the woman for any and every job, Jaime Pine," he said, with the hint of a smile. "Have dinner with me. Tonight. Hell, right now. I'll cook. Let me feed you."

She swallowed over a sudden lump in her throat because the look in his eyes said it wasn't only food he was offering. As she licked at her dry lips she wondered if he could tell that her body was hungry. She hadn't dared to risk her heart or her body since Graham. For years, work had been her focus and her vibrator her sexual release.

Luc was tall and slender with keen features and a fair complexion. Where his skin peeked from his clothing, she could see his body was mostly covered with tattoos. She noticed that about the record executive as soon as he opened the front door to let her in to their appointment.

"I don't mix business and pleasure," she explained as she clutched her briefcase and looked down at the tips of her high-heeled shoes.

"Good, then this will be the first time," Luc said, as he pushed off the wall and came toward her. "And I promise you I will never make you regret it."

It took weeks of working together for him to wear her down and he had been right. He had never made her regret it. Not once.

Not like Graham...

Jaime took a breath as the elevator slowed to a stop and she stepped onto the Jersey City, New Jersey rooftop. Briefly, she allowed herself a moment to take in the view of

Manhattan in the distance. The day winds blew, causing the flowing one-shoulder pantsuit she wore to press against her body as she made her way around the pool to reach Graham standing with his back to her. He was just as dazzling in clothes as he was naked with his muscled, six-foot-nine frame and waist-length dreadlocks that framed a face that was both masculine and beautiful.

She first met him when he went by the name Pleasure and performed at a friend's bachelorette party when she was in college. In the first four years of their dealings, they went from a stripper and loyal customer to her paying him for a sizzling session of sex in one of the private rooms at the strip club to help her forget her joyless marriage. Six months later she turned to him as she fought hard to reclaim independence in the months following her divorce. His body had been her playground. Every inch of the length and width of his dick had been her salvation. Until it ended with a few reminders that the only bond between them was hot sex and money. Two years later, after he left his scandalous work—and many disappointed clients behind—he'd sought her out and professed to want more from her than sex. For six months, he curled her toes with sex and dug his way into her heart with his attention and care.

Graham turned on the rooftop and smiled at her. Her heart swelled with love for him. At that moment she could almost forget that just two weeks ago a crazed woman from his past broke into his penthouse apartment, drugged him, and threatened his life at knifepoint. Almost. Happening upon the crime scene and having rage and a knife hurled at her ensured Jaime would never forget.

"Hello, Graham," she said, holding out her hands to him as she neared.

"Hello to you," he said, taking her hands in his and pulling them around his back as he bent his head to taste her lips.

A greeting that was leading to a goodbye. A reluctant one but a goodbye none the less. Not even that familiar chemistry humming around them, and creating an ache within her, would stop it. No man had ever created such hunger in her. So much that she set it all aside. His past. Hers. Theirs together. All of the drama. For the most exquisite heat and passion.

Just the whisper of his breath against her body could make her almost cum. His kisses? Easy climaxes that were explosive. His strokes? White-hot bliss that left her dazed.

Jaime leaned back first and reached to wipe her gloss from his supple lips. "You're not making this easy, Graham," she said, trying hard to smile but failing as she closed her eyes and tilted her head back to shake it as if to clear it. "Why are you so damn fine?"

"There's more to me than that," he said.

"You're right. You are smart and funny and deep, and you are the most amazing lover. You are strong and good and . . . and . . . you are leaving me," she finished sadly, reaching to stroke the neat edges of his locs and then the side of his handsome face.

"I need some time alone to get my shit together and—"

"And I need to decide if I can ever get past your past," she finished for him, knowing her jealousy of his former career and the attention he drew from women had become a major issue for them.

He nodded as he rubbed her wrist with his thumb. "I love you, Jaime. I swear I love the fuck out of you," he told her fiercely.

"I believe that," she said confidently. "And I love you too."

"I know that," he said.

He pulled her close and lifted her body against his to hold her close as he pressed a dozen kisses to her face . . . and then her lips before he set her back down.

"Until we meet again?" she asked softly, forcing a smile even as a tear raced down her face.

Graham nodded and stepped back from her. With one final kiss blown to him, Jaime turned and walked away.

One year later, without hearing from him, Jaime had still held out hope they would both heal the wounds of their pasts and reconnect, until Jessa, in a drunken rage, cruelly revealed that Graham and she had slept together that very day. That had been five years ago.

No, he's not Graham to me. Not anymore. He's Pleasure. Always been Pleasure. And always will be Pleasure 'til the day his treacherous heart stops. I was a fool to ever think he loved me.

"Jaime, what's wrong?" Luc asked.

She focused on his face on her phone and offered him a smile. "Not a thing. I'm headed in to enjoy my surprise," she said, walking back over to Aria.

He chuckled and smiled. "Perfect. Call me when you're done?" he asked.

With a soft wink, she ended the call.

"Was that Luc?" Aria asked as they made their way toward the private terrace.

Jaime gave her a look that said: "Who else?"

There was no one else for her.

Not anymore.

Chapter 2

"Jaime."

"Huh?" she asked in a whisper as she was lightly shaken from sleep.

"Ja-mie!" the voice urgently whispered to her again.

"What?" she snapped, lifting her head from the plush pillows to open her eyes. Aria was barely visible in the darkness. "What time is it?"

"If you would wake up and listen, it's clearly dicking down time," Aria whispered.

"What!" Jaime exclaimed with a frown.

"Ssssshhhh!"

What little she could see of Aria faded into the darkness. Jaime sat up and reached for the lamp.

"No, don't turn the light on!" Aria exclaimed in a whisper. "Come over here."

She rolled her eyes and flung back the covers. "Over where, you *nut*? It's pitch dark," she snapped in annoyance.

"Ssssshhhh!"

Jaime pressed her feet against the warm wood floor as she just made out Aria's figure by the door to the left of the bed. Her queen-sized bed faced glass doors leading to the beach, but the curtains were drawn. She reached out and patted her nightstand for her phone to turn on the flashlight. She had barely taken a few steps when muffled cries sounded off.

"Yessssss. Yes! Yes! Yesssssssssssssssssss!"

Jaime's mouth fell open in surprise. "What in the entire hell was that?" she asked in a harsh whisper as she swung the beam of light onto her friend's face.

Aria's eyes were wide with shock and glee. "That is somebody—some man—fucking the hell out of Renee," she said, before widening her eyes even more and cringing comically.

Thud-thud-thud-thud.

"Well damn," Jaime exclaimed at what had to be the headboard—or maybe just somebody's head—banging against the wall.

A deep guttural moan and a high-pitched squeal echoed together.

They both covered their mouth with one of their hands in shock.

"Well, now she is fucking the hell out of him," Aria said. "Go, Renee."

"What time is it?" Jaime asked as she shone the light on her face before switching it back to Aria.

"I already told you," she said. "It's—"

"Dicking down time," they said in unison.

Thud-thud-thud-thud-thud-thud-thud-thud-thud-thud-thud-thudthudthudthudthudthudthud.

"Uh oh," Aria said as the pace of the pounding sped up.

"Yesssssssssssssssssssssssssssssssssss!" Renee screamed.

"If they keep that shit up, I'm going home to my damn husband and get me some thud-thud-thud," Aria said with a deadpan serious expression.

Jaime took the light off Aria's face as she bit back a laugh. "How long have they been at it?" she asked.

"Long enough where Renee will be walking with a wide leg spread," Aria said. "That's a promise."

They both tensed as the roars of Renee and her lover filled the air. Rough. Animalistic. And seeming to outlast the Energizer Bunny.

Jaime was relieved when it finally came to an end and silence reigned from Renee's room down the hall.

"Can I have my room and my privacy back now?" Jaime asked, feeling the need for a shower…and maybe a cigarette?

He really did fuck the hell out of her.

"I'm going to call Kingston and get my happy ending via FaceTime," Aria said, opening the door and peeking out before leaving with a funny face.

Jaime turned the flashlight off and tossed her phone onto the middle of the bed as she moved over to press the button to open the automated curtains and sliding glass doors revealing the beach and ocean. She stepped out onto the terrace. The moon and the surrounding darkness were being replaced by the break of day as the sun rose. It was beautiful. Streaks of rich oranges, reds, and yellows dominated the retreating darkness, creating deep lavenders and blues where they merged. She eyed the digital clock on the dresser. It was just close to half-past five, but she was done with sleep.

With Aria in the middle of having virtual sex and Renee probably sleeping off what sounded to be one hell of a climax, Jaime knew she was left on her own. "Their nuts won't kill my show," she said, reentering her room to remove the black satin short set she wore to bed. She made her way past the head of the bed to reach the adjoining bath behind it for a quick shower.

Thirty minutes later, she was dressed in a black strapless bikini with sheer black wide-leg pants, her braids up in a dramatic topknot. It was a lot for so early in the morning.

"Fuck it," Jaime said as she turned this way and that in the mirror before leaving her suite.

She paused in the doorway at Renee and her lover sharing a kiss at the end of the hall. He was still in his white swim trunks and she was naked as the day she entered the world. Coolly, she cleared her throat as she leaned in the door jam. She gave them a tight smile and a little wave as they both looked at her in surprise.

"We were just saying our goodbyes," Renee explained, not bothering to hide her nudity as she looked up at him. "This is Sanders."

"Mornin'," he said with a toothy smile as big as his island accent.

"Good morning," Jaime said, looking away as they shared another kiss with a deep moan.

"Maybe we'll see each other again before the week is out," Renee said.

"Maybe," he agreed, with his voice sounding more like "most definitely".

Renee chuckled lightly. Flirtatiously. She whispered something to him. He laughed.

Jaime felt as if she was intruding.

His footsteps sounded against the wood floor before he walked past her.

"It's nice to put a face with the... *sounds*, Sanders," Jaime called behind him as Renee walked down the hall to stand beside her.

He glanced back at them with a smile and shake of his head before walking across the den and out the French patio doors toward the beach.

"What a night," Renee sighed.

Jaime arched a brow as she looked down at Renee's nudity. "I have seen—and heard—way more of you than I needed to, friend," she drawled dryly.

"I might stay naked all week long," Renee said, running her hands over her close-shaven head before spreading her arms wide as she walked backward down the hall.

"Stay ready so you don't have to get ready, huh?"

"There is no getting ready for the goodness—*the hardness*—of a thirty-year-old dick."

Jaime's eyes dipped. "Well on behalf of your thirty-year-old one-night stand and myself…thank you for waxing," she said, reaching back to pull her bedroom door closed.

Renee took a bow.

"I'm off to explore. Be back in an hour," Jaime called over her shoulder before she made her way across the suite to the front door. Immediately, the wild blend of sweet tropical flowers, succulent spices the islands were known for, and the crisp scent of the nearby ocean was intoxicating. She took a deep inhale as she appreciated the beauty of the land and the colonial architecture of the white structures against the pale beach, the towering almond, palm and lemon trees, turquoise waters, and green mountains in the distance.

It truly was beautiful. Relaxing. Serene.

After the last few years of growing her business and outgrowing drama of the past, this week was just what she needed. She was looking forward to the vibe, surroundings, amenities, and excursions. And Luc gave it all to her without asking for anything in return.

She eased her phone out of her pocket to call him, knowing he was up—maybe even still in an all-night studio session with one of his newer artists. She paused as she eyed the large beachfront wooden yoga pavilion. Yesterday, upon their arrival, Charmaine had taken them on a personal tour of the resort and the large rear wall of the structure had been covered by curtains. But those were now opened revealing a mural in the works.

Peaches, turquoise, and blue abstracts served as the backdrop for serene-looking people in varying shades of brown with bright eyes that on second glance showed more defiance than humor.

It looks so real. More like a photo than a painting.

Slow steps carried her up the stone-paved path to the steps. Somehow the mural was skillfully muted enough to not overpower the yoga studio or the surrounding island but still vibrant enough to draw and hold the eye. Tantalize. Intrigue.

It was masterful.

And although incomplete she took out her phone and captured several shots.

"So beautiful," she said aloud, fighting an urge to stroke it but knowing by the strong smell of oil paints that it was still wet.

"Thank you, Jaime."

She froze. Her phone fell from her hands. She trembled. Her heart pounded wildly. "No," she whispered with a lick of her lips.

But she knew—her body knew—even before she turned around and laid eyes on Graham Walker standing at the foot of the steps that it was him. Her entire body felt like one open and exposed nerve. Raw and vulnerable. Their eyes held and she hated the tears that rose with a quickness as each inhale and exhale of her breath echoed harshly. It had been six years since that day on the rooftop. And of course, the time had done nothing to dull his beauty. Not one thing at all. Instead, it had enhanced it.

Long, waist-length dreads framed a face that used to haunt her. The hardness of his high cheekbones and jawline were softened by supple lips and bright eyes surrounded by long and lush lashes that she knew firsthand grazed his face when he slept. Still tall, muscular, and fit. That was clear even in the loose, paint-stained shirt and drawstring pants he wore.

As they continued to stare at one another, she raced through so many emotions. Feeling each one. Swiftly. One after the other.

"And when I saw Pleasure–I mean Graham—today I told him to stop hiding from you and reach out. Didn't he call? He might be busy, being back in business and all," Jessa had said with a lick of her lips.

"You're a liar," Jaime replied.

"No, I saw him today. It was good to see him . . . and feel him . . . and fuck him."

That memory of Jessa Bell taunting her six years ago landed her on anger.

"It's good to see you, Jaime," Graham said, wiping his damp hands on a cloth as he climbed the few steps into the open-air building,

She bit her bottom lip and stepped back from him as she shook her head. "No," she whispered, feeling strangled by his betrayal, and hating how the pain lingered even after all the years. It was visceral. And deep.

Damn.

He smiled and his dimples deepened as he walked over to where she felt frozen. "I can't believe it's you," he said, his voice still deep and strong as black coffee. The scent of his signature Tom Ford cologne still warm and intriguing.

"To hell with you," she said snidely, before moving past him.

She nearly stumbled as she took off down the front steps, running from him and everything she felt at seeing him again. This man she once loved. This man who swore off being a manwhore. This man who slept with her worst enemy.

A strong hand clasped around her wrist to stop her retreat. She grimaced and grunted as she snatched away from his touch and turned to land her free hand solidly against his cheek. "Stay the fuck away from me, *Pleasure*," she spat.

His face hardened and their eyes locked again as he held her in place with just inches between them. His jaw clenched and unclenched and the look in his eyes changed as he wrapped an arm around her waist and lifted her with ease up against his body. Her struggle against his strength was futile.

"Put me down, Graham!" she shouted, not caring who heard.

But the area of the beach around them was empty.

With long strides, he walked them to the rear of the palladium where there was an attached small shed. It was filled with shelves of yoga mats, blankets, towels, and bolsters. The scent of candles was overwhelming in the long and narrow space, but not more so than her body being pressed against the closed door by Graham's.

She tilted her chin up as he looked down at her. Her eyes searched his when he stroked her cheek with his finger. The anger fused into hurt, but she clung to her fury. "A grown ass man still selling dick for a living?" she said, meaning to be snide and cruel. "That's all you got going for you?"

A coldness entered his eyes. "There was a time you couldn't get enough of all I had," he volleyed back.

"I was a fool to think you had anything more going for you than that," Jaime said, her voice soft but her intent to strike out against him very clear.

Graham squinted as he looked at her and his grip on her upper arms tightened a bit. "If sex was all we had then why are you so angry I didn't reach out to you?" he asked, his eyes searching her face.

She released a bitter laugh, keeping her eyes on his. "It's you reaching back out to Jessa Bell that has me pissed."

He frowned in confusion. "Jessa Bell?" he said, releasing her and taking a step back. "I haven't seen her since the day her ex-father-in-law tried to kill her."

"Yes, I know."

"No, I don't think you do if the fact that she appeared out of the blue, tried to seduce me, said some cruel shit, and then flew out of there when whatever the hell she was hoping to go down did *not*," Graham stressed, resting his hands on his hips as he looked over at her.

"Liar," Jaime said, fighting the childish urge to mush him in the face. "She told me you fucked her, Plea-sure."

He shook his head in disbelief. "I've never fucked that lady. When does she claim I did?" he asked.

"That night."

"What!" he exclaimed in surprise.

Jaime rolled her eyes. "Save the masterful performances for the bedroom, Graham, because I'm not buying it," she said.

In one large step, he was back before her and gripping her upper arms to hoist her body up a bit off the floor. "And I'm not selling a damn thing but commissions of my art," he said through clenched teeth.

"Once a whore…always a whore," she said with deliberate slowness.

If she was honest with herself, she wanted him to make her believe he no longer sold his body and that he never shared it with her enemy.

"That could go both ways," he returned in a cold voice, reminding her that she was married to another man when she used to pay for his sex.

Jaime gasped in shock and eased her hands up between them to press against his chest before she used all her might to put space between them with a push. Her might was nothing against his strength because he barely budged and was still in her personal space, sucking the very air from around her with his presence.

Just like always.

"Look at me," Graham demanded, giving her arms a little shake.

She did, casting her eyes up at him.

He leaned down. "I am many things, Jaime, but I'm not a liar," he said, his voice hard. "Am I?"

She said nothing, denying him the confirmation he sought more out of stubbornness than disagreement. She felt the coolness of his breath against her face and the heat of his body against her own.

"I *never* slept with Jessa," he insisted.

I believe him.

Jaime grunted in derision. "Too bad you can't say that for all the other women you've screwed over the years," she said, holding on to her anger because any other emotion—at this moment—was dangerous.

As hell.

Silence reigned. Her breathing increased pace and depth. Each exhale seemed to echo. Her pulse sped and the pounding of her heart was thunderous. When his eyes dipped down to her mouth with longing and caused her nipples to tighten, she roughly pushed against his chest trying not to take in the familiar hardness of it as she did. He gave her a slow and wicked smile that caused her clit to throb with renewed life. She jerked her hand up to pop against his cheek.

WHAP.

Graham captured her hand, keeping it pressed against his face before he turned his head and pressed a kiss to her palm. "Jaime," he said softly.

Just the sound of her name being whispered from his lips sent every one of her senses into high alert. The scent of his warm and spicy cologne. The touch of his hand against her pulse. The very sight of his beautiful face. The sound of their rushed breathing that blended in the brief space between them.

He lowered his head and she hungered for the taste of his mouth.

It had been seventeen years since she'd first laid eyes on him and had felt undeniably drawn to him. At that moment, her awareness of him was just as strong—maybe more so.

The kiss never landed. Her disappointment stung.

"Damn," Graham swore, pounding his fists against the door before he turned their bodies so that his back was braced against it as he guided her back from him, outstretching his arms.

Jaime fought to slow her breathing and steady her pulse as she took several more steps back. She closed her eyes, feeling freed from the draw of him. At his continued silence, she opened her eyes to find him staring at her as he raked his fingers through his dreads and bit his bottom lip.

The look in his eyes?

Hunger.

She shivered.

"What are you doing here, Graham?" Jaime asked.

"Trying not to strip you and make love to you on the floor."

I believe him.

Her heartbeat was fast and wild as she swallowed over a lump in her throat while he took her in from head to toe. Slowly. Deliberately. She thought of the bikini and sheer pants she wore but felt naked. He knew her body. Intimately.

And she knew his, remembering it well. Every pleasure spot. Each nuance to make him roar like a lion.

Like massaging his inner thighs while I licked the pulsing vein running the length of his thick and long dick.

"I better go," Jaime said, pressing her fingertips to her neck and finding it heated.

"That might be best," Graham agreed. "You are tempting me and it's getting harder to fight the urge."

She nodded several times before walking toward him.

Graham remained leaning against the door, blocking her retreat.

Their eyes locked once more.

The tension in the small space was thick and heavy. Pulsing between them and around them. A creation uniquely their own.

"It was good to see you, Graham," she said.

"You too, Jaime."

She reached past him to grip the doorknob. "Excuse me," she said, looking out one of the glass panes at the beach.

"Don't go," he implored, covering her hand with his.

Jaime gasped at his electric touch.

"The very sight of you makes me want to throw it all away," he whispered down to her.

She made the mistake of glancing up at him. It was her undoing.

And with one final shake of his head, Graham slid his arm around her waist and pulled her body in front of his before he buried his face against her neck. "Jaime. Jaime. Jaime," he moaned against her skin.

Madness set in quickly.

She felt transported back in time and closed her eyes as the wave of pure desire poured over her. "Graham," she gasped as she dropped her head onto his shoulder.

"Fuck it," he said before he gripped the back of her neck and turned her face to capture her mouth with his own.

The first stroke of his tongue against hers brought up a cry of hunger from deep within her. She splayed her fingers on the sides of his face and kissed him back with fervor as he turned them again to press her back to the door. She brought each of her knees up to clasp his side and rolled her hips as he pressed his hardness against her belly.

Everything was so familiar. Time meant nothing. The hum of their chemistry was steady and their passion blinding. Every pulse pounded. Her head spun.

This was an addict feasting on their drug.

It was damn good. Glorious.

Graham kissed her deeply as he grabbed the rims of her pants and bikini bottoms into his fist and jerked them down over her hips and buttocks. She felt it all. The trembling of his hands against her soft skin. A rush of desire that made her heady as she lowered each leg for him to finally remove the garments. The draft of air when he flung them away blew against her. The mix of its coolness against her skin. The heat of his kisses that caused her to whimper.

As he shifted his pants and boxers down around hips and buttocks to pool around his bare feet, she cried out as he hitched her up higher against the door to level her breasts with his face. Graham used his entire tongue to lick one taut nipple and then the other before dragging it up the deep valley of her breast and her entire neck with a wildness that thrilled her.

"Graham!" she gasped, arching her back from the door.

He turned her body, pressing her breasts against the warm glass of the door. "Bend your legs," he ordered.

She did, bringing each one up with her inner thighs against the door and her knees as high as her waist. She didn't know his plan for her. She did not care.

Graham held her up with his arms as he bent his body to lick and bite each buttock.

She cried out when his tongue licked at her core from behind. Quivering in heat, she curved her back, raising her bottom and giving him access to more of her intimacy to taste and suckle. "Shit," she swore with a moan from the back of her throat as she closed her eyes at the first wave of her climax.

He moaned and grunted as he sucked at her sweet juices as if thirsty and starved. "So good," he moaned against her flesh. "So. Good."

Jaime fought the urge to hotly lick at the glass plane of the door.

With one last deep bite of each of her soft buttocks, he rose and guided his hot and hard inches inside her as he gripped her hips to slide her down against his upward thrust.

They gasped.

Jaime dragged her fingers against the door into a fist that

she pounded against the wood at the feel of him pressing against her inner walls. Hot. Hard. Throbbing. Filling her completely.

Graham clenched his square jaw and licked at her back. He held her up with his body and used his now free hands to grab each of hers to bring up over her head. When she began to circle her hips, causing her pussy to tightly slide up and down his tool, he cried out roughly. He loved her freedom of inhibitions.

She bit her bottom lip and smiled, remembering so well how she loved the effect she had on him. With a look over her shoulder, she saw his head was back and his mouth was open wide. Every muscle in his body was strained. She went still. He looked at her. His eyes were wild and dazed with pleasure. She returned his stare as she worked her pussy muscles to squeeze and release his hardness.

Graham folded their entwined left hands against the door and released her right hand to press his own down between her body and the wood. His fingers sought and found her clit.

Jaime's body went tight when he worked the swollen and damp flesh as he delivered hard thrusts up inside her. Again. And again. And again. "Damn," she swore, pressing her eyes closed tightly as she lightly tapped her forehead against the door.

The combination of his deep thrusts, his hand holding one of hers in slight bondage and the other stroking her clit was driving her mad. Would his sudden reappearance, their clash, and now their explosive sex drive her fully out of her mind? She wasn't sure.

His thrust came on fast, furious, slick, and deep.

Against her back, she felt his heart pounding. His sweat dampened her. His moans and grunts echoed in her ear. And she knew before she felt his inches stiffen inside her that he was going to come and that brought on her climax.

With a cry that echoed around them and seemed to rise from deep within her, Jaime's head fell back against his broad shoulder when explosive, white-hot spasms took her over, as she cried to God to save her from the torture of this pleasure.

His roar mingled with her cries. His thrusts slowed with each rough grunt. His body was stiff and his grip on her hand and clit was firm as he enjoyed his own waves. "Jaime. Jaime. Jaime," he groaned into her ear between jagged breaths.

She licked at her parched lips and took deep breaths as she fought to hold on to her sanity. Raising her head, with her eyes open, she looked out at the beach blending into the edges of the turquoise water of beautiful Grenada. A treat. But nothing to rival what just happened between—.

Jaime went stiff from panic and not pleasure. "No, no, no," she whispered with a hard wince as she finally thought of Luc.

What have I done?

"Let me down. Let me down. Letmedown. Letmedown," she said, pushing back against Graham to put distance between their bodies and to break the fiery organic connection between them.

"What?" Graham asked, sliding his spent inches from inside her as he set her on her feet and stepped back.

Still feeling the effect of her climax, she stumbled a bit on her feet.

Graham reached to steady her.

"No!" she roared, panicked as she avoided his touch.

Graham withdrew his hand and eyed her oddly.

What have I done?

Passion was dominated by remorse.

"I have to go," she said, bending to pick up her bikini bottom and sheer coverup pants to clumsily slide on without a bit of grace.

"Jaime, talk to me," Graham implored, picking up both her shoes to hand her.

She snatched them away from him, shaking her head as she fought back the tears rising like a morning tide. She rushed into her shoes before turning to snatch the door open.

"Jaime."

She paused and closed her eyes as she inhaled the smell of the ocean.

He did nothing wrong. I did.

"This was a mistake," Jaime said softly, not looking back as one tear raced down her cheek.

"Jaime—"

"Goodbye, Graham," Jaime said, adding firmness to her tone before she closed the door and raced away from the site of her betrayal.

Chapter 3

"Money!"

With his shooting arm still raised, Luc watched the basketball from his spot on the three-point line of his court as it sailed through the net with a swoosh. He looked over to his assistant, Kendell, and smiled broadly. "Like I said... money," he said, holding up his hands to catch the ball Kendell lobbed at him. "You got the vid?"

The twenty-something man, fresh out of college and looking to earn his break into the music industry, nodded as he moved his thumbs over the keyboard of his phone. "Just sent it," he said, his raspy voice lending him more to an artist than a hopeful future music executive.

Luc stuffed the ball under his arm while he posted the vid to his Instagram before sliding the device into the back pocket of the oversized shorts he wore sans shirt.

"Time to go, Luc," Kendell said, reminding him of the upcoming call time for the Summer Jam rehearsal.

One of his artists was performing for the annual concert hosted by one of the top radio stations in New York. He liked to have the personal touch for his small, carefully curated roster of artists. If he could be on-site for any of their performances, studio sessions, and photo/video shoots then

he made it happen. His dreams to conquer the music industry deserved nothing less.

From his days growing up in Brooklyn with hip-hop
narrating his life while he struggled like hell with a drug-
addicted mother and father in prison, to working his way
through college where hungry days had been the cost for his
Bachelor's in Communication, and then using money left
from an insurance policy after the death of his beloved
grandfather to open a small music studio, Luc had a love affair
with music that would not be denied. His ear for good music
and eye for a star was unequaled and five years ago those
innate skills landed him an artist and repertoire position at one
of the "Big Six" major record labels. He loved his work as an
A&R exec, but his recent talks about acquiring his own label
would be the beginning of his empire if he could get the deal
done. Ten years from working as an unpaid intern to even
being considered to run his own label was huge.

With one last shot of the ball, Luc turned and walked
beside his assistant to leave the sports center of the Midtown
West apartment building where he called his three-bedroom
condo on the sixtieth-floor home. His smaller condos in
Atlanta and Los Angeles were more for business. New York
would always be home base.

"You changing?" Kendell asked as they stepped onto the
glass-enclosed elevator.

Luc looked at his reflection in the glass, leaning in to
smooth his hand over his neck as he took in the plain V-neck
tee and red-and-white shorts he wore with Jordans. "Yeah,"
he said, pulling his phone back out to check Jaime's Instagram. "When I leave there, I have a meeting at the label and
then dinner—"

"At Jue Lan's," Kendell provided.

He frowned a little. Jaime hadn't posted all day. She was
an Instagram junkie and a luxurious vacation in the Caribbean was the right locale to overshare.

Is she okay?

He felt so protective of her, especially with her out of the country. He didn't know what he would do if anything happened to her—especially on a trip he orchestrated to spoil her the way she deserved.

Maybe she was too busy loving life to focus on posting about it.

The elevator slowed to a stop.

"Hi, neighbor. How are you doing?"

But she didn't call me this morning either . . .

Luc's heart beat a little faster in concern as he pulled up Jaime's contact info. A photo of her filled the screen. She was in a beautiful strapless gold gown and swamped by his tailored tuxedo jacket after they left a charity dinner at Cipriani's for a foundation of music executives raising money for cancer research. It had been their first date and they had clicked right away. He smiled at the memory of the night.

"Luc," Kendell said, gently nudging his elbow.

He looked over at him. "What?"

"The young lady spoke to you," his assistant explained.

What young lady?

"Me," a feminine voice said as if reading his thoughts—or maybe just his facial expression.

He looked to his left. A pretty woman with wide eyes and a pouty mouth stood beside him. He recognized her from around the building. Clothing clinging to reality-defying body parts made her hard to miss, but he was avoiding catching the obvious vibes she was always throwing him when they briefly encountered each other.

"How you doin'?" he asked politely.

She smiled. "You tell me," she replied, turning this way and that in the white strapless jumpsuit she wore with heels.

He fought not to wince.

Miss Too Much.

It was all too obvious, and she was too done up for it to feel real. The long hair, makeup, boobs and hips, tight clothes, and wide-eyed blinks with super long lashes was too much. Pretty? Yes. Sexy? Of course. Regardless, the very last thing he was looking for was another woman in his life—side or main. Jaime Pine was *more* than enough.

"You have a good day," Luc said with cool cordiality, turning his back on her before calling his woman via FaceTime.

"Savage," Kendell said softly in awe with a shake of his head.

The call went straight to voice mail. He frowned deeply as he checked his gold watch. It was close to one in the afternoon. He called again. Same result. He'd just feel better hearing her voice or seeing her face.

Was her phone dead? Out of good range?

The elevator slowed to a stop.

"Everything okay?" Kendell asked as they stepped off onto the sixtieth floor.

"I hope so," Luc said, gripping his phone tightly enough to snap it.

Guilt was heavy.

Jaime felt the weight of it profoundly. Not even the hours that had passed since she had sex with her ex had lessened her culpability. Not one bit.

"Shit," she swore as she closed her eyes and squeezed the bridge of her nose between her fingers as she drew her knees to her chest where she sat in the middle of her bed covered by nothing but a towel. The long and hot shower she took as soon as she entered her room that morning did nothing to erase the memory of Graham and what they had shared. She was soiled by guilt and nothing could wash that away.

Luc did not deserve what she'd done.

With an ex she had not seen in years.

With no protection.

Without care to how much her betrayal would hurt Luc.

She set her head down upon her knees and set free the tears she held back. Silently. Painfully. Her regret was palpable.

I love him. I adore him. Luc is amazing.

"Why did I do it?" she asked herself softly as she raised her head to look out the open doors of the terrace at the beach.

Because Graham wasn't out of my system.

That truth settled and lowered her shoulders more.

"Hey, you."

Jaime looked over at the door of the room at Renee leaning in the frame and not quite sure how long she had been there. She used the sides of her hands to erase her tears, wishing she could handle her guilt and remorse in the same manner.

"Everything okay?" Renee asked, walking into the room in a turquoise woven cotton sundress with her phone in hand.

No.

"Yeah," Jaime lied, giving her a waning smile.

"Luc called," Renee said, holding up her phone. "He was worried that your phone was going straight to voice mail."

Jaime's stomach felt stung by acid. She knew the stress of her guilt would cause an ulcer at that rate. "I'll call him in a little bit," she said, not wanting to at all.

She already cheated and now she would have to lie.

"I told him you were sleeping off a late-night drinking session."

Jaime looked into Renee's eyes and saw concerns and questions, but she had no truth for her friend. As badly as she wanted to reveal her dalliance, the last thing she needed was to be lambasted for cheating—and in particular, cheating with Graham. For Renee and Aria, he would always be Pleasure the manwhore.

They weren't concerned, believing, or understanding of his redemption.

For years, the thought of Jessa's lie about sleeping with Graham had tortured her. Discovering it wasn't true had been such relief. But why had she cared so much?

Still?

She was over Graham Walker.

Or so she thought.

"Fuck," she swore again.

That was the problem.

A hot and dirty fuck.

She looked at her phone at the foot of the bed. Charmaine, their concierge, had brought it to their suite saying someone was kind enough to turn it in at the front desk. "Someone my ass," she muttered, reaching to pick up the device.

It was powered off but not dead, and she didn't doubt that it was Graham who did it as soon as he found it during the aftermath. He hadn't been the type to snoop or invade privacy and she doubted that had changed.

And I shouldn't have doubted him when Jessa lied.

More guilt.

"Aria and I thought we'd all do that sightseeing tour and really take in Grenada," Renee said, moving over to the bed to pick up Jaime's phone and plug it into the charger near the lounge chair.

Soon it will ring, and I will have to look Luc in the face and lie or break his heart and tell him the truth.

"You game?" Renee asked.

Jaime eyed her as she moved over to look out the open

patio doors. "You're mighty energetic after that workout you had early this morning," she said, running her hands through her hair.

Renee smiled. "He must have blessed me with the spirit of his youth," she said.

"I think it was more than *just* his spirit," Jaime drawled.

"It was just sex. No big deal. Right?"

Wrong. So very wrong. There was no such thing as "just" sex.

Jaime's eyes shot to her phone when the apple icon filled the screen as it was powered on. "Did Luc say anything else?" she asked.

Renee glanced back over her shoulder. "Something about a rehearsal and he'd call you back later tonight."

"Okay."

Good. That gave me time.

To do what exactly?

Aria sailed into the room in a white tank and floor-length cotton skirt with a bright print pattern. "Hey, Jaime. Where'd you go this morning?" she asked, as she plopped down onto the end of the bed.

Heaven and hell.

"I walked around the resort," Jaime said.

And cheated on Luc.

"How was it?" Aria asked as she smoothed her hair up into its curly topknot.

A vision of Graham holding her body against the door as he tasted her core flashed. "Amazing," she said softly and honestly as her clit throbbed to life at the memory.

Silence was normally his refuge.

In the few days since he made love to Jaime, it had failed him. Just as much as he had failed himself. "Shit," he swore, turning off the steam before leaving the glass-enclosed shower, nude and wet.

He didn't bother to dry off as he stood before the mirror over the marble bathroom double sink and snatched off the cap protecting the dreads he'd been growing since he was just twenty. With a deep breath, he studied himself. It'd taken him a long time to look at himself—really look at himself—and like what he saw. For so long he'd used his appearance, tall athletic frame and big dick, to run through women. Their attention fed his ego, wet his dick, and made him a lot of money as first a stripper then a high-class escort.

It took therapy to realize all of it was him trying to prove his masculinity after reckoning with his childhood abuse.

"I was violated by an older boy when I was six," he said, his eyes on his reflection as the carefully guided advice of his therapist played out in his head.

"Release it so that it doesn't control you."

There was a time when he didn't even allow himself to think about it. He even let that haunting memory turn him against attending church—in particular, the one where he was fondled in a closet by Lionel.

Graham tensed. He rolled his shoulders and gritted his teeth. That one act had peppered his life. Still did.

Even his relationship with Jaime.

Seeing her today had brought back all the old feelings he had for her and made him feel young again. Being buried deep inside of her—thrust after thrust—and seeing the same spark he brought to her eyes had enlivened him. He'd been with plenty of women—more than he was proud to admit—but no other woman made him feel like Jaime did. Today proved no woman probably ever would.

To be with her he had said "Fuck it" and thrown away years of celibacy as a part of controlling his sexual addiction. It seems, with Jaime as the lure, he was better suited to fight his year-long cocaine addiction of the past and not his sexual one. He still remembered the exact moment he lost the will to cling to his abstinence...

"The very sight of you makes me want to throw it all away," he whispered to her as he looked down at her. *Feasted on her beauty. Lost in her allure.*

And then she looked up at him, and in her eyes, he saw the same desire he felt. Wild. Unable to be bridled.

And with one final shake of his head, Graham slid his arm around her waist and pulled her body in front of his before he buried his face against her neck. "Jaime. Jaime. Jaime," he moaned against her skin.

Everything after that was a blur of heat and passion.

He had sworn he would not have sex again without being in a long-term relationship. No more one-night stands where the head of his dick reigned over the head on his neck. He'd lost control. For that, he was disappointed in himself.

But Jaime was no stranger. He once loved her deeply. The only woman he had ever given his heart. And she still owned a huge piece of it. And seeing her again—having her body again—had opened up the door he'd closed on his feelings for her. Now it ached.

Will I ever get over her?

"Jaime damn Pine," he muttered with a shake of his head and yet another clench of his jaw.

"Yes."

Graham whirled, already surprised by the sound of her voice, and shocked to see her standing at the open doors to his beachside cottage. It was at the end of the resort's property on a secluded part of the beach. He left the bathroom, still nude and damp, and came out to the bedroom to stand behind the woven seagrass headboard.

Her braids were now flowing down her back and her face was free of makeup. Just the sun's kiss deepening her brown complexion. Her high cheekbones spoke to her African heritage and her feline shaped eyes hinted that her mother was

Black and Asian. The full and plump softness of her mouth rounded out her features.

Beautiful.

"We need to talk," Jaime said.

His chest filled with that same joy and hopefulness and excitement at seeing her again. "In here?" he asked, eyeing the bed that faced the open doors to the terrace. He moved from behind the bed, exposing his nudity. "And like *this*?"

"No," Jaime said as she quickly turned her back to him.

Graham chuckled. "I'll get dressed," he said, taking in the sight of her buttocks in the peach wide-leg jumpsuit she wore. The spaghetti straps and draped fabric exposed all of her back.

He cleared his throat and ignored the slight hardening of his dick as he walked to the carved wooden armoire to remove white linen drawstring pants from the stack of folded clothes. "I'm dressed," he said, letting the rim of the pants settle low on his hips.

She turned to him and watched him as he walked over to stand beside her in the open doorway. Her eyes dipped to take in his abdomen, and she licked her lips before darting her eyes away to some focal point down the length of the beach.

It was late afternoon and a little of the summer heat had begun to fade. A draft of wind blew, causing the thin material of her jumpsuit to cling to her body. His eyes smoldered at her hard nipples pressing against the cotton. He licked his lips. His desire for her was far from sated. And again, his resolve disappeared like a fine mist in wind.

Graham walked over to her. Her eyes widened and her breaths deepened with each of his steps. "Are you back for more, Jaime?" he asked, stopping just an inch from her and snaking his arm around her waist to jerk her close.

She rested her hands on his bare arms and tilted her head back with her mouth just slightly ajar.

He shivered from her touch and hungered to taste her lips.

"No," she said with an adamant shake of her head that caused the ends of her braids to tease his arm.

With regret, Graham released her, remembering that he should be as strong as her in resisting the attraction between them. *But she feels and smells so damn good.*

He offered her the patio chair under the large umbrella and instead chose to sit on the hammock across from her to enjoy the tropical sun.

"Congratulations on the commission," Jaime began, removing the shades hanging from the front of her jumpsuit to slide on her face. "When I asked my concierge about the mural, she said you had been on the island for the last couple of weeks painting it."

"I only work on it during the off-hours," he said. "Another week or so and I'll be done and headed off to my next painting adventure."

Her smile was wan as she looked down at her hand and then back up at him. "Winning major awards for your art, having acclaimed shows, and being commissioned by high-ranking political figures and celebrities have kept you busy since the rooftop, huh?" she asked. Softly.

Graham nodded. "Yes, but is that your way of asking why I haven't reached out since then?" he asked, his deep voice defeating the echoes of the crush of the waves in the oceans.

Jaime removed her shades and matched his stare. "Yes, Graham," she said. "I figure the universe saw fit for us to meet here and at the very least we owe each other one last conversation before we say goodbye this time and know that when we're done, neither of us will hold onto hope that we will see each other again."

He heard the finality in her voice and the pang it caused was deep and radiating. "I don't think either of us can ever outrun our past. We know too much about each other," he said, revealing why he had fought himself every time he felt the urge to reach out, resolving himself to releasing his love for her once and for all. "I don't think I can ever be what you need, or understand, or fully forgive. Our past together is the very reason I just don't believe we can have a future."

Jaime looked over at him for a long time. So many emotions crossed her face until finally there was peace. "I had a dozen other questions, but you answered the one I needed most," she said, rising to her feet to walk over to stand before him. With the hint of a smile, she stroked his cheek. "You are right, Graham, because there is no future for us."

He turned his head quickly and pressed a kiss to her palm and was rewarded with a shiver—a telltale sign that she was just as affected by him as he was by her. "Goodbye forever?" he said, knowing it sounded more of a question than a statement.

"Goodbye, Graham," she said, easing her hand away before she turned and walked onto the beach without looking back.

Goodbye, Graham.

From the backseat of the black SUV, Jaime remembered the look in Graham's eyes when she said farewell. They lacked the finality of his words. She saw his doubts. His regrets. His wish that things between them could be different.

It both scared and thrilled her.

No. No more Graham.

Two days ago, had been the last time she would see him. Going forward she was done thinking about him. She didn't need him. She had Luc—a man who had no doubts about their future together. She smiled, thinking of seeing *him* again. Being with *him* again. She would keep her betrayal to herself, more not to hurt him than anything else.

Graham Walker was in her past.

"I am exhausted, but I know after a week of not having pussy on hand that Kingston ain't thinking about sleep," Aria said, following it with a yawn from her seat on the third row of the SUV.

Jaime glanced back at her over her shoulder. "You should be ready for some," she teased.

"Hell, you too. Only one wore out and probably tore out is Ms. Island Fling over there," Aria said, lifting her chin in Renee's direction where she sat on the second-row seat with Jaime.

She imagined just what Graham's buttocks had looked like, clenching and unclenching, as he thrust inside her. Mid-thrust she closed her eyes and shook her head to free herself from the steamy recollection. "Yeah. Right?" she said weakly, casting her gaze out the window as they pulled up to the guard booth of Richmond Hills, their affluent New Jersey subdivision.

"Don't hate because Mama got fed," Renee said.

"Really, *Ma-ma*? Considering he's younger than your son that's a *really* bad choice of words," Aria drawled.

Renee just chuckled.

"Home sweet home," Jaime said, meaning to change the subject. The very last thing she wanted in her life—especially this particular week—was another dick. She didn't even want to think about or discuss anyone's penis.

"Jaime, you get dropped off first since Aria's in the rear seat and your luggage went in last in the back," Renee rationalized.

"Fine with me," she said, even though they had to pass both Renee and Aria's home to reach her spacious European-styled house.

Like all the homes in the massive subdivision, it spoke of

affluence and wealth. Somehow at night, it was even more luxe, with beautiful landscaping highlighted by towering metal streetlamps and the exterior lighting fixtures of every home.

"Alright ladies," Jaime began, gathering her items as the SUV slowed to a stop at her address. "I will be off the grid tomorrow getting my mind right for work on Monday."

"Same here," Renee said.

"I'll be on dick duty all weekend so don't call me and I won't call you," Aria said.

Jaime smiled and climbed from the SUV once the driver held the door open for her. "Thank y'all for an awesome girl's trip," she said, heartfelt and warm.

Both ladies smiled at her. "Same here," Renee said again.

With one last glance back to make sure the driver had the right luggage to bring to the porch, Jaime climbed the stairs. As she slid her key into the lock, she regretted not letting Luc meet her there. Only the safety and security offered by the guards gave her the confidence to open the door and have no fear of an intruder waiting and lurking.

"Surprise!"

Jaime hollered out as her foyer and living room was illuminated revealing people, party décor, and her Luc in the center of it all in a tailored all-black tuxedo kneeling with his hand outstretched revealing a spectacular diamond engagement ring inside the black box of his favorite jeweler. She gasped in surprise and covered her open mouth with her hands.

"Surprise, Jaime."

She heard Renee and Aria whisper that together but didn't turn, knowing they were in on the surprise as well. She was thankful they pressured her to wear a nice sundress to travel home in. One of them took her bag and keys from her trembling hand as she slowly walked the rose strewn path that led to him.

He was so handsome in all black with his fair complexion

and jet-black hair. He smiled and her heart skipped a beat. Her parents were beaming, showing every tooth in their mouths right behind him as Jaime came to stand before him, surrounded by friends, employees of her business, and neighbors. She loved that he wore his heart on his sleeve.

Luc bit his bottom lip and smiled—charming as ever—and she remembered the night they spent together before the trip. Her belly warmed in desire and her clit throbbed to life. She was thankful that recent events had not dulled her desire for Luc.

Before he could speak, she reached for his hand and with a little tug, he rose to stand tall before her. She eased her arms around him and pressed her hands to the strength of his back as she tilted her chin up to kiss him. First a soft suckle of his bottom lip and then lightly stroking the tip of his tongue with her own. He jerked her body closer to his with a moan as he deepened the kiss as everyone sighed, oohed, or applauded. She missed him and was truly glad to be back in his arms and her senses.

She fought back her tears of guilt as he broke their kiss. "Is that a yes before I even got to pop the question?" he asked, his deep voice seeming to rumble near her ear.

She nodded and nuzzled her face against his neck as he lifted her with ease off her feet.

Forgive me, Luc. Please forgive me.

Chapter 4

One month later

Jaime was awakened with a start but remained lying on her side. Through the floor-to-ceiling window, the hot summer sun was just rising above the metropolis and in the distance, she could see its gleam atop the water of the river. It was a beautiful view. She allowed herself a few precious moments to relish it before the hustle and bustle of her day—their day—began.

She looked over her shoulder to find Luc sitting up in bed watching something on his laptop with his AirPods in. Her hustle was only outmatched by his. She loved how hard he worked for his dreams. Where most men would be satisfied, Luc was only determined to have more. Do more. Be more.

He was so fixated that his laser focus on the laptop did not waver as she slid the sheet off her nude body and moved on the bed to sit behind him. Massaging his arms, she pressed kisses from one of his broad shoulders to the other inhaling the scent of his soap still clinging to his skin. They had shared a quick shower after making love last night against the windows of his bedroom.

Wanting his attention, she removed one of the earbuds. "What's that?" she asked before sucking his earlobe.

Luc brought one hand up to take the one she pressed to his shoulder to kiss the palm. "The new sneaker commercial for one of my artists," he said, using his free hand to rewind the video.

He squinted as he studied it frame by frame.

"The one dropping next week?" Jaime asked.

He nodded.

With eyes twinkling with mischief, she eased her hand around his waist to take his dick into her hand and slowly stroke him to hardness. He hissed from her touch and let his head fall back against her shoulder as he bent his legs to thrust his hips forward, sending his laptop over onto its side on the bed.

"I got the music summit today," he reminded her, with his eyes closed and his pleasure clear.

"Then I better get on top."

She came around his body and flung the sheets back as he gripped his thick inches and guided them inside her. She swiped away his hands and twirled her hips as she slid down on his hardness until all of him was planted deep within her. She released a cry and dug her fingernails into his shoulders as Luc slapped her buttocks and then brought his hand up to twist in her jet-black bob to jerk her head back. He pressed his free hand to her back and brought her body forward to taste her hard nipples.

"Lick them nasty," she gasped.

He did with a deep moan as she worked her hips back and forth to glide her core up and down him, striking the hard base against her clit and stoking her climax. And his.

"Come on baby," he begged in a fevered whisper. "Let's get this nut."

She picked up the pace, gripping the headboard as she rode him fast and hard as he sucked deeply at her nipples. She loved that. He knew it. The internal explosion came with ease and they both cried out as she pushed herself to keep riding him through the waves of their white-hot spasms until both their bodies went slack after their release.

"Shit," Jaime swore, releasing a heavy breath as she raised her arms above her head and looked down at him, sweaty and spent.

"Move...in...with...me," Luc said in between breaths.

Jaime smoothed her wayward bob back from her face as she too took large breaths that caused her full breasts to rise and fall. "Huh?" she asked.

Luc chuckled and sat up higher in bed with her still straddling his lap with his spent dick now limp against her thigh.

She looked down into his keen handsome features before pressing her hands to his tattoo-covered chest as she tilted her head to the side. "When I said I was thinking about selling my house in Richmond Hills I wasn't trying to woo an invite for us to live together," she said.

"And when I asked, I wasn't feeling manipulated to do so, Jai," he said reverting to the nickname he used when he was really putting on the charm.

"Luc," she began with a slow shake of her head.

"Besides," he said, holding up her left hand to show the five-carat diamond ring on her third finger. "We're getting married."

She smiled. "We're getting married," she agreed, glad that her guilt about Grenada had truly begun to fade.

Somewhere along the line, she convinced herself that those stolen moments with Graham were a goodbye to ensure he was completely flushed from her system and thus making her able to fully love Luc Sinclair the way he deserved, forevermore.

She looked about the room with its modern design in shades of pale gold. "I honestly didn't know when I designed this place that I would live here...until we find our own home."

"Or condo," Luc inserted.

She nodded in agreement. "That we purchase together. My first marriage taught me to be present and visible in every aspect of my next marriage," she said, locking her eyes with his to show it was important to her.

"I'm not Eric," he said.

"And I'm not the Jaime I used to be," she countered.

Luc sat up straight. They were face to face. Eye to eye. "Deal."

With a wiggle of her nose, she leaned in and covered his mouth with her own to suckle slowly and deliberately with a soft grunt as she kept her eyes joined with his.

"Damn, Jaime," he whispered against her moist lips as his dick stirred to life against her thigh before standing tall and erect as she continued.

"What goes up must come down," she teased.

Luc swore before quickly grabbing her around the waist to fling her onto her back and dive his body atop hers as he entered her warmth and moisture with a hard thrust of his narrow hips. "My turn," he moaned against her neck as he fucked her swift and hard.

Jaime spread her arms wide across the king-sized bed and closed her eyes in pleasure.

Later that evening, after a final walkthrough of a home she redesigned in Tribeca, Jaime pulled her convertible onto her double driveway. The summer sun was hot, and she was thankful for the shade of the trees lining the sidewalks as she moved to the street to look up at the house. For more than a decade, it had been her home and most of that time it held the secrets of a miserable marriage. She thought of the way Eric would degrade her during sex. Tragically, his humiliation and snide remarks had stung deeper than the strokes of his dick.

She'd redecorated since reclaiming the home after his death, but the misery inside it was built in the foundation and still clinging to the framework like a stain. "It's time," she said aloud.

"Time for what?"

With her arms crossed over her chest, Jaime looked back at Aria now standing behind her with her curly afro pulled back from her face with a black band. "I'm selling my house," she admitted, curious to her reaction.

Aria's eyes widened in shock. "You're moving?"

Jaime looked back at the European-styled home with all its bedrooms never filled with children. It was Jessa Bell that bore a child for her husband. "Yes," she said. Firmly.

"Well shit," she said.

Jaime arched a brow. "Didn't you help plan my surprise engagement party?"

Aria twisted her mouth before sucking air between her teeth. "I didn't think that shit through," she said, stepping closer to wind her arm through Jaime's.

She frowned. "You thought we would move in here?"

"Like, I said I didn't think it through," Aria repeated with sadness clear in her tone.

Jaime let her head rest on her shoulder, so thankful for her friendship and that the ways of her past had not put distance between them that couldn't be forgiven. "I had more miserable days here than good, Aria," she reminded her.

"I know."

She refrained from letting her know that upon the sale she would split the money with Delaney, Eric's daughter with Jessa Bell. She knew that neither Aria nor Renee would agree, but Jaime felt Eric owed his only child something in this world regardless of what Jessa was able to financially offer her. With the house being valued in the high six figures it would be quite an inheritance for Delaney one day.

At the echo of a car door, they both looked down the winding street just as Renee's first ex, Jackson Clinton, pulled off in his silver pickup truck. Jaime and Aria's eyes widened as they looked at each other and then back down the street at Renee in a blue caftan watching her first love drive away—back home to his wife.

Uh-oh.

"Say what now?" Aria quipped, already headed in that direction and tugging Jaime by the arm behind her.

"That is none of our business, Aria," she insisted.

"Says who?"

"What are you going to do when I move?" Jaime asked as she finally fell in step with her friend.

"Video call to fill you in on all the Richmond Hill drama."

Jaime frowned. "Did people used to chit-chat about all *our* drama years ago?"

"Please. We made the newsletter...*several* times."

Jaime's frown deepened. Some old habits of wanting privacy were hard to break. "See, that's why I'm moving," she said.

"Maybe moving isn't such a bad idea."

Jaime stopped, suddenly causing Aria to get jerked back as she held on to her arm. "What's going on?"

Aria turned her head to eye her and Kingston's Mediterranean home. Gone was the wear and tear it had begun to show with its need of fresh paint and landscaping. Two years ago, they had done a major renovation and now it sparkled with new windows, shutters, paint schemes, and a sun porch. "I wanna go home," Aria said with sadness.

"Okay," Jaime said, giving the other women a peculiar look at the melancholy in her voice as she released her arm.

"You go ahead home. We can jump Renee on her business another time."

"Not home," she said, motioning her hand toward her house across the street. "*Home.* Newark. Brick City. I miss my Moms. My family. That vibe and energy. The burbs are for the birds, Jaime. Now you're leaving. Renee is on some sort of dick crusade. My kids barely know my side of the family. Kingston is busting his ass to make sure we never fall in the hole about money again. If we move to Newark, we could buy something the same size, much cheaper, and a little closer to my crazy ass, fun ass, ready to fight ass family and... and... I can get my husband back."

"Back?" Jaime asked, feeling concerned.

Of the fallout in 2010 by the vindictive words of Jess Bell, only Kingston had been proven to be free of any misdoings with her or any other woman. It was the marriage of Aria and her sexy Black doctor that gave Jaime hope that happily ever after was possible. They were couple goals.

Aria released a heavy breath. "He works so much. The kids and I don't really see him until Sunday and even then, he's charting or planning or catching up or..."

"*Or?*" Jaime led, deciding to give her the push she was hesitant to give in Grenada.

"Not fucking me," Aria said in a rush with the words almost blending.

Jaime winced. "At all?" she leaned in to whisper.

Aria gave her a hard stare. "Don't be silly. It's not the quantity, it's the quality. More of the wham and bam and less of the licking and flicking. You know?"

No. Not at all, Jaime thought, not making matters worse by admitting she and Luc did the dirty twice that morning. Back to back.

"Quickies before kids wake up just ain't getting it," Aria said, her face serious. Very serious.

Jaime knew Aria's past dealings with men left a lot to be

desired. Her teenage and college years had been wild. Real wild. So much so that she feared she was infertile because of it. Two babies later that myth was finally debunked, but Jaime worried if Kingston didn't step up his dick game that Aria would find a side-boo who would.

Wait. Who am I to judge?

First, she cheated on Eric, and then she cheated on Luc.

And both times—more than a decade apart—with the same man.

She remembered Graham burying his face against her neck as he moaned her name. The memory echoed, both mocking and titillating her.

"Jaime. Jaime. Jaime."

"What's wrong?" Aria asked.

Jaime blinked hard before focusing her gaze on her. "Huh?"

"You looked weird just now. You good?" Aria asked.

Jaime swallowed over a lump in her throat and nodded. "Gas," she said with a weak laugh.

Aria leaned back.

"*Anyway*, what does Kingston think about the move?" Jaime asked.

"I haven't told him yet that's what I would like for us to do."

Jaime spotted Kingston's black BMW Roadster coming up the street. "Right now, seems like a good time as any," she said, nudging her.

Aria's eyes took on laser focus. "To do what?"

Jaime smiled as she smoothed her finger across her shaped brow. "Whatever you want," she said. "What we want in a relationship matters."

When she said the words, she envisioned the look of horror on her mother's face that it would cause. Virginia Osten-Pine was of the old guard of dutiful wives whose main priority was her family—both husband and children equally as long as the children did not disobey whatever was needed for the father to thrive.

Aria turned to look at her with wide eyes. "Well, Jaime Pine, where is Jaime Hall?" she asked.

"That fool is dead and gone," Jaime said. "Now hopefully I don't lose myself again when I become Jaime Sinclair."

"That's up to you," Aria advised. "And this fuck session I am going to have is up to me."

"You want me to watch the kids for a little bit?" Jaime offered.

She went stiff and pointed at her. "An offer to babysit? You done fucked up now. Hold that thought," she said before turning to fast walk across the street to meet her tall and handsome husband as soon as he climbed from the low-slung sports car.

Jaime smiled and continued down the street to reach Renee's home three houses down from Aria and Kingston. As she climbed the stairs she glanced back just as Aria pressed Kingston against the now open front door with a deep—almost inappropriate kiss—before leading him inside the house and giving Jaime a thumbs up.

God help Kingston.

She rung Renee's doorbell as she waved to her new neighbors. A young Latino couple, the Hernandezes, who were expecting their first child. *And from the look of her belly, it was any second now.*

"Hey, Jaime," Renee said around a yawn.

Jaime eyed her. "Girl, stop faking like I woke you up. We saw Jackson just leave here," she said, bending her frame onto one of the lounge chairs on the porch before she crossed her legs in the green linen pants she wore with a crisp white V-neck tee and gold wedge sandals.

Renee sighed as she closed the front door and claimed a

seat as well. "Go ahead. Let me hear it," she began as she tapped her fingernails against the arm of the chair.

Jaime hid a smile. "I'm moving," she said.

Renee's facial expression quickly cycled through relief, shock, confusion, acceptance, and then sadness. "Jaime," she said softly as she settled back against her chair and crossed her arms over her chest as she looked down the street at Jaime's house in the distance.

She remained silent and let her friend—the analytical chief executive officer—process that bit of truth.

"We did not think this one through," Renee said with a shake of her head.

Jaime chuckled.

Renee's eyes shifted over to her. Hard. "What's funny?" she asked.

Jaime held up her hand as she continued to smile. "Aria said the same thing. I mean word for word," she explained.

Renee mustered a grin. A brief one. "Everything is changing," she said softly before she held her caftan out enough to pull her knees to her chest beneath its cover.

"Hey," she called over to her, worried that Renee had renewed her affair with alcohol. "You good?"

Renee shrugged one shoulder. "I should be," she began. "Kieran is firmly settled in Atlanta with her husband, and Heather is living the life she always wanted in Cali, but I miss my kids. I...I miss my life the way it was...before everything. But that makes me a horrible mother. Right?"

"No. It makes you human," she said, leaning forward to set her elbows on her knees.

Jaime was well aware that Kieran's pill addiction and Aaron's full transition to become Heather had taken a toll on her friend years ago.

"They're my kids. I loved and supported them through it all and they both hauled ass once they got their shit together," she said, pursing her lips and releasing a long breath as she blinked away rising tears. "I want them here with me."

Jaime sat back in her chair again. "Or," she began slowly. Softly. "Are you afraid of being alone?"

Renee looked reflective. Her eyes dropped to take in the Hernandez couple walk by with a wave as the wife, Leela, splayed her hands on her round belly. "Maybe," she said with the hint of a smile that spoke to remembering her days of carrying her babies in her womb. "Or maybe I'm more afraid of being forgotten."

A tear broke free and raced down her cheek.

Jaime jumped up and quickly took the steps to sit on the arm of the chair to pull Renee's head to her chest as she rubbed large circles onto her back. "Is that what Jackson being here was all about?"

Renee scoffed as she swiped her tears away with her thumbs. "I'm just paying back the bitch for what she did to me," she said, speaking of the mistress who became Jackson's wife and the mother of his outside child. "Fuck her."

They shared a chuckle. "Isn't it more like fuck Jackson?" Jaime drawled.

"That, too."

That caused a belly laugh that echoed through the quiet neighborhood.

Renee released a long sigh as she clutched Jaime's hand. "What are we going to do without your bougie ass around here making us all step up our game?" she asked.

"Take a moment and think, 'What would Jaime do?'" she suggested.

Renee leaned back to eye her. "That is *not* what 'WWJD' means!"

Jaime shrugged a shoulder and held up her hands. She gave Renee one last hug around her shoulders before moving back across the porch to reclaim her seat. A door slammed. They both looked up the block and their mouths fell open as Aria marched across her porch and stomped down the steps before eating up the distance between the two homes with long strides down the middle of the street that spoke of her annoyance. Her 'fro bounced up and down with each step and the fading summer sun highlighted the brown tips.

She looked glorious, even if she was fueled with frustration.

"What's going on here?" Renee asked as she rose to her bare feet.

Jaime rose as well and leaned against the banister. "That was quick?" she said to Aria.

"Exactly!" Aria snapped as she stepped up on the curb.

"What was quick?' Renee asked.

"Kingston's nut," she replied as she climbed the steps.

"Oh," Renee said.

"I thought I was babysitting," Jaime said lightly.

Renee arched a brow. "You? Babysit? That's not WWJD. Okay?" she said with a chuckle.

True.

Aria's children, beautiful ten-year-old Nehru, and handsome six-year-old Nyheim were her godchildren, but she kept her duties to encouraging conversations, keeping their secrets, and buying them expensive gifts for birthdays and holidays. The kids loved it that way and so did she.

"I already breastfed and put the biggest baby in my house to bed," Aria drawled with an eye roll.

They all laughed.

"How about dinner out somewhere? My treat," Jaime offered, not ready to end their time together for the night.

"I have some quarterly reports to read through for an early morning appointment," Renee said with obvious regret.

"I gotta get back to the kids and finish an article I'm editing about the current state of police reform," Aria said. "I just wanted to see what Renee had to say about the news."

"Disappointed," she offered. "At least we have until the house sells."

"Right," Aria agreed, using her phone to check the nanny cams in her kids' room.

Better now than later.

"Actually..." Jaime began.

Renee and Aria shared a look.

"Luc asked me to move in with him," she admitted smiling as if showing her teeth to her friends would make it great news. "We're not waiting for the sale of the house or the wedding."

Renee and Aria shared another look.

"When are you moving?" they asked in unison.

Jaime slid her hands into the pockets of her pants. "I'm going to try to sell the furniture along with the house and the movers are coming this weekend to get my clothes and things," she said.

The women shared another look before Renee opened her arms and motioned for both of them to step into an embrace. They did, with Jaime weaving her arms around Renee's and Aria's waists with all three of their foreheads touching.

"This will not be the last time we see each other," she said.

Neither Renee nor Aria said anything, but their doubtful faces spoke volumes.

Luc took a sip of his cognac on the rocks as the bright, colorful lights of the strip club played against his face and the bass-driven music seemed to thump against his body. Over the rim of his glass, he didn't watch the gyrations of the dancers in their booth. He was with a group of well-known rappers who had tons of money and tons of fans, and the dancers wanted both. Strip clubs were not his scene on the regular, but he knew from his days running the studio that the wild environment was one the best gauges if a song was a banger or not. So his focus was on the men in the crowd.

Their eyes might be on the nearly nude women, but their heads and shoulders rocked to the music while their lips mouthed the hook.

"I told you it was hot."

Luc fought not to frown at the whisper close to his ear. His nostrils were assailed with the hot smell of weed and liquor that tinged the breath of his rap artist Blaze as he raised his glass in a silent toast to him. "So, is this the new single?" he asked.

"Told you," Blaze said, his mouth filled with diamond-encrusted gold teeth. "The streets already love it."

Bzzzzzz.

Luc reached for his cell phone in the back pocket of his sweatpants just as a stripper removed her bikini top and leaned in to jiggle them in his face. He leaned back from one of her nipples almost poking his eye as he checked his phone.

A text from Jaime.

She was at his—their—apartment. He was ready to get home to her.

"Lonely," he read.

The next text was a picture of her naked in the middle of his—their—bed with her legs spread wide. *That* stirred his dick to his life. "I'm out," he said to Blaze who nodded as he ogled two nude dancers twerking for their life to get his attention.

He eased past the eager dancer and left the VIP section, shaking hands or giving daps to those he knew as he made his way toward the door. When he was finally standing outside, he took a deep breath of the fresh air, glad to be free of the smell of body oils, weed, fried food, and dude sweat.

Luc dialed Jaime. "On the way, baby," he said as he climbed behind the wheel of his Bentley.

She laughed softly. "That's what I thought."

He smiled broadly and accelerated out of the parking lot toward home.

Graham couldn't sleep.

He sat up in his king-sized bed and looked out the large bay windows of his massive loft condo in the DUMBO section of Brooklyn. The moon was full and high and lit the front half of the space with a silvery blue haze. Naked, he climbed from the bed in the center of the loft and walked over to look over at the Manhattan Bridge over the East River and then down at the cobblestone streets below.

It wasn't a desire to see the city nightscape that kept him awake; he was used to that.

He turned and look to the rear of the loft where dozens of his paintings and framed sketches leaned against the wall. Far more than that had been sold over the years and one even hung on the wall of the Museum of Fine Art. Never had he imagined when he turned to art during his stay in rehab that it would become his life's work. He did it for love, but the acclaim and the wealth were nice.

Very nice.

Thoughts of his art career weren't on his mind either.

He turned and crossed the room to flip through the stacks until he found the one he sought. A large realistic drawing of Jaime he sketched during his days using the rear room of the Bedford Community Center in New York as his studio. He'd painted her from memory months after they said goodbye on that rooftop. His love for her was in every stroke of his charcoal to paper. His longing in every shadow. His regret that love was not enough in every smudge.

That was his sketch of both his love and his heartbreak.

As he held it in his hand, remembering how his thoughts of her had plagued him in the two weeks since he returned to the States, he knew it was time to let Jaime—both the painting and the woman who served as its muse—go for once and for all.

Chapter 5

One week later

Jaime tapped the stylus against the iPad as she studied the mock-up for a kitchen redesign in a mansion in Alpine, New Jersey. She used the tablet to reconfigure the layout of the custom cabinetry. "What do you think of this instead?" she asked, turning the screen to hand it across her desk to Hamilton Fuqua, one of the three design consultants at her firm.

She shared a look with Madison Archer, her head design consultant and her second in command.

Hamilton was young, stylish, and beyond creative. Although he'd only been with her firm for the last few months, she loved his aesthetic and was constantly testing him to see his growth. He looked more like a football player than a designer, and that made her respect his eye even more. "Much better," he said with a nod as he picked up a large white binder on the corner of her desk and flipped through swatches of tile. "There's more room under the cabinets and this pattern won't seem as busy if you use it now."

Madison gave her a surreptitious wink as she tapped her stylus against her Kente cloth-covered iPad.

Jaime looked at the navy subway tile fashioned into a herringbone pattern. "This is the first tile I considered," she said, stroking it with her fingertips before cutting her eyes up to him. "You remember that?"

Hamilton nodded. "I thought you should design the entire kitchen around it," he said.

He was right.

"Let's put it on the virtual board with the second color palette for the client to choose from," she said firmly to Madison.

"Right away," she said, rising from her seat.

Hamilton did the same.

Jaime pulled up her calendar on her private iPad. "What time is their appointment?" she asked, furrowing her brow as she looked at her busy schedule for next week.

"Tomorrow at three," Madison said, pausing at the door with her hand on the handle.

Madison was taking lead because Jaime and Luc were leaving for an extended weekend in Miami. "I won't be off the grid so keep me updated to their choices and definitely if something goes wrong," Jaime said.

"Absolutely," Madison said, before opening the glass door and leaving.

Jaime glanced up when Hamilton paused, and she saw the hope in his eyes. "Not yet," she said with a gentle smile meant to be encouraging.

She generally didn't allow new design consultants to attend appointments—where they might be unexpectedly asked by a client for input—until six months of employment.

He nodded in understanding before leaving.

Jaime began checking emails, swiftly swiping her fingers across the touch screen to delegate them to trash or to respond.

"Knock-knock."

She glanced at the door to find her administrative assistant, Katie. "How much of my time do you need at this exact moment?" Jaime asked as she directed her gaze back to the screen.

"Less than a sec," Katie promised, wearing a fuchsia pantsuit and bright green glasses that somehow worked. "You have a delivery."

Jaime looked surprised. "I wasn't expecting anything," she said.

"And your mother is on line one."

Jaime frowned as she rose from her seat behind her desk, an A-frame base of wood with a glass top. She smoothed her hands over the bright red pencil skirt she wore with a red silk tank and heels. "Package first, then my mother," she said taking long strides across her glass-enclosed office situated in the middle of the two-thousand-square-foot office space.

Katie reclaimed her seat at the glass desk in front of Jaime's enclosure while Jaime continued to the front doors to find a large, flat box. "How are you today?" Jaime asked the uniformed delivery man as she looked down at the package now leaning against the chairs in her reception area.

She gasped and paused for a second as she recognized the slashing handwriting.

"I'm good, and you?" he said.

Normally she opened packages upon delivery to ensure nothing was damaged and it was the correct item she had ordered for clients. She decided to forgo that as she took the machine he offered to sign for the delivery. "Thanks," she said, even as her heart continued to flutter.

For a long moment after he walked back out through the glass doors etched with her name, Jaime eyed the package.

"Everything okay?" Katie called over. "Should I get it taken down to the warehouse?"

She rented two storage areas in the basement to keep

design elements that she owned and used for staging or to sell at a fair price to clients.

Jaime clasped her hands together and shook her head. "No, this is for me," she said, picking it up and finding it not too heavy for her to manage as she carried it into her office to sit on one of the four easels she kept for design presentations with her staff.

She felt silly for how her hands trembled as she undid the tape running along the seam on the side of the box. For some reason, she thought it might be a nude Graham painted as he remembered the heat fueled sex they shared against a door in Grenada six weeks ago.

His raw and rough cry as he climaxed seemed to echo around her.

She grunted a little and gave herself a shake to release the memory while she opened the lid with trepidation. To prevent her employees who were working at their stations around her glass office from seeing the wrong thing, she leaned in. The sight of her face surprised her, and her mouth fell open at the beauty of the sketch. Not her beauty—this wasn't about ego—but the exquisiteness of his artistry. His skill.

Graham was truly a master.

With bated breath similar to what he evoked in hot passion, she removed the framed sketch from the box and held it in her hands as her eyes devoured it. Missing not one detail. Not even the effort he placed into a strand of hair that tended to fall over one of her eyes. The pout of her mouth as if ready to be kissed. The softness of her shoulders before the charcoal faded, leaving the viewer to imagine what should come next.

And her eyes.

So haunting. So full of raw emotion she recognized as the vulnerability of love. The sweet mix of fear and excitement.

"Oh, Graham," Jaime whispered, unable—or unwilling—to accept the cause for the tears that rose.

Beneath her right thumb was his signature. G. Walker. She stroked it and felt an odd energy course through her body. She couldn't explain it and didn't want to accept it. That awareness of him continued to pulse even in his absence.

Raising her thumb, she eyed the date. 2016. Sometime after the rooftop farewell. A lifetime ago.

She settled the frame back on the easel and walked backward away from it as she continued to study herself in the sketch. All of her that he saw and captured. Long after she reclaimed her seat and leaned back in it as she crossed her legs, she turned to face the window. But even in the reflection, her eyes sought the picture. Got lost in it.

Wondered just what it meant for Graham to send it to her. No message was included.

Or was she missing it?

"It doesn't matter," she said. "*I'm* done. *It's* over."

She eyed the picture again. He was so talented. And this was a piece from years ago. She thought of the mural that she loved at just half its completion. Curiosity nipped at her. Unable to fight it, she turned to her computer.

"Graham Walker," she said as she typed his name into her favorite search engine.

There was an article announcing the mural but no full photo of it. Would she have to go back to Grenada to see the final product?

And was Graham back in the States?

A click of his upcoming events link revealed he had an art show coming up in a couple of weeks. In New York. Her heart raced at that.

"I don't think I can ever be what you need, or understand, or fully forgive. Our past together is the very reason I just don't believe we can have a future."

He was right.

Had she loved him? Without question.

Had she struggled to see a future for them? Absolutely.

Just seeing a woman eye his good looks and towering physique led to her fear they were an old client—someone who had shared the body of the man she loved. There had been plenty of heated arguments and frigid cold silences.

"Jaime? Your mother," Katie reminded her.

She leaned forward and pressed the button to talk. "Put her through. Thanks," she said, answering the call and placing it on speaker. "Hello, Mother."

"I hate calling *there*," Virginia said, her tone haughty.

Jaime arched a brow. "And she's off to the races," she muttered with sarcasm.

"What's that?" Virginia asked.

"When you say *there* like that, do you mean calling me at work?" Jaime asked. "At the business I own that has employees who rely on me to provide salaries so that they can contribute to society and feed their families? Is that the *there* you speak of?"

Virginia sighed. "Now that you're getting married... *again*," she whispered.

Jaime rolled her eyes.

"I don't see why you need to keep doing *that*."

The *that* was as condescending as the *there*.

She tensed and rolled her neck to relieve it. Every time her mother would show a sliver of growth in changing her antiquated views of gender roles, Jaime held out hope that a tiger could change its stripes.

And every damn time I'm wrong.

It was her mother's hand in her raising and mother-to-daughter chats when out of earshot of their husbands that had molded Jaime into the Stepford wife willing to take mental abuse behind closed doors as long as the façade stayed pristine. Even after his affair with Jessa was revealed and

Jaime left, her mother had formed an alliance with Eric's parents to convince them to remain married using everything from his Catholic religion to shaming her for wanting more for her life than a marriage that had been framed with disdain and coldness.

And so much hate after that misdial led to him overhearing me and Pleasure having sex . . .

Pushing aside the hurt that still lingered over her mother's choice of marriage by any means over her own daughter's happiness, Jaime settled her gaze on the sketch. There in her eyes was also the sadness of never feeling good enough for her mother. With a shake of her head and lick of her lips, Jaime closed her eyes. "Mother, the influence you had on me during my marriage with Eric will not be the same with Luc and me, please know that," she said, not caring that her tone was clipped.

"The influence?" Virginia asked.

Jaime was sure she was clutching the string of Tiffany pearls around her neck.

Miss Prim and Proper Pearls.

She smiled, remembering Graham's old nickname for her during his days as Pleasure the stripper, when his sultry dick-slinging performances awakened desires in her and caused sensitive spots to tingle like she never knew they could in her innocence.

"You know, Mother, you need a little *pleasure* in your life," Jaime said with a chuckle.

"I have my bridge tournaments and charity work for the church," Virginia insisted, ever the wife, mother, and socialite extraordinaire.

The chuckle grew to a laugh.

"What's funny?" she snapped.

"Nothing, Mother," Jaime said tucking her jet-black blunt bob behind her ear.

"I like Luc—"

"You also loved Eric, who was horrible to me and tried to kill his pregnant mistress after stalking her, while he was trying to reconcile with me," Jaime interrupted, so desperately wanting her mother to see the error of her own ways. "You also loved his parents, and one is now serving time for the attempted murder of Jessa's daughter. You liking Luc is most definitely *not* a selling point, Mother."

The line went quiet.

Jaime dropped her head in her hands. She wasn't sure if Virginia Osten-Pine's feelings were hurt or if she was feigning that they were. The master manipulator. Virginia's little stunts had taught Jaime how it felt to be manipulated by others. She wasn't here for it anymore.

Not from her or anyone else.

So she remained silent, adamant to no longer play the "Mother, I'm Sorry" game.

Virginia surprised her by just ending the call, causing Jaime to eye the phone.

Hmmm That's new.

She twisted her mouth as she tapped the phone against its base, fighting the urge to call her mother back before she finally hung up the receiver. "Nope," she said, determined not to fall for her mother's newest chess move.

"And my obedience is the queen she's trying to capture," Jaime said dryly.

Knock-knock.

She looked up from logging off her computer and smiled at Luc standing in the now open doorway. "Hey, you," she said, surprised and pleased to see him like they hadn't just had breakfast in their kitchen that very morning.

Things were good. Damn good.

Rising from her desk, she crossed the room to reach him, loving the way his dark eyes missed nothing about her body as she came to stand before him. Her heels raised her height, and it was so easy to press her hand to his chest and kiss him. "You would think we didn't live together," she whispered against his mouth before giving it a quick lick. "Why are you *sooooo* fuckable, Luc Sinclair?"

He pressed his hand against her lower back. "Why is your office glass?" he asked, dipping his head to press a kiss to the spot behind her earlobe. "Because I would fuck you right now."

Warm with desire, Jaime looked at him. "On the jet then?" she asked.

His eyes darkened. "On the jet," he promised before gently sucking the tip of her tongue into his mouth.

"Shit," she swore in a gasp when he freed it.

They both had been so busy clearing their schedules for their weekend getaway that they hadn't made love in a few days. It was clear they were more than ready. "Let's roll," she said, turning to cross the office and gather her purse and briefcase.

"No briefcase," Luc said.

"No briefcase," she agreed, putting it back inside the short wooden file cabinet near her desk.

"Damn, this is dope as hell."

Jaime froze and cut her eyes over to see Luc—her beautifully sexy Luc—standing before the easel studying the large sketch of her. "Yes, it's pretty cool," she said lightly as she tucked her designer clutch under her arm and grabbed her keys. "Did you get my luggage?"

"Yeah."

She trailed her glossy almond-shaped nails across his back as she passed him to reach the door. "Babe," she called to him, willing him to turn from the sketch made by her ex. She still couldn't explain why he had sent it to her.

The same ex she'd fucked during the trip the man staring at the drawing had paid for.

"Where'd you get it?" he asked, glancing over at her.

Fuck.

"I commissioned it," she lied. "Years ago. I forgot about it 'til recently."

Luc reached out and stroked the glass before sliding his hands into the pockets of the vintage denims he wore with a crisp striped button-up shirt.

Jaime felt uncomfortable as he continued to stare at it. Her nerves felt shot. "Luc, you ready?"

"Yeah. Yeah, I'm ready," he said, finally turning to join her outside the office.

She turned off the overhead lighting before closing and locking the door.

"Have fun this weekend," Katie said with a wave.

Luc's phone vibrated with a call and he reached for his phone from his back pocket. "Luc," he answered.

"We will," Jaime said, sliding her hand into his free one.

He squeezed it even as he began giving sharp instructions to his assistant. She raised his hand in hers and pressed her nose to his wrist to inhale the scent of his crisp and cool cologne.

I like the warm spiciness of Graham's better.

Her eyes widened at the impulsive thought just as Luc brought his arm up to wrap around her shoulders and bring her body back against his, their hands still entwined as he continued his phone call. She worried about where the comparison between her past and her present came from. She nibbled on her bottom lip, her eyes finding and locking on the drawing until the elevators closed and blocked it from her view.

Jaime leaned against the railing of the yacht as she sipped a flute of La Fête du Rosé, a Black-owned rosé made in Saint-Tropez, France. The South Beach Miami sun was hot, but the speed of the vessel caused a cool draft to blow against her body as she took in the view of the water and the lavish beach homes lining the shore. Another surprise from Luc. The private jet landed but instead of being chauffeured to the home she thought they were renting, they spent the weekend aboard a luxury yacht complete with staff.

The setting, atmosphere, food, and vibes were good, but things were off between them.

She turned and leaned against the rail, her sheer cover-up pressed to her body by the wind, as she eyed him sitting on a deck chair swiping away on his phone. Their argument that morning still lingered between them. They'd spent most of the day in the same room or area of the yacht but pointedly on other sides of the space.

"Excuse me, Mr. Sinclair."

Jaime looked over at the steward, a fit man in his mid-thirties with a bald head and full beard in a navy polo shirt, cargo shorts, and deck shoes.

"Lunch is served on the aft deck," he said.

"Thank you," Luc said, turning off his phone to look over at her. "Hungry?"

She nodded. "I could eat," she replied.

Ever the gentleman, Luc rose and waved his hand for her to go up the stairs before him.

She had to admit with his black aviator shades on and tattoo-covered chest bared, Luc's sexiness could not be denied—even in the coolness of their annoyance with each other. Instead of going straight to the stairs, Jaime sauntered up to him and ran her fingers along his stomach.

Luc grabbed her wrist and held up her hand. "Stop playing games, Jaime," he said. "I didn't like them much as a kid and I damn sure don't give a fuck about them now."

"I'm not playing games, Luc," she said, leaning toward him as she looked up at him. "I need to make up for this morning."

He snatched off his shades and tossed them onto the deck

chair beside him. "This morning," he scoffed. "Don't you mean all damn weekend?"

True.

She reached down between them to grip his dick. "I like to have sex when I'm in the mood," she began, rising on her toes to lick at his lips. "I wasn't in the mood...so no sex. That's my right. I'm not fucking any man on his demand."

His lean face filled with annoyance as he clenched his jaw.

"I don't owe you my pussy for this trip or this engagement ring," she continued, her voice barely above a whisper but still clear with her intent to establish her rights within their relationship. "Even when I tell you during sex that it's yours...it's still *mine.*"

"Yo, Jaime," he began.

She continued to stroke him to hardness inside his shorts. "Now you want to eat whatever the chef cooked for lunch *or* you wanna eat me and help keep me in the mood?"

Luc flexed his broad shoulders as he looked away into the water and then back at her. "I'm going to fuck the shit out of you," he promised before he snatched her hand from his dick and then picked her up.

She snuggled her face against his neck and sucked away his sweat, wrapping her legs around his waist as he walked them across the deck and down the stairs. She missed the heat of his hard dick in her hand and longed to have it inside her.

"Hold lunch," Luc said to someone before he opened the door to their cabin and entered, locking the door with a nudge of his foot.

He dropped her onto the middle of the bed before working his shorts off to kick away with his foot.

Graham's dick is curved.

No. No. No, she thought as she pressed her eyes closed.

All weekend long her thoughts betrayed Luc. Comparing him to Graham in every way. Height. Weight. Length of dick. Stroke maneuvers. Amount of sweat. Kisses. Nipple licking. The climax face. Clit strokes. All of it.

In bed and out.

Laughs. Taste in clothes. Music choice. Politics.

Anything. Everything.

Focus, Jaime. Focus. This is Luc. You love him. You love fucking him. Focus!

Luc undressed her.

Graham would taste every part of my body he exposed. Focus!

She spread her legs as he climbed onto the bed between them. Her clit throbbed with life as he opened her plump lips and licked the swollen flesh. She arched her back and dug her fingernails into his shoulders as she cried out. "Luc," she gasped as she rotated her hips.

But that wasn't real.

Between her guilt at letting the spirit of Graham invade their sex and her anger at not being able to control the direction of her thoughts, Jaime's desire had faded. Sex with Graham had opened the door to feelings she thought she had long since left behind. That drawing of her kicked the door wide open.

Shit.

It was wrong to judge one man against the other. Luc was everything she could wish for in a mate: loving, sexy, stable, passionate, loyal, and kind. And now everything felt shadowed by memories of Graham.

And this man she loved deserved more than that.

Focus, Jaime. Get your shit together.

But she didn't. She couldn't. Even with her grand speech of having control over her body she went through the motions, pretended to climax, and then turned over onto her knees so that she could bury her face into a pillow as Luc entered her swift and hard. She pretended to moan and clutch the sheets. She talked dirty. She clutched her walls against his tool with each of his deep thrusts. And when she was ready for the performance to end, she took the lead and worked her hips back and forth to pull down on his hardness.

That was a guaranteed quick nut, and she was soon rewarded with his.

Luc flattened their bodies onto the bed with him lying on her back and his dick still inside her. "Am I too heavy?" he asked.

"No," she rushed to say, grabbing his arm to keep him there. With her. On her. In her.

Everything had changed and she knew *she* had to fix it to save her relationship.

The question was: How?

"Baby. We're home."

At Luc's nudging, Jaime awakened with her head leaning against his shoulder in the rear of the car service SUV. Rapidly blinking with a grunt, she saw their apartment building. Last she remembered they had boarded the private jet at the airport in Miami. "Damn, I blacked out," she joked.

Luc chuckled. "The boat must have worn you out. I had to carry you off the plane," he said as she raised her head and he looked outside the window to make sure traffic was clear before he opened the door.

The familiar sounds of New York traffic flooded the interior of the car before Luc exited and solidly closed the door behind him.

Working the kinks from her neck and shoulders, she gathered her designer tote and shades from the seat as the driver raised the rear door to remove their luggage and Luc came around the vehicle to open her door and hold out his hand. She gave him a little smile as she slid her hand in his hand and accepted his help down onto the sidewalk. As he moved to take their rolling luggage, she looked up at the rays of the sun glinting off the glass of the towering buildings.

"I'm glad we came back early enough to rest up for work tomorrow," she said as they entered the building together.

"Let's order in something to eat," he said as they crossed the marbled floor to the elevator.

"Cool," she said, eyeing their reflection in the polished elevator doors.

She and Luc looked good together. Young, polished, and stylish, surrounded by wealth and affluence in the heart of Manhattan, fresh from a weekend trip aboard a yacht and a jet. The woman she saw was a successful professional with a thriving business and staff who respected and relied on her. A woman in control of her destiny, standing just as tall and equal to her man.

So different from her suburban life as the perfect wife in Richmond Hills.

She felt emotional at the thought of her growth. Her reemergence. Her claim over her own life.

The doors opened and the image disappeared. Her resolve to stay true to her own wants, needs, and desires did not.

Inside their condo, she immediately stepped out of the heels she wore with a white sundress. She pressed her bare feet to the hardwood floors and raised her arms wide to playfully turn, causing the skirt to rise like a parasol around her waist and expose the sheer white thong she wore. "It's good to be home," she said.

Luc paused in shifting through the mail to look up at her. His eyes darkened as he unceremoniously dropped the stack back onto the side table. With two long steps, he was beside her and picking her body up against his. She wrapped her arms and legs around his neck and waist as his hands cupped her buttocks beneath the skirt.

"I thought we were hungry," Jaime said, as he walked them to the rear of the condo to the owner's suite.

"Hungry. Horny. Same difference," he said as he pressed delicious kisses to the valley of her breasts exposed by the V-neck of the dress.

"Let me help you," she said, sliding the straps down and exposing fast hardening nipples to his clever tongue.

"Hmmmmm," he moaned as he circled each brown tip.

She looked over across the distance of the spacious room and she froze as she eyed Graham's framed sketch of her on the wall above their bed. Her stomach tightened. Her eyes were wide. Her heart beat fast. And hard.

As Luc sat down on the edge of their large bed with his mouth greedily licking at one of her nipples Jaime kept her eyes on herself in the sketch. "Luc, how did that picture get here?" she asked.

He looked back over his shoulder. "Nice surprise? I had it shipped here and hung while we were in Miami," he said, before turning back to reclaim her nipple.

But her thoughts were elsewhere. For her, as she stared at the strokes of Graham's charcoal against the paper to recreate her image, she felt an energy glide over her body. A thrill.

A dirty little secret.

She rubbed Luc's back and pressed kisses to his brow as she kept her eyes sealed on the drawing—this representation of a past she shared with this other man. Her Graham. Her pleasure.

In truth, it was intriguing. Invigorating.

Her desire came on in a rush. Her nipples hardened. Her clit throbbed. Her belly warmed. Her juices made her wet. Ready.

Luc slid his long fingers beneath her panties.

"Rip 'em," she whispered in his ear as she felt plugged into a new energy source.

He did with a grunt.

"Fuck me," she whispered near his ear with a hot lick of his lobe that caused him to shiver as she eyed the drawing of

Graham's and saw the love he once had for her sketched in her eyes.

Her gasp was deep—from the very pit of her belly—when Luc raised her and entered her wetness to fill her.

"Aaaah," he cried out against her throat. "Damn it's wet." Wetter than ever. Hotter than before.

She could believe it. For her, Luc was there in body but so was Graham in spirit. And she rode them slowly, inch by inch, to the most explosive climax ever.

Chapter 6

"I have to speak my truth."

Graham clasped his hands in the space between his knees where he sat in the circle of people at the Bedford Community Center. Their chatter died down to silence and twelve sets of eyes landed on him. He cleared his throat before bending slightly at the waist to pick up his bottle of water.

"Stop stalling, Graham," Olive said teasingly with an encouraging smile.

He returned the smile of the full-figured woman with a milk-white complexion. She, along with the majority of the people gathered there with him, had become a family of sorts. They had helped each other to embrace the reality of their addiction and then fought to not let it control or overcome their lives. This group of people he proudly led was his salvation and they deserved the truth.

"I am Graham Walker, and I am a sex addict in recovery...for six weeks," he finished, glancing down at the polished wood floors before looking back up at them.

Some eyes were filled with surprise and many more with understanding.

Just last week he had proclaimed himself in recovery for over five years.

"I've avoided admitting that to you, which is a lie of omission," Graham acknowledged. "I apologize to you all for it. This is a system built on truth and trust. I violated both of those. Forgive me. I was ashamed of my relapse."

"Talk about it."

Graham eyed Bob, a tall and thin man of sixty with long salt and pepper hair, a kind face, and wise eyes, who ran the group when his travels kept him from doing so. "I happened upon a woman from my past whom I hadn't seen in years but thought about often," he said, glancing up at the overhead bright lighting. "Someone I loved but couldn't be with because of my past as a stripper and consort. But here she was suddenly. Just as beautiful, sexy, and her eyes filled with just as much desire for me as I had for her. I fought it, but I couldn't resist having her again."

He closed his eyes and shook his head at the stark memory of being deeply planted inside Jaime once again. "But my issue with it was whether it was my attraction for her or just pure horniness once the door to my desire was opened," he continued with a deep breath. "At that moment I didn't care. I didn't give a shit about anything but sexing her. Pleasing her. I needed it."

"Whoo," Olive exclaimed, fanning herself with her hand.

"You okay, Olive?" he asked with a hint of a smile. She was always the most raucous in the group. With her came lots of levity.

"Continue," she said, crossing her legs.

"Thanks," he replied.

Graham chewed on his bottom lip as he gathered his thoughts. "I fought hard to overcome my past and not repeat it. Hopefully, by being honest tonight with you and myself I can get back on track."

They applauded him and he nodded in thanks.

"I think I was the last to speak, but would anyone else care to share anything?" Graham asked.

Everyone remained silent. A few shook their heads.

"Then let us all stay strengthened this week in our fight to maintain control over our minds, our bodies, and our lives," he said, closing out their weekly session.

As everyone folded their chairs to place them back on the racks lining the wall, Graham focused on grabbing the oversized rolling garbage can and gathering up the trash from their refreshment table.

Bzzzzzz...Bzzzzzz...Bzzzzzz...

"Night, Graham," several of the SA members called to him before leaving.

He gave them a hand wave as he reached for his phone and answered. "I'm on the way," he said before she could speak.

The call ended.

He chuckled and finished cleaning up before he left the red brick building and locked it with the key that had been entrusted to him years ago. Looking around at the quiet streets of one of New York's suburban towns, he put his keys in the pocket of his running shorts and placed his Air Pods in his ears to fill them with Jay-Z's "4:44" before he took off at a run. This sprint from the community center after their weekly meetings always reminded him of his nightly runs where he called the town of Bedford, New York home.

First his careers—selling dick, and then art—led him all over the world. He'd seen and experienced more culture than he ever dreamed about through his struggles in life. And he loved the times he would rent a loft in a European country or connect with the history of his ancestors somewhere on the African continent. Graham was most at peace in other lands. His creativity soared.

He slowed to a jog on the tree-lined street and lightly tapped the rear of his shiny blacked-out SUV parked on the street where he'd left it to run to the community center. He glanced up at the two-story French colonial-style house with wrought iron railings. He continued across the mowed lawn to take the steps of the brick wraparound porch two at a time to ring the doorbell.

It was here that he felt most at home.

The door opened and he was blessed with the warmth of his mother's smile.

"I thought you were headed back to Brooklyn without stopping by," Cara said, as she stepped back to let him enter. "And I made lasagna, too."

Graham hugged his mother before touching the gray hair at her temples with a wink. "You'll be sixty this year," he reminded her.

She playfully slapped his hands away. "Gray hair is a crown of splendor; it is attained in the way of righteousness," she said. "Proverbs 16:31."

His mother always had just the right Bible quote on the tip of her tongue, ready to slide in any and every conversation. Once he had resented her and the religion she loved. He'd felt unprotected by the walls of her church and her God. What used to be a source of tension between them for years he now accepted as her way of finding and keeping her place in the world. "Where's Pops?" he asked.

"Outside with that motorcycle," she said.

Graham immediately headed through the kitchen and over to the side door to open it. His father knelt on the other side of the Harley Davidson he purchased after his heart attack over a decade ago. Just the top of his silvery hair was visible and the clank of metal on metal battled with the raspy soulful voice of Teddy Pendergrass singing "Love T.K.O." playing from his phone.

It was while he was in the hospital recovering from the attack that a nurse unknowingly revealed to his father that Graham was the stripper known as "Pleasure." Tylar, a reformed lady's man, whose affairs had led to his parents' divorce, had advised him to make the money dancing while he could, and then to move on. Their relationship, and how freely they talked to one another, would shock most people, be it worked for them. No one, outside of his therapist, knew him better than his father from whom he inherited his towering height, good looks, and love for women. Not even Graham losing his virginity to one of his father's many girlfriends—Essie Nunes—as a teenager had come between them. Tylar Walker used to see women as expendable receptacles for his nut.

Thank God he changed.

Since his parents re-wed twelve years ago, Tylar was proud to let people know the old dog happily sat on the porch and watch the cars go by. He had come on in. Tylar and Cara had found their happily ever after. As he leaned in the doorway and listened to his father sing along to R&B classics while he tinkered with his ride, Graham remembered advice his father gave him from what they thought was going to be his deathbed:

"Love over sex always wins at this game called life."

A marked difference from the advice of his whoring days.

Love.

"Takes a fool to lose twice. And start all over again," Graham mouthed along with his father and Teddy, thinking of Jaime and wishing he didn't feel so foolish.

★ ★ ★

"Congrats on selling the house."

Seated at a round table in the center of the crowded high-end soul food restaurant with Aria, Kingston, and Renee, Jaime smiled at Luc over the rim of her glass as she took a deep sip of sparkling water. "Thank you," she said to Kingston.

"So, when's the wedding date?"

Jaime froze but forced her body to relax before anyone caught it. "We haven't set it yet," she answered Renee.

Luc shifted in his seat when two pairs of feminine eyes landed on him. "I'm ready. It's on your girl," he said in that deep voice of his.

"Damn right, get that pressure off of you," Kingston said.

The eyes shifted to Jaime.

She ignored them and motioned to their waiter. "More sparkling water," she said when he reached the table.

"Anyone else need anything?" the young man asked with his eyes constantly going back to Luc, who was oblivious as he and Kingston discussed last night's baseball game.

"No, we're all good," Jaime said, not quite sure if he was gay or a fan of Luc's many top-charting rap, pop, or R&B artists. "Thank you."

The server walked away.

She turned her head to find the two sets of eyes still on her. "What?" she asked with a frown.

"The wedding?" Renee reminded her as she smoothed her hand over her close-shaven head, looking stunning with oversized jewel tone earrings and a satiny emerald V-neck pantsuit.

"As soon as we decide, I'll let y'all know," Jaime said, leaning back in her chair to give the waiter room to set a fresh glass of ice and a small bottle of sparkling water on the table.

Aria reached with her fork to pierce a piece of Kingston's perfectly cooked, medium-rare steak. The cost was her husband leaning over to press a kiss to her neck. She looked as delectable as the meal in the bodycon print dress she wore with her curly afro in full floss mode.

Luc set his elbows on the table before leaning over to Jaime. "I'm gone eat you on the ride home," he promised for her ears alone.

Jaime stroked his square jawline and softly giggled.

"Really, y'all? Really?" Renee snapped.

Both couples looked over to where she sat. "My date for the evening is the bag chair," she said, waving her hand toward Jaime and Aria's pocketbooks. "And everyone else is clearly in a pregame mode for sex tonight while I'm Only the Lonely. Real-ly?"

"Uh-oh," Luc said, before straightening up in his chair.

"Last time I saw Jackson he said y'all was still kicking it," Kingston added, putting his muscled arm behind the back of Aria's chair.

He was rewarded with one of Aria's soft elbows jammed into his side.

"What?" he asked in confusion.

Renee arched a brow. "Really? Jackson told you that?" she asked, her tone deceptively soft. "And did he, by chance, *Kingston*, tell you that I ended things because his dick bends in the middle when it's as hard as *he* can get it?"

"Oh shit," Aria swore.

Jaime's cat-shaped eyes went wide and round with shock.

Luc covered his mouth with his hand—so he could be laughing or frowning. Who knew?

Kingston's eyes were on Renee and he seemed afraid to blink.

"Huh? Did your best buddy Jackson tell you that, Kingston?" Renee asked. "Huh? Did he ask for your medical assistance, *Dr.* Kingston, to make it more like wood...than *fudge*?"

"Great God," Aria gasped.

"No, ma'am," he said to Renee, although he and she weren't very far apart in age.

"You do me a favor, Kingston, since you're toting news like you work for TMZ. You tell Jackson's snitch-bitch ass that in Grenada I met a man with a younger, harder, thicker, and longer—"

"Whoa!" Jaime and Aria said in unison holding up their hands.

Renee crossed her arms over her chest and sat back in her seat.

"O-kay...so, there's a cigar station upstairs," Luc said, rising from his seat to look down at Kingston. "Maybe we should go check it out."

"Yeah. Yup. Yes. *Yes,*" Kingston stressed as he rose as well.

The men headed across the restaurant to the elevator.

"Renee. Renee. Renee. Re-neeee," Jaime said with a wince as she pinched the bridge of her nose.

"What?" she asked, relaxing her stance and reaching for her glass of non-alcoholic fruit punch.

"Why'd you get so mad?" Aria asked. "You knew Kingston and Jackson were still friends and that they talked...the same way you talk to us about stuff. Right?"

Renee shrugged.

Jaime eyed her friend's drink. "Is that alcohol-free?" she asked.

Renee looked offended. "Being single won't be enough to make me relapse," she assured them of her recovery from alcoholism years ago.

"You and Jackson are done?" Jaime asked.

Renee nodded. "I need to get on with my life, and figuring out what it looks like these days," she said, tapping the tip of a coffin-shaped nail against the cloth-covered table. "And I can't do that with one foot stuck in the past."

"True," Jaime said, thinking of her own quandary.

Luc was in her heart, but Graham was in her head.

"You know I'm going to hear about your fudge analogy again later, right?" Aria asked as she picked up a slice of honey-coated cornbread from the napkin-covered basket in the center of the table.

"Seems to me Kingston should be more worried about fucking the hell out of you then what Jackson and I are up to?" Renee said with a slick side-eye.

Aria's mouth fell open and a piece of cornbread threatened to tumble from her tongue. Thankfully, she kept her decorum and swallowed it before responding. "Well damn, what got into you besides Jackson's fudge?" she snapped.

"I owed your husband that one," Renee countered.

Jaime nodded in agreement.

"Okay, yes, you did," Aria agreed. "All these years of marriage and he still doesn't know what to chew and what to spit out? *Damn.*"

"Are things—or his thing—back to normal?" Jaime dared to ask before a sip of water.

"Wait a minute. It's not his thing that's the problem. Kingston is still delivering wood. Thankyouverymuch. It's the lack of *time*," Aria rushed to explain. "Not erection."

Jaime bit back a chuckle. Aria really was funny without trying. She did not let her Ivy League education keep the Newark out of her.

"And no, not yet," she added with a suck of her teeth.

"Sanders hit me up on Facebook," Renee revealed, with her eyes suddenly twinkling with glee.

"Who?" Jaime and Aria asked in unison.

"Chocolate Angel."

Jaime and Aria shared a look.

Renee shrugged.

"I thought that was a vacation fling," Jaime said.

"A hit it and quit it," Aria expanded.

"Maybe it's time for another vacation," Renee said. "Just a little refresher course. He's game if I am."

"Does he want to come here?" Jaime asked.

"No," Renee said after a pause that felt meant to tease them.

The waiter came back to their table. "Would you ladies like to see the dessert menu?" he asked.

Jaime looked down at her half-finished plate of stuffed pork chops and braised collard greens. "No thank you," she said, picking up her phone from the table. "I am stuffed."

Renee looked up at him and eyed his engraved name tag. "I will, Colin," she said with a sultry smile as she extended her hand. "What to do suggest?"

Jaime had been catching up on Graham's Instagram from her fake account when the huskiness of her friend's voice caused her to look up with her brows slightly creased. *Welp. He's not gay*, she thought as he gave Renee a lingering look.

"Do you have *fudge* on the menu?" Aria asked.

Colin eyed the women as they each snorted with laughter. "We have a fudge brownie a la mode," he said.

Aria turned to Renee, barely able to hold in her laughter. "What do you say, Renee, do you want fudge, or have you had enough?"

Jaime felt for the young man as he looked on innocently.

"No more fudge," Renee said, fluttering her fingers at Aria as if to shoo her. "Do you like sweet things, Colin?"

"Jesus," Aria drawled.

"I suggest the sweet potato pie," Colin said.

Deciding to mind her business as her friend stepped fully into her cougardom—or pre-midlife crisis—Jaime returned to Graham's feed. There was a time-lapse photo of a sketch he was doing of a ship during the Atlantic slave trade. She double tapped it to give it a "like".

She had convinced herself that she followed him on social media to keep up with his career and his career alone. It was conceivable since he rarely posted himself. Only his art. His one true love.

She exited the app and then lightly tapped the corner of her phone against her chin. "This was nice," she said, before sitting her device face down on the table. "We need to do this again...if you and Kingston can make up."

Aria chuckled. "Got my man all shook up and shit," she teased.

"Kingston and I are fine," Renee assured them. "And I agree this was fun. Maybe next time I will be dating—"

"An adult, hopefully," Aria inserted.

"And," Renee continued. "I can bring him along."

Aria raised her glass of wine. "And I much prefer Luc to Pleasure."

"I will toast to that," Renee agreed, lifting her glass of fruit punch as well.

Jaime didn't join them and instead settled her chin in her hand as she stared at them. "I've said it a dozen times over the years and I'll say it once more—because I'm not sure why my relationship with *Graham* is stuck in your craw— neither of you knows enough about him to continuously judge him," she said, her annoyance clear.

"What little we know of the manwhore is enough," Renee said.

"Amen to that," Aria agreed.

They touched glasses.

Ding.

Jaime nodded as she reached for her glass and took another sip. "It's a good thing everyone's past and secrets aren't out on front street to be judged so easily," she said. "Glass houses and all that. You know?"

She thought of Renee's affairs and Aria's scandalous sexual past.

Renee and Aria frowned.

She felt so protective of Graham because she knew his story and she ached for everything he had to overcome. And to see him thriving in his career, having left the sex work behind, she was proud of him, even if the future they hoped for together didn't manifest. They had both evolved, and some of the past they shared played a role in that. And maybe the space they gave each other to heal also led to the room to grow.

For damn sure I am not who I used to be...

Aria held up a hand. "Wait, the last time we discussed Graham you were riding him just as hard," she said, her tone suspicious and accusing.

Renee nodded in agreement. "Especially after he screwed Jessa," she added.

"That didn't happen," Jaime said before she could stop herself.

"And *how* do you know that?" Renee asked, sounding more like a mother than a friend.

"Jessa lied," was all that she said.

The men returned and she was thankful as that line of questioning faded away.

It was at that moment that Jaime acknowledged the shift in their friendship, and she wasn't quite sure if it was just a divide forming between them or a relapse of her old self. She hadn't shared her secret about Graham, and she doubted at that moment she ever would. The one lesson they all could take from what happened with Jessa Bell all those years ago was to not give *anyone* the ammunition to judge or destroy you.

Because friends could become foes.

★   ★   ★

Luc glanced at his watch.

It was coming up on four in the morning. He was beat and ready to go home, climb in bed, spoon Jaime, and sleep through the morning. He pulled his phone from his pocket and checked the view of the security cameras in the apartment. Everything was still and quiet with darkness broken up by small pockets of light throughout the condo. In their bedroom, Jaime was fast asleep on her side with a hand resting on his pillow. He chuckled when she released a little snore.

"Okay, Kevin, let's get a playback," he said to the sound engineer as he turned off his phone and set it back down on the armrest of the leather sofa where he sat.

"Right up," the man said as he began to punch buttons on the digital mixer.

Luc stood up and motioned for Zhuri to come out of the booth. He eyed the petite woman with a bright pink curly 'fro and skin as dark as midnight whose voice seemed bigger than her slight frame. And she was a dynamo, able to sing opera, pop, soulful R&B, and even rap. She played five instruments and wrote her lyrics. She was poised to be the next Alicia Keys or John Legend—with the right positioning, marketing, and rollout. In the music business sometimes talent wasn't enough.

"I think I got it," she said, her voice raspy.

"I hope so, the meeting at the label is at one," he said.

Her eyes played out her nerves. This was her debut album, and everything mattered.

Luc hugged her to his side. "Listen, talent isn't the issue. It's how much talent you have and how to find your voice in the market that is filled with plenty of talented people," he said trying to reassure her as he had a thousand times since a video of her went viral.

"I trust you, Luc," she said, before taking the seat next to

Kevin who used that as his cue to let the music—her music—fill the room.

That made him happy. He was a label head still acting as A&R and he knew it, but there was no one's ear he trusted more than his own.

He closed his eyes and slowly began to get lost in the bass blended with a playful piano riff as she sang about heartbreak. He had so much banking on her and securing his new label, so when she hit a raspy riff, then went low and then easily transitioned to a high note, the chills he felt made him emotional.

Failure was not an option.

He came from nothing. His grandfather had to die for him to even get a foothold in a country where there was no easy path for men like him. He had to use his grief and misery to find hope and fuel his dreams. He pressed his hand to his chest where a tattoo of his Pop-Pop was over his heart.

And when she eased right into the pocket as she sang about being hurt but overcoming, Luc looked over at her with pride. The song ended with notes from the piano. "That's a hit, Zhuri," he said.

She smiled. "We got it?" she asked, sounding hopeful, happy, and sleepy.

"Most definitely," he said. "I think it's the first single. It most captures who you are. The thing about your talent is its broadness, but we want to make sure to stick to the right path where your creative voice—what best represents who you are—is heard throughout."

Zhuri yawned as she nodded in understanding.

"Alright that's it," Luc said, feeling a yawn of his own coming. "Zhuri, see you tomorrow at the office. One sharp. Kevin, get that to me."

"Right away," the sound engineer said.

He and Zhuri left together discussing their big meeting the next day.

"Goodnight, Mr. Sinclair."

Luc stopped and looked back. "Good night, Daniel," he said to the twenty-something young man sitting at the front station of the studio with his schoolbooks spread out before him as he worked his shift.

A far different picture than when Luc first saw him a year ago when he stopped at a red light and saw him sleeping in a glass bus stop shelter with his head atop his knees that were pulled up to his chest. Luc had gotten him the job at the studio and advanced him money to get a small apartment. Now Daniel was in college and living up to everything he promised Luc he would do with the help he offered him.

With one last smile and a nod of encouragement, Luc left the building and made sure Zhuri was safely in her ride before he climbed into his vehicle. He checked his email and then opened the file Kevin sent as he connected his phone to the Bluetooth system. Driving through the near-empty streets of New York with one hand, he lightly pounded his free one against his thigh as he listened to the song again and sang along with it. Off-key and not caring. He kept it on repeat, fighting off the fatigue that made every move feel weighted down with sandbags.

When he finally crawled into bed, Jaime moved closer to him and pressed a hand to his bare chest. He covered it with his own, thankful that his days of being alone and coming home to an empty bed were over.

Chapter 7

One week later
6:08 AM

Jaime sat on the side of the bed alone. Luc was in the Hamptons at a gathering for music representatives at the home of a retired executive still respected as a mentor in the music industry. He would return later that night. She wore one of his monogrammed dress shirts and when she raised the collar to press it to her bare face the scent of him clung to it and caused an ache deep in her belly. Although she missed him over the last couple of days, she was glad for space. It was needed more than ever.

I need to clear my schedule.

She picked up her cell phone but set it down again at the early time. She looked down at her bare feet and wiggled her toes with their white-painted nails that matched her fingers. She'd gotten a mani-pedi at the salon downstairs just the day before.

Time for a color change. Maybe a glossy black.
Fuck it. Who cares?

Jaime released a breath and stood to walk over to the

window and look out at the city awakening as the sun rose in the sky. It appeared white amid the deep oranges and yellows of the skies above steel, concrete, or glass-front buildings. It was the money shot that many New Yorkers paid the cost to live high above the streets below to see when they rose from their privileged beds every morning.

Her reflection was pensive in the mirror as she released a breath that fogged the glass. With a sigh, she turned and pressed her back to it. Across the divide, her eyes fell on the sketch still above the bed and now seeming to mock her. Jaime frowned and pushed off the glass to storm across the polished floors. She stepped up onto the bed to walk across it until she and her likeness were eye to eye.

Jaime released short panting breaths, feeling bereft and adrift.

Making a fist, she swung up above her head until she felt the hem of Luc's shirt raise against her thigh, she felt the need to destroy it. She closed her eyes instead and let her fist softly land against the glass before she splayed her fingers to press against it.

I can't.

It is too beautiful. It is skillful and masterful. It is my very essence.

Having it hanging above the bed I share with another man is wrong.

That also was true.

Jaime dropped to the bed and buried her face in the pillows as she brought her knees up to her chest. She smelled Luc either on his shirt or the sheets. Tears rose, beginning with a slow fall and then swiftly escalating to sobs that racked her body.

8:01 AM

Jaime dialed her office and then placed the call on speaker before setting the phone on the top of the dresser.

Brrrnnnggg. Brrrnnngg. Brrrnnngg.

In the large frameless mirror above the furniture, Jaime pressed her fingertips to the puffiness beneath her eyes before she smoothed her eyebrows and then raked her fingers through her bob. "Get your shit together," she told herself.

How?

"Good morning, Jaime Pine Design. How many I help you?" Katie answered the line.

"This is Jaime. I need all my appointments rescheduled for the day," she said, opening the top drawer to eye all of her silk and lace panties perfectly folded. She selected a black one and bent slightly at the waist to pull them on under Luc's shirt.

"Everything?" Katie asked after a moment of hesitance. "You have the walkthrough of the music hall at nine and—"

"I know my schedule, Katie," she said in clipped tones.

Calm down.

Jaime pressed her bare feet to the floor and rolled her shoulder before stretching her arms high above her head and releasing a long breath. "Katie," she said with a calm that she held on to with a hair-thin thread. "Reschedule everything. Thank you."

She tapped the screen to end the call.

Bzzzzzz. Bzzzzzz. Bzzzzzz.

She eyed the phone. A picture of Luc filled the screen. She picked it up but did not answer as she left the bedroom and made her way down the hall to the open living space. Finally, the vibrations stopped.

I love him. I do.

She lay belly down on the modern sofa and then extended her arm to look at the brilliance of her diamond engagement ring. "Mrs. Luc Sinclair," she said.

She frowned remembering how important being Mrs. Eric Hall had once meant to her. *Maybe I'll just keep my name this time. Or maybe there won't be a wedding at all.*

"Shit," Jaime swore, closing her eyes.

And there, against her lids like a movie, so many memories they shared in the last ten months played out. She softly smiled at one remembrance . . .

"Open your eyes."

Luc removed his hands from her face, and she did as he asked to see they were at a racetrack in Las Vegas and standing before a red McLaren sports car. "No!" she squealed in excitement as she whirled to jump up and wrap her arms around Luc's tattoo-covered neck to kiss him.

He chuckled as he wrapped a strong arm around her waist. "Happy?" he asked as his eyes studied her face.

"So happy!" she exclaimed with excitement and looked over her shoulder at the racecar and the driver standing by ready to take her for a ride. "I've wanted to do this for a long time," she said, one of her hands clutching his navy V-neck T-shirt in her fist.

She had confessed to him once during a late-night phone call her fascination with racecars.

And he made it happen for her.

"I remember," Luc said, sitting her down on her sneakered feet. "Okay, first you gotta register and then do virtual training before you drive your fifty laps."

"Drive?" she asked. "I get to drive."

With his arms crossed over his chest, Luc nodded as he looked down at her.

Jaime grabbed his forearms. "I am going to give you the absolute best blow job ever," she promised in a low voice.

"I haven't had that already?" he asked, his voice deep and low.

"No," she admitted. "I've been holding it back for this very reason."

"Tonight?" he asked.

"To-night," she stressed with a wink.

And she had kept her word.

His roars that night as he filled her mouth with his seed seemed to echo around her.

That was Luc. Forever making her happy. Forever reliable. Consistent. Constant. Loving.

And the sex? Pure delicious sexy icing on the cake.

Luc was the complete drama-free package.

He doesn't deserve this.

11:11 AM

Jaime pushed the plate of fruit away as she sat in their dining room and vaguely listened to the news playing from the television in the den. She hadn't eaten all morning, but her appetite was gone and replaced with so many emotions. Guilt above all. Leaving not much room for anything else.

She picked up her phone and swiped to pull up her contacts. Her thumb hovered over the screen.

Tell them. No more lies. They are your friends. Your sistahs. They would not betray you. Ever.

With a tiny bite of her bottom lip, a small reveal of her nervousness, Jaime called Renee's cell phone first.

It rang just once.

"Jaime. Hold on one sec," she said.

Jaime rested her chin on her knee as she listened to Renee giving someone succinct instructions.

"Okay, I'm back. You up for lunch? I'm starving," Renee said, sounding as if she was still busy as she spoke.

"Let me add Aria real quick," Jaime said, before adding her to the call.

"Hey, Jaime. What's up?" Aria asked, mumbling slightly.

"Take the pencil out your mouth," Jaime said dryly, knowing it was a quirk of hers.

Aria just laughed.

"Okay, this is all three of us—"

"Aria, I'm starving. Are you in the city?" Renee asked. "Jaime and I were just deciding on lunch."

"I'm home," Jaime inserted before talks of lunch could continue.

"Why?" Aria asked.

"That's why I wanted to talk to y'all," she said. "I have something to tell you. I need to tell you."

"Can we do it at lunch?" Renee asked.

"Renee, eat a fucking Snickers and get over it already," Jaime snapped. "Sorry. I got a lot on my mind."

"What's going on?" Renee asked, her tone serious and concerned.

"Yeah, what's up?' Aria added.

Jaime put her foot down and rose to make her way down the hall to their owner's suite. She eyed the frame sketched on the wall as she came around the bed to stand at the foot.

"Jaime, you still there?"

I saw Graham in Grenada.

And . . . fucked him.

And . . . and . . . it destroyed my relationship.

He was there. Unseen but *seen.*

Tell them. Share the burden. Release the cage your deeds have created for you.

"What is it, Jaime?" Renee asked.

The traits of old resurfaced and she was ashamed to be anything but flawless. Especially when Luc was so damn perfect. So utterly and completely perfect. She closed her eyes and pressed her phone to her face as she turned to sit down on the end of the bed.

It's a good thing everyone's past and secrets aren't out on front street to be judged so easily. Glasshouse and all that. You know.

Her own words mocked her as well.

"I...uh...was thinking about a business move," she lied with a wince. "But let me work out some more kinks before I run it by y'all."

"You sure?" Aria asked.

Not at all.

She hung her head. "Yes," she lied once more.

"Okay well, let me get to lunch," Renee said. "I got an afternoon meeting after that."

"I'm working from home, Renee, so no haps on a meetup," Aria said.

I fucked up, y'all. Help me.

A tear fell.

Long after they ended the call and hung up, Jaime sat with her regrets that she didn't have the strength to confide in her friends.

5:08 PM

Jaime opened the double glass doors and stepped out onto the balcony. The day was beginning to turn to night. Rush hour traffic sounded and bounced off the towering buildings with the unique timbre of the city.

Luc had texted her hours ago to say he would be home before midnight. No studio. Straight to her. And she knew as surely as she knew even a broke clock was correct twice a day, that he would be there just as he said. If not earlier. That made her smile as she gripped the wrought iron railings and looked up the length of the street. She was thankful for the time as she grappled with revealing her truth.

But I don't want to lose him.

I can't.

The thought of hurting him, hurt her. And he would be hurt. And angry. And betrayed. And she could have prevented that if she had stood strong in her love and respect for him that early morning in Grenada instead of getting lost in the haze of lust.

Or was it more than that?

She looked down at her toes.

Lust was easy.

The truth was Graham had silently been in their relationship long before Grenada. Even one of her fondest memories of Luc's had Graham's unseen hand in it . . .

"As a kid, what did you want to be when you grew up?"

Naked and sitting astride Graham's muscled thighs, she looked down at his face. The moonlight cast him with silvery-blue shadows from the large windows of his penthouse apartment where they lay on the floor in the living room in front of the fireplace. Rain poured outside, keeping them inside from the bad weather.

"No one has ever asked me that," she admitted as she trailed her finger through the grooves of his abdomen and up to his chest to circle one brown nipple.

It tightened to a bud.

"I feel blessed to be the first," Graham said, his eyes on her as the blazing embers of the fireplace were reflected in the dark brown depths.

Jaime sat up straight as she looked into the fire, drawing a blank. "I don't remember," she said, looking down at his handsome face again. "That can't be. Every child has dreams and wishes. Right?"

He sat up straight and gave her a wink before he raised his hands from her hips to gently close her eyes with his thumbs. "Go back to it. That time. Remember. Because it's important. She was important then and you're important now. She's still there and wants to be heard."

Jaime opened her eyes and rested her forehead against his. "You have no idea about growing up with my mother. She is . . . all-encompassing," she whispered to him, feeling the sadness of her childhood rise. "She eclipsed me. Her wants. Her demands. I love her . . . but I also—"

Jaime's eyes widened in shock as she pressed her mouth closed, not wanting to give voice to that feeling as a tear raced down her cheek. She shifted the hand that stroked his back to lightly press to her lips as she shook her head.

Graham kissed her lips before shifting his mouth to her ear. "Stand up for her now like you couldn't then," he said, deeply and with meaning. "It matters. She matters."

She shivered.

"Find her," Graham said as he closed her eyes again with his thumbs.

As he massaged her shoulders and then her back, Jaime forced herself to relax and remember the dreams of a little girl before the wants of her mother could outweigh them. And then it came to her and she gasped slightly.

His hands fell away from her body as if leaving her free to feel every bit of the memory.

Hers rose to her cheeks as she remembered at age six when she found her beloved racecar missing from beneath her pillow to be replaced by a Barbie doll and a crown. "I had loved that car," she said in a whisper. "My grandfather gave it to me. I would push it around my room for hours imagining I was driving it."

"You wanted to race cars?" he asked.

She opened her eyes and theirs held.

"Yes," she said, smiling as something she tucked away resurfaced like a bloom. "Even after the car disappeared, I would use shoes and pretend."

Graham crossed his legs around her and settled his hands on her buttocks. "Have we found the secret of why you speed?" he mused with humor.

She shrugged one shoulder and then looked off a moment in wonder. "I forgot all about that," she said, surprised by the feeling of nostalgia.

"Look at that smile," he said, nuzzling her jawline with his nose.

Jaime leaned back to eye him. "She thanks you," she said.

"Nice to see you,*" he said with emphasis.*

An evening wind rolled past, sending her hair back from her face and lifting the edge of the shirt around her thighs. It could have exposed her panties and she didn't care because she was facing—and accepting—an indelible actuality. Graham had *seen* her—made the effort to know her—deeply. Completely.

And forced her to find every part of herself that she forgot or denied. For that, she would always have love for him.

Always.

5:55 PM

"What you doing, Mother?" Jaime asked as she lay atop the area rug in between the low-slung massive coffee table and the sofa.

As a kid, she loved being on the floor. Sitting. Playing. Napping. Pushing her little red racecar.

"Look at the time, Jaime," Virginia said.

She did.

"Dinner is always at six," they said in unison.

Virginia chuckled.

Jaime rolled her eyes.

"How's Luc?" Virginia asked.

She stiffened. "Mother, *I'm* here. *I'm* calling. *I'm* on the phone. Ask me how *I* am."

Virginia sighed. "Jaime, must everything I do lead to a confrontation between us?"

Nice to see you.

"I just want you to see me," she said, feeling as if she gave voice to the little girl she used to be and the woman still hungry for her mother to accept her importance in the world.

"See you? Then hang up and call me on FaceTime," she said.

Jaime turned her lips downward. "Not what I mean, Mother," she said, sitting up to press her back to the seat of the sofa as she picked up the remote and flipped through the channels on the television over the unlit fireplace. She paused at a replay of the NASCAR race from the weekend at the Bristol Motor Speedway. She upped the volume to hear the roar of the engines as the racecars circled the track at high speeds.

"What's that noise?" Virginia asked.

She smiled. Her mother would faint to know she watched NASCAR races on television and had even driven a racecar herself. "Why did you throw my car away?" she asked, as she lowered the volume.

"Your what?"

"Granddaddy gave me a little red racecar that I loved when I was five or six," she explained.

"I don't remember that."

Possible. It meant nothing to her so why would she?

Jaime eyed the car of Bubba Wallace, the most successful

African-African NASCAR driver to date. She was #Team-Bubba. "I loved that car. I slept with that car under my pillow. I took it everywhere."

"Jaime, did you really call me right before dinner to talk about a toy?"

No.

"I wanted to talk to you about something—"

"Hold on, Jaime. Your father is calling my name to the heavens."

Jaime's shoulders slumped as the landline phone was set down.

I need you, Mama.

The phone rustled when it was finally picked up. "Jaime, your father is ready for dinner," Virginia said, sounding rushed. "Call me tomorrow and we'll talk."

"Tell Dad I said hello," she said.

The call ended.

She let her head fall back on the seat as she released a breath that was heavy with her disappointment.

10:04 PM

Luc or Graham?
Graham or Luc?
Neither?
Both?
Don't be silly.

She hit the home screen on her phone and looked at Luc's picture. "Good dick. Good job. Good heart. Good man," she said, before going into her photos and looking at the picture of Graham she screenshotted from his website. She twisted her lips as she went back and forth between their photos.

"You can get with this or you can get with that," she rapped.

She froze and lowered her phone realizing the lyric from Black Sheep's "The Choice is Yours" had come out of nowhere. And it didn't fit because the choice was not hers.

Or is it?

"You can get with this…" she said, looking at Luc's picture…

> *Luc gripped her neck with one hand and her ass cheek with the other as she bent over the back of the sofa as he delivered deep stroke after stroke inside her.*
>
> *"Harder, Luc. Fuck me harder," she begged into the cushions of the sofa.*
>
> *He delivered as the front of his thighs slapped against the backs of hers.*
>
> *"Yes!" she screamed, feeling the slick back and forth motion of his inches against her walls.*
>
> *"You want this nut? Huh. You want it."*
>
> *She rolled her hips. "Yes, give me that nut. Gimme. Gimme. Gimme."*
>
> *"It's y-y-y-y-yours," he roared.*

"Whoooo," she said at the memory before swiping over to Graham's photo. "Or you can get with that…"

> *"What's my name?"*
>
> *"Pleasure."*
>
> *"And what do I give?"*
>
> *"Pleasure."*
>
> *He laughed huskily as he pushed his dick deep inside her with one swift thrust from behind on the floor of the private room in the strip club.*
>
> *Jaime felt the pressure of him against her walls. She felt the heat of him deep inside her. "Fuck me," she ordered, hardly believing her words or her actions.*

"My pleasure," he told her thickly as he stroked deep and fast inside her before switching up to a slow grind.

Her pussy walls throbbed against the length of him as her juices drizzled around his dick and down to wet the cleavage of her buttocks.

"Say you my nasty bitch," he ordered.

"I'm your nasty bitch."

And she was.

That was Graham when he was Pleasure the stripper and she had gladly paid him two hundred dollars for the service, but that was also the past Graham felt they couldn't overcome. Those days when she wanted his sex and paid the price for it.

She shook her head. "How did we think we could make it more?" she asked aloud.

But they had, for six months. He'd given up the sex game for her. He made her feel loved. And seen. He did the work to convince her that she was special to him.

"Our past together is the very reason I just don't believe we can have a future."

Jaime swiped over to Luc's picture. "I'll think I'll get with this, 'cause this is where it's at," she said.

Decision made.

With a heavy breath she unfollowed Graham's Instagram account and then deleted his picture from her phone—and her life—once and for all.

11:24 PM

Jaime took a deep inhale of the steam in the charcoal slate shower before turning off the water and opening the fogged glass door. She jumped when Luc suddenly appeared in the doorway. "I didn't know you were home," she said, taking in how sexy he looked in all black.

"I just got back," he said, removing his gold watch.

"Early," she said. Softly.

He shrugged one shoulder. "I was ready to get home."

To me.

Her eyes shifted to the corner of the vanity table.

And he'll do the same for us.

Luc's eyes followed her line of vision and then widened in surprise. "Jaime, is that—"

"We're pregnant," she announced, pressing a hand to her damp, still flat belly.

Luc dropped his head and his hands. His watch hung loosely around his wrist and the breaths he took quickened. "A baby," he said, looking up with eyes filled with black boy joy.

"A baby," she repeated, giving in to the joy she denied herself all day.

She suspected she was when she missed her second cycle and just prayed it would be late. It wasn't. Early that morning she finally had the nerve to use the pregnancy test she purchased.

Luc walked into the bathroom and slid a hand around her waist to pull her naked body against his. "Our baby."

She closed her eyes with her chin atop his head and wrapped her arms around his neck, quickly praying she had made the right choice.

Chapter 8

Graham took a sip of his champagne as he looked down about the room of the world-renowned art museum for the closing night of his exhibit—the largest and most prestigious of his career. Nearly all of his work over the years was on display. From his spot on the balcony, he surveyed the faces of the elegantly dressed people who were observing his pieces right before their eyes—perhaps for the first time.

Certainly, different than the days when women considered his body the piece to be goggled, pawned, and paid for. In his immaturity, and still reeling from the trauma of his youth, he thought sexually satisfying women had been his vocation. Now he knew his art was his true calling and his passion. He chuckled into his flute of champagne at the irony.

Over the rim of his glass, he caught sight of a woman paused in the entrance to the room. He lowered the glass, finding the sight striking as she stood with her hair up in a sleek topknot as she was surrounded by the elaborate gold brocade framing the entrance. It was regal and majestic. Deserving to be captured for eternity in oils. The brown of her skin and the white of the deep V-neck sleeveless top she wore with a massive satin skirt in citrine. The large gold medallion she wore was snuggled atop her cleavage and matched her heels.

When she stepped into the room, the movement of her body was familiar.

His heart hammered as he watched her like a hawk as she looked about the room, leaning this way and that. The further she moved into the room the more his suspicions were confirmed. And then his chest felt light and excited all at once.

"Jaime," he whispered.

What is she doing here? A coincidence? It can't be.

Steadying himself, he smoothed his hand over his tailored tuxedo jacket and his grip tightened on his glass as he watched her intensely. Absorbed her. Enjoyed her. Her beauty. Her regal grace. The way she moved with just a hint to the passion he knew he could bring out of her.

His Miss Prim and Proper Pearls.

That nervous and unsure person was gone and in her place was a confident woman. The years had aged her well. Jaime Pine was and would always be one hell of a woman. He knew from studying her movement through the room that she finally knew it. Not the façade she had learned to portray but a true discovery and self-awareness.

It was sexy as hell.

And many men—a few women—took notice. One even tried to stop her by lightly touching her wrist. She eased away from his touch with a polite smile as she continued moving through the crowd.

With another sip, he looked on as she began to stop and study his paintings. Tilting her head this way and that. Sometimes she gave a soft smile. Other times the art evoked sadness.

And then he remembered the painting she would soon

come to and he felt alarmed. He crossed the carpeted floor to leave his solace. As soon as he reached the bottom of the steps, he stopped a server and placed his still half-filled glass on her tray. With large strides he fought hard not to appear to be rushed and politely ignoring those who tried to gather his attention. Graham neared her just as she came to a stop in front of *Not What It Seems*.

She gasped a little and pressed her hand to her throat.

At first look, it was just a painting of a beautiful couple in an apartment, but with the use of darker hues and shading in the shadows was a faceless person with a knife ready to pounce. Some people never picked up on it.

He took another step closer to her.

Jaime turned as if she sensed him. "Graham," she said softly.

The sight of her up close took his breath away. Even when she snuck away from her boring life in Richmond Hills to come to his shows when he was stripping, something about her had drawn his eye and made him feel a thrill even with a hundred more women vying for his attention.

His eyes dipped to her gloss covered mouth and he hungered to kiss her. Clearing his throat, he stepped up beside her. "I wasn't expecting to see you, Jaime," he said, as he clasped his hands behind his back.

"I wasn't expecting to see a reminder of...of that day," she said, using her hand to smooth her perfectly coiffed topknot as she looked back at the painting.

Graham eyed the painting and was taken back to when a crazy person from his past drugged and trapped him at knifepoint. A surprise visit to his apartment had pulled Jaime right into the melee. "I thought you were going to get hurt that day and it took everything out of me," he admitted, feeling tightness across his chest at the memory.

Jaime glanced up at him. "You saved me—*us*," she stressed. "I thought you were going to kill her."

"I would have to save you," he said without a doubt.

They locked eyes.

"We've been through a lot together. Haven't we?" she asked.

He towered over her by nearly a foot as he looked down to see his reflection in the brown depths of hers. *Where I belong.*

Graham closed his hand into a fist to keep from stroking her face.

Something in her eyes said she too wanted to feel his touch.

"Jaime," he warned in a low voice.

She nodded in understanding and broke their gaze, returning it to the painting. "Whatever happened to . . ."

He clenched and unclenched his jaw. "Still in jail. I made sure of that shit," he promised her.

The memory of almost losing her touched something deep in him. It was not to be denied.

She fell silent and slid her hands into the hidden pockets of her elaborate skirt.

"Jaime."

She turned to face him.

His eyes took in her face as his heart thundered. "Regardless of anything. I will *always* love you, Jaime," he said, unable to contain the emotions inside him.

He saw it. There in her eyes. Unable to be hidden.

"You know what, Graham?" she asked. "I will always love you too. Nothing can change that."

His gut clenched.

Jaime's breath quickened when Graham's eyes dropped to her mouth. He wanted to kiss her. Taste her tongue and mouth. She wanted the same.

Forgive me.

The child she carried could be his and by her foolish choice, she had taken the right and privilege to be a father from him. There was a choice. Just the truth. Whether Luc or Graham was the father was up to genetics. And nothing else.

And now here he was in front of her declaring his love and fucking her right on up until she poured out her heart as well, even as she twisted her engagement ring on her finger in her pocket.

The tug of war between her past and her present continued.

And now a baby was in the mix.

She hung her head, needing a break from their connection because the thought of having made a child with this tall, muscled, handsome, and enigmatic man standing before her was thrilling.

But then there was Luc.

And she was just as happy at having a baby with him as well.

I love them both.

I want them both.

She felt overwhelmed. By her actions. Her pregnancy. His love. Hers.

The truth would destroy everything.

What about Luc?

Now she felt panicked.

Shit.

"I have to go, Graham," she said, stepping back from him.

He took one stride toward her.

She shook her head and held up her hand before she turned and walked away from him once again. When she reached the door, she felt a hand at her wrist and turned just as Graham wrapped an arm around her waist and guided her down a long and narrow dark hall until he opened a door

and swept them inside a dimly lit storage room to close it and
press her against it.

He captured her body to his and kissed her like he was
starved as he fed her hunger.

If she was honest it was what she came for. Him. It.
Their chemistry.

She arched her back as he wildly licked her neck, her
chin, and then her mouth. It was selfish and reckless, but so
fucking glorious as she shivered everywhere. And when his
hand rushed to lift the volumes of her skirt until he pressed
his hand against her pussy, she opened her legs for him
against a door once again.

"Jaime," he moaned against her ear as he eased her sheer
panties to the side and stroked her clit with his thumb.

She cried out and he swallowed it with his mouth.

"You don't understand, Jaime," he moaned against her
lips. "I could fuck you forever."

Caught up in his heat and lost in his words she was able
to run and hide from her lies and her deception.

"Shit!" he swore, stepping back from her with deep
gulping gasps for air.

She eyed him, dazed by passion, and confused by him
withdrawing it.

With a small shake of his head, he raised the finger that
had been inside her to suck deeply.

This man. This man. This motherfucking man.

"I'm celibate," he said as if the words were torn from
him. "I want to fuck you. And I know damn well that I
could, but I can't. Not like this. Not when there is no future.
Then it's just sex and I don't do just sex anymore."

He stood before her a man battling his convictions and
his desires.

And she was a woman looking back at him as her desires
battled her obligations to Luc.

When the words to beg him to make her cum started to tumble from her lips, she turned and flung the door open to run away.

This time he let her go.

Luc bopped his head as he listened to the reggae-influenced rap song of one of his artists who wanted to touch base with his Jamaican roots.

"What do you think, Luc?"

He looked down at the laptop with the open Zoom conference with his artist and his producers. "I don't know. I feel like it's missing something," he said, sitting back against the sofa. "Maybe a girl to do the chorus."

The front door opened, and he looked back over his shoulder, giving Jaime a wave. "Something. I don't know. I just know it's not ready yet," he continued.

He heard a rustle of material near him a second before Jaime climbed onto his lap.

Her eyes were glazed. "Tell them you'll call them back," she whispered to him.

Luc put his hands on her waist and tried to lift her from his lap. "I'm in a meeting."

"Then they can watch," she said as she grabbed the hem of her white top to begin to pull it over her head.

"Whoooaaa!" Luc exclaimed before leaning past her to slam the computer closed. "Baby, what's up with you?"

She kissed him. Deeply. With a guttural moan.

He broke the kiss and leaned his head back against the sofa. "What has you stirred all up?" he asked with a nervous laugh, "How was the art show?"

Jaime pulled the top over her head, exposing her lace-covered breasts to him as she took his hand and pressed it beneath her citrine skirt. He hissed at her wetness and his dick rose to life. "Damn, Jaime," he said, raising one hand to her back to jerk her forward to suck her nipples through the lace before removing it to fling away.

She was in heat and it led him straight to the fire with her.

With a twist of her hips, he felt her clit strike the base of the middle finger he had deeply planted inside her. "Damn, Jaime," he said again, looking at her in wonder as she lifted one of her breasts high enough to bend her head and lick the brown tip.

"Make me cum," she begged. "Please."

He ached as he fumbled through sliding his gray sweatpants and boxers down to free his hard and long dick. She wrapped her fingers around it and swiftly stroked the tip as he grabbed her panties and tore them with one hard pull.

Fuck it.

She rose on her knees and quickly eased her core down onto his hardness. They both cried out. "Damn, Jaime," he gasped.

She rode him with fervor. Fast and hard. Each hard thrust of her hips sent her sliding her back and forth on his inches as sweat beaded across her body.

"Damn, Jaime. Damn!" he swore, looking up at her in wonder as he licked his lips.

She pulled him forward and buried his face against her breasts, nearly smothering him as she kept at it until her heart pounded like drums against his ear.

He had never seen her like this before. Never.

And when she cried out, rough and harsh, with her climax as her walls spasmed around his dick and her wetness coated him, he watched her ecstasy and felt her body shudder from deep within her.

It was a sight to see. She arched her back and thrust her breasts forward as she raised her arms around her head, her face glowing from her climax.

"Damn, Jaime," Luc gasped before flinging his head back and thrusting his hips upwards as he fell headfirst into euphoria. "Damn!"

She continued to ride him until his dick was spent and limp. "I needed that," she gasped in between breaths before she rose.

He looked down at his dick lying on his side and then up at her standing there, breasts free with her medallion still hanging in her cleavage, wearing nothing but her dramatic skirt and gold heels, with her lips gloss smeared across her mouth and strands of her hair freed from her topknot.

Wild and beautiful.

I love her.

She walked out of the living space and came back with a warm and soapy washcloth to kneel before him and cleanse their juices from him. "You can get back to your meeting while I take a shower," she said, rising to her feet when she was done.

His eyes dropped to her bared belly. "Does being pregnant make you so horny?" he asked.

She looked shocked, before smiling at him. "Probably," she said, picking up her torn panties, bra, and top before leaving the living space again.

He stood and pulled his sweatpants up over his flaccid dick. "How was the art show?" he asked, following behind her into their bedroom.

She was stepping out of her skirt, leaving it in a brightly colored puddle on the polished wood floors, removing her necklace as she moved across the room to her walk-in closet. "It was nice. I left early," she said over her bare shoulder.

Luc frowned a bit. "What's wrong?"

Jaime turned as she removed the gold ball stud earrings she wore. "Huh?"

"Is something wrong?" he asked.

She shook her head before turning to place the earrings

in her large jewelry case atop the center of the dressing island. "Just gonna grab a shower and go to bed," she said.

He frowned a little bit. Something was off. Even during sex, something was different. Damn good. But different.

"I'm going to warm up the rest of the salmon you made," he said as she moved over toward him to reach the adjoining bathroom. "You want some?"

"No, I'm good," she said.

He reached for her wrist. She stopped and looked up at him. "What was that about out there?" he said, motioning his head back toward the hall leading to the living room.

She looked confused. "Sex?" she asked.

"It was...intense," he said.

She smiled, but it didn't reach her eyes.

"I never saw you like that, Jaime, that's all," he explained when she continued to stare at him.

"Me coming home to fuck you is a problem?" she asked. "I won't do it again."

Their eyes met and held.

"I didn't say that," he rebuked.

They laughed.

"Luc," she said, her joviality fading. "Why do you love me?"

See. I knew it.

"Do you doubt that I do?" he asked, hating the unease he felt.

Jaime looked down and then up at him with a glossiness in her eyes that could only be tears welling up. "Never," she stressed, as she forced a smile. "I know you love me but *why* do you love me?"

Where is this coming from?

"Don't you know you deserved to be loved?" he asked her.

Again, she looked down. She shrugged her shoulders.

"Jaime, what is this about?" he asked, his deep voice even darker with concern.

"For my one question you asked a bunch more," she said, sounding tired. "Just forget about it, Luc, I'm going to wash."

She eased her hand from his grasp and walked away. He watched her retreat. "Jaime," he called over to her.

When she turned, he imagined her flat belly soon swelling with his child and he felt devotion for her. "I pictured the kind of woman I wanted at my side. A smart one. A strong one. A loyal one. Someone to have my children and be devoted enough to our family to hang around. Someone passionate. Someone fun. I knew what kind of woman I wanted in my life. I just didn't know what she would look like until I met you, Jaime Pine."

Her mouth opened a bit and her eyes softened.

"You are everything, Jaime. Every fucking thing," he swore to her.

She pressed her left hand to her belly and the sight of her engagement ring against reminded him of their family to come. The life he never had as a kid he would have as an adult. He pressed his hand over his heart, knowing his grandfather was proud in heaven. "Let's set a date," he said.

Her hand dropped from her belly. "Right now?" Jaime asked.

"Why not?" he asked.

"Why now?" she countered.

"Why not now?" he volleyed back.

Jaime leaned her naked body against the door frame. "Luc, I'm tired and I really would like to wash. Can we do this...tomorrow over dinner?" she asked. "I'll cook and we'll sit down and get to it. Okay?"

"I would like a date before the baby is born," he suggested as he turned to leave the room.

"You and my mother both," she muttered before disappearing into the bathroom.

He paused at the doorway and looked back at her skirt

on the floor. Moments later the steam from the shower swirled out of the doorway. Luc believed in his gut instincts. He relied on it. His success was in large part to it.

And something was wrong.

Of that he was sure.

"You've made a mistake."

"Regardless of anything. I will always love you, Jaime."

"You are everything, Jaime. Every fucking thing."

"Jaime. Jaime?"

She had been staring out the window of her office, but she cut her eyes over without shifting position, to see her lead design consultant, Madison, looking at her with a curious and concerned expression. "What?" she asked, clearing her throat and picking up the stylus to her iPad.

"Jaime, the wood floors ordered for the Connecticut house is wrong and you signed for its delivery," Madison explained, leaning over to sit her tablet in front of her.

She frowned at her signature on the invoice and then at the amount. "Shit," she swore.

"This isn't like you," Madison said. "Everything okay?"

I'm just pregnant and not quite sure who the father is. My life is fucking Paternity Court right now.

But she wouldn't dare to reveal that. Even the new Jaime had boundaries.

No secrets. Just boundaries.

"I was crazily distracted, and I goofed," Jaime admitted, reminded of the day her focus was on her pregnancy and the week she slept with both Graham in Grenada and Luc at home.

"Do me a favor, call the distributor to see if we can be granted some favor and swap out for the right materials," Jaime said.

Madison nodded. "And if not? This was a custom order."

Shit.

"See what you can do for me. Get me some info and I will call the client, cop to my mistake, and persuade them not to fire us for fucking up the timeline," she said.

"On it," Madison said, giving her a consoling look as she stood and left the office.

"My life is a fucking mess. Deadass," she said, imitating Aria's Newark accent.

Releasing a lengthy breath, she dropped her stylus and scratched her eyebrow with the tip of her almond-shaped fingernail. She needed her friends. To talk to them. Confide in them. Be berated and judged by them. But in the end, they would help her navigate the shit.

She pressed the intercom.

"Yes," Katie said.

"Get me Aria and Renee on the line," Jaime said, pushing back in her chair as she rose to her stiletto covered feet.

I want to be happy with my pregnancy.

Turning, she looked out the window.

"You have another call on the line. Should I put that through first?" Katie asked via the intercom.

"Who is it?" Jaime asked, hoping it wasn't the Rogans about their house in Connecticut.

"Graham Walker."

Jaime looked back over her shoulder. A shimmy of awareness floated over her and her heart's beat changed in an instant. "Put him through and hold the calls with the ladies," she said, looking down at her engagement ring.

"Okay."

"I will always love you, Jaime."

She turned to her desk and eyed the flashing light on her phone. "What could he want?" she wondered aloud in a whisper.

There's only one way to find out.

Clearing her throat, she picked up the headset. "Jaime

Pine," she said in her most professional voice as she rolled her eyes at herself.

Just last night you were tempted to beg him to make you cum.

"Yes, I know, Jaime. I called you," Graham said, his voice deep and throaty.

"How did you get my number?" she asked as she retook her seat and pretended not to be affected by the closeness of his voice to her ear.

"Google."

"Right," she said. "How can I help you?"

"I can't stop thinking about you, Jaime."

She felt what could only be excitement. "Graham—"

"Over these years. Since Grenada. And all last night," he continued. "I don't know what to do about that. I'm pretty fucked up right now."

"Just ignore it," she said, even though she couldn't.

"I can't."

"You have to. Our past won't let have us have a future, remember?" she reminded him.

"But I'm not ready to say goodbye."

She wrinkled her brows and sat up straighter. "Huh?"

"I love you, Jaime. On some real shit. I love you."

Jaime tingled as she looked up to the ceiling and shook her head, denying his feelings and her own as she twisted her engagement ring around her finger.

"I miss talking to you. Seeing you. Kissing you. Sharing with you. Laughing with you. Traveling with you. Loving you. I miss it," he stressed with raw and real emotions that were clear. "What if Grenada wasn't just a coincidence. What if..."

It was meant to be.

She pressed a hand to her belly.

What if we made a child?

"Look, I don't know. Maybe I'm living off the past and making assumptions on what could or should be. Maybe my head is up in my ass or the clouds about this, but I have been trying to get over you since Grenada and I am failing like a motherfucker."

Same.

The line went silent as she released breaths meant to ease the turmoil rising in her.

"Jaime, last night drove me crazy."

She pressed her thighs together hoping to ease the bloom of her clit as she remembered how he left her so hot and bothered that Luc had benefitted from her desire. She looked down at her ring.

Forgive me.

"I want to see you again," Graham admitted. "Look, let's have dinner. I can cook the jambalaya you used to like."

"At your place?" she retorted. "How would that help your celibacy?"

He chuckled.

She tingled all over some more. Graham made her feel giddy and light.

"Okay, dinner wherever you choose," he offered. "No strings."

"How can there be when you're anti-sex?" she mused.

"I'm not anti-sex. I'm anti-casual and reckless sex," he explained.

Like Grenada.

She spun in her chair, twisting the phone cord around her body, as she looked at her reflection in the glass and saw the excitement at having Graham back in her life in any way. It wasn't right. But she couldn't explain why he made her feel the way he did.

Fuuuuck.

Because she also had Luc and he made her feel things as well.

Forgive me.

But the woman in the reflection was not ready to say goodbye to Graham Walker. Not yet.

"Jaime."

She winced and hung her head as her torture played out across her face and a tear fell because it was wrong—so very wrong—but it didn't feel that way.

"Dinner," she agreed.

"Tomorrow at eight?"

"At the Red Rooster in Harlem," she said.

"Jaime."

"Yes?" she said, closing her eyes as she pressed her phone closer to her ear.

"I love you."

"I believe that," she whispered.

Click.

Chapter 9

Two weeks later

Jaime eyed Renee and then Aria as she cleared her throat.

These are my confessions . . .

"I'm pregnant!" she announced with bright eyes.

They both showed surprise, shock, and then joy before they exclaimed and jumped up from the patio lounges to come toward her.

Jaime took a quick inhale. "And I'm not sure who the father is," she exhaled.

They both froze mid-step.

"Oh shit!" Aria gasped with shocked eyes.

Renee flailed her arms and knocked her glass of ice water onto the patio. "What!" she exclaimed.

Jaime closed her eyes to avoid their stares. When silence reigned, she dared to look at them. They had reclaimed their seats and looked unsure of how to react. "It's either Luc or . . ."

Renee and Aria shared a brief look before they both leaned forward.

"Graham," she finished.

"Oh, *helllllll* no!" Aria exclaimed, throwing both of her hands up in the air dramatically.

Renee's shoulders slumped, but her face was unreadable. "Jaime," she said with disappointment.

Get it all out.

"When we were in Grenada—"

"Grenada!" they exclaimed in unison.

Jaime nodded. "Graham happened to be at the resort painting a mural, and well, things—*sex*—happened."

"Oh. Okay. I was the *only* one not getting dick in Grenada," Aria declared, looking from one friend to the other.

Renee shook her head before she stood up and walked into the house to return with a small brush and dustpan. "Anything else?" she asked as she bent down to clean up the shards of glass.

"Graham and I have been back in touch for the last couple of weeks."

Renee hung her head for a few moments before looking back at Jaime over her shoulder in her squatting position.

Aria opened and closed her mouth a few times, but no words came.

Sometimes silence was able to convey more than words.

"What are we supposed to do with all of this, Jaime?" Renee asked as she slowly rose to her feet, leaving the dustpan and brush on the ground. "What do you want us to say about this...this...?"

"Living breathing Maury Povich level of drama," Aria supplied before scratching her scalp.

"Aria," Renee said with a serious tone even as she continued to look down at Jaime. "Where are you with all of this, Jaime?"

Jaime pressed a hand to her still flat belly. "Regardless of the father, this is my baby and I'm going to be a mother and I'm happy about *that*," she said softly.

Renee's expression changed and she offered the hint of a smile. "When are you due?" she asked, coming over to sit beside her outstretched legs on the patio.

"April."

"An Aries," Aria offered. "And it figures your child would have a diamond as its stone."

They all laughed.

"Right," Jaime agreed.

"And what do you want? A girl or a boy?" Renee asked as she reached for Jaime's hand to clasp with her own.

"A girl," she said, picturing a plump, brown cherub who looks like...

Me? Luc? Or Graham?

"Of course," Aria drawled, coming to sit on the other side of her legs on the patio lounge.

"And who do you want to be with silly, silly girl?" Renee asked.

"Luc or Graham?" Aria added.

Jaime licked the dryness from her mouth as she looked at one friend and then the other. "One is my past and the other is my future but right now both feed a different hunger in me...and I know it's wrong. I know after what Eric did to me with Jessa that it's bizarre and crazy for me to do the same to Luc—who loves me, but I...I..."

"You what, Jaime?" Renee urged. "What in the hell are you doing?"

"Fucking up her life," Aria supplied.

Jaime leaned back against the lounge and closed her eyes. Soon her belly would swell with life and she would have to face her secrets.

"What do they know?" Renee asked.

"They know I love them," she offered, with her eyes still closed as she gave in to a fantasy where she continued to have the best of both worlds.

Aria sucked air between her teeth. "Cut the bullshit, Jaime," she snapped.

Jaime winced.

She's right.

"Luc doesn't know anything about Graham and Graham doesn't know about Luc or the baby," she admitted.

"Jaime," Renee admonished.

"Damn girl. You lying here. Lying there. You lying *everywhere*," Aria stressed.

I am.

She opened her eyes and eased her knees up to her chest.

"Who do you hope is the father?" Renee asked.

She pictured Luc holding their baby and then Graham doing the same.

With a shake of her head, she pushed aside her thoughts of both.

"The answer should be the man you are going to marry," Aria said.

Jaime eyed her. "Right. Yes. In a perfect world it will be Luc's child," she said.

"Are you going to have a DNA test?" Renee asked, rising to finish cleaning up the glass.

Another question I'm not ready to answer.

Renee paused in the doorway. "Cut it off with Pleasure and build your life with Luc, Jaime," she advised before entering the house.

She looked to Aria who gave her a helpless one-shoulder shrug.

"If nothing else, everything that happened with Jessa Bell taught me that everything done in the dark comes to the light," Aria said. "Everything. Every time."

Jaime gave her a nod as she looked off at the gentle movement of the water in the pool.

Everything. Every time.

"Now let me get this right, Ma'am."

Jaime stood at the podium and nodded as she looked up at Lauren Lake sitting on the bench with her gavel in hand and makeup flawless per usual.

"You were dating this man?"

The judge pointed at Luc sitting in a chair to the left of her.

Jaime nodded.

"And then you had sex with this man?"

Her finger swung to Graham sitting in a chair to the right of her.

The studio audience of Paternity Court *all gasped in shock.*

Jaime looked over her shoulder to glare at them.

Luc jumped to his feet. "We're engaged, Your Honor."

Graham jumped up as well. "She never told me that."

Jaime looked from one to the other.

"Sounds like you need us when you're done here."

She looked at the bench and her eyes bugged out of her head when Lauren Lake's head spun and became the faces of the Cutlers from Couples Court.

"The fuck!" Jaime exclaimed.

"We're waiting for you," the Cutlers exclaimed before the heads spun again.

"Steve! Steve! Steve! Steve!"

Jaime turned and all the faces of the audience had transformed into the bald-headed host of the Steve Wilkos Show.

"Turn around and get these results, Ma'am."

She pivoted again to find Lauren Lake's head back in

place as she shook a manila envelope in her hand. "I have the DNA results . . . but y'all know I am revealing nothing until after a commercial. Right?"

The audience applauded and agreed knowingly.

"Right!"

"Yup!"

"We know that shit!"

Luc wrapped his arm around her waist. "Jaime."

She looked up at him.

"Jaime," Graham said as he held her hand, entwining their fingers.

She looked over at him.

"You could have gotten your results on my show, Jaime!"

Cringing she looked at the television screen next to the bench at Maury holding a beautiful brown baby with pink bows. "Mama," she cooed.

"Maury! Maury! Maury!" the studio audience chanted loudly.

Lauren Lake banged her gavel. "Not on my show, Povich."

"Jaime?" Luc tugged at her waist.

"Jaime?" Graham squeezed her hand.

"Mama."

"Maury! Maury! Maury!"

"Jaime?"

"Jaime?"

"And the results are—"

Jaime released a high-pitched scream just as her head exploded into fragments . . .

She awakened from the nightmare with a cry and sat up straight in bed cloaked by darkness, looking around in alarm. Luc's side of the bed was empty. She reached out and grabbed his pillow to snatch to her chest and bury her face into the softness, wishing he were there and not at the studio.

That was the craziest dream ever. I don't even watch talk shows. The fuck?

Guilt was a hell of a thing.

And so is my messy ass life.

She reached over to turn on the sconce on the wall on her side of the bed before she flung the sheets back and sat on the side in her eggplant satin slip. She picked up her phone and started to send Luc a sexy text to motivate him to come home, but decided against it. Instead, she opened up the app where some of her text messages were delivered—those she would never want Luc to pick up her phone and see.

She scrolled through old texts Graham had sent her over the last two weeks.

G: I CANT FORGET THE WAY YOU LOOKED IN THE DRESS YOU WORE TONIGHT. I CANT SLEEP BECAUSE OF IT. THINKING OF YOU IN AND OUT OF IT. DAMN.

That had been a form-fitting yellow sundress she wore to that first dinner. Even when she pulled the dress on her body and eyed herself in the mirror, she had imagined just what he would think of it. The look in his eyes as she walked across the restaurant to reach where he sat had not disappointed.

Even then, weeks later, the dark hunger in his eyes made her shiver still.

G: THANK YOU FOR GOING TO THE MUSEUM WITH ME. ENJOYING YOU ENJOYING ART MADE IT DOPE AS HELL FOR ME. IVE BEEN THERE A DOZEN TIMES BUT NEVER SAW IT THE WAY I DID THROUGH YOUR EYES.

She smiled, remembering the moment he came up behind her as she studied African artifacts to regale her with details of a particular item's history or little-known details he knew from his position on the museum's board. She had been amazed at the growth in him from the man she first met in a hotel room to strip down for horny women at a bachelorette party and earning a living by selling himself to women hungry for his touch and his skill.

Like me.

The man who got his GED at twenty and hadn't finished his first year of college until twenty-six—three years after becoming a sought after manwhore.

And now years later, he was still growing beyond who he used to be.

G: HAVING YOU IN MY HOME BUT NOT MY BED WAS A BIG TRIUMPH FOR ME TODAY. IM FUCKING PROUD OF MYSELF. YOU JUST DON'T KNOW. LOL.

"Oh, I know," Jaime said aloud, thinking back on the last time she'd seen him just a couple of days ago.

She had walked around his loft in her bare feet and sifted through his art as she sipped wine and listen to Coltrane serenade them on his vintage record player as he cooked a seafood and vegetable dish for her. Graham had given up eating red meat ten years ago. And when she wandered into the kitchen to look around his towering body, he fed her a bite from the pan as their eyes met. Instantly her body had hungered for him instead as her nipples hardened and her clit begged for attention. From his touch. His lips. His dick.

Not once had they fucked in the two weeks, but the desire to do so lingered between them with a pulsing life all its own.

She admired his dedication to his continued recovery from a sexual addiction brought on by a desire to defeat a violation in his past. But she knew if he had just made one damn move to have her, she would have hungrily served up the pussy. Being lost in him all of her guilt and doubt faded to nothing.

G: I LOVE YOU. I WILL ALWAYS LOVE YOU. I WILL HATE THE MAN WHO WINS YOU. WHO CAN LOVE YOU WITHOUT A FUCKED UP PAST TO OVERSHADOW IT. MY GUT SAYS STOP THIS. DON'T DO THIS. I WONT LEAVE THIS WITHOUT SCARS BUT MY

HEART SAYS HAVING YOU BACK IN MY LIFE FOR EVEN A LITTLE
WHILE IS WORTH EVERY RISK.

She heard the front door open and close. She set her
phone and her feelings for Graham aside just as Luc came
down the hall and entered their bedroom, looking handsome
in the handmade black shirt and slacks he wore with his
beloved diamond jewelry.

"You're up?" he said, removing his watch as he strode
over to his walk-in closet.

"Silly dream," she explained as she smoothed her hand
across the silk scarf she wore around her hair as she rose to
walk over and lean in the doorway.

He glanced at her with fatigue hooding his eyes.

"How's the album coming?" she asked as he placed his
diamond watch, necklace, and bracelet on the island before
he began to unbutton his shirt. She stepped over to him and
eased his hands away to finish the task.

"Which one?" he asked with a chuckle.

He had a lengthy roster of clients as A&R.

"When can you take a break?" Jaime asked, sliding the
shirt off his strong arms.

He looked down at her. "Whenever you need me to,"
he assured her. "You good?"

She folded the shirt and slid it into the container for items
to be dry cleaned. "I'm worried about you. Not me," she
said with honesty.

"You know what would help me?" he asked from
behind her as the sound of his belt hitting the floor echoed.

She looked over her shoulder. He was naked. Strong.
Tall. Dick long. "What?" she asked, still feeling her arousal
awakened by the texts and her memories of desire denied.

"I need to eat," Luc said.

"Oh," she said in surprise. "Okay. There's some leftover
shrimp in garlic butter from Spark's—"

Luc shook his head and walked over to gently guide her

to sit down on the padded leather bench in the corner where he normally sat to put on his shoes. He knelt as he eased the lace edge of her delicate satin slip up her thighs and spread her knees.

"Oh," Jaime sighed as she thrust her hips forward and pressed a hand to the back of his head as he lowered it to suck the lips of her clean-shaven pussy.

She gasped and arched her back as he licked her clit with a moan. She raised one foot to the edge of the bench when he turned his head sideways to really get at her with his tongue. She shivered and rolled her hips, lowering her hands to open her lips and expose the fleshy bud to him. "Suck it," she begged. "Suck it, baby."

He did. With pursed lips. Slowly. In and out. Pushing her over the edge as he pulled on the swollen bud. Her explosion came quickly. It was hot and forceful as she cried out from the back of her throat, enjoying every moment of her climax.

Luc stood up and looked down at her through his barely open eyes as she released heaving breaths. "Good?" he asked with moist lips.

She nodded weakly, with her legs still spread open and her clit slowly pulsing.

He smiled and walked out of the closet, leaving her there just like that.

Jaime sat up, placing her elbows on her thighs as she dropped her face into her hands. Fatigue hit her hard. "Shit," she swore, trying to get her shit together.

"Jaime."

She awakened with a start and looked up from her hands to find Luc standing before her with a plush black towel draped around his still damp body. "You washed?" she asked.

Luc chuckled and bent to pick her up. "You fell asleep," he said as he carried her out of the closet and across the room to lay her on her side of the bed.

Well damn.

She squeezed one of her plush pillows to her chest as she lay on her side. "What about you?" she asked, raising her head from the pillow.

"Nah, I'm good," Luc said as he removed the towel to dry off. "I gotta get right back up at nine for that summit in Miami, remember? A nut would have me fucked up in that closet right along with your ass."

"Just gone," she joked. "Whoo."

He tossed the towel into the bathroom and came around to the right side of the bed. "Trust me. I was tempted," he said with a yawn and stretch.

Jaime reached to turn off the sconce and took the light from the room as he climbed into bed naked. "I will meet you at the door on my knees when you get in tomorrow night," she promised.

"Word?" he asked.

She chuckled. "Word," she agreed.

He spooned her and pressed kisses to her nape. They were delicious. Her smile spread easily, and her moan was of satisfaction. "Luc," she warned.

"This helps me sleep," he said against her nape before another round of warm kisses.

"Yes, I know, but it makes me hot and you have to get up in a few hours," she reminded him as she reached behind herself to take his dick into her hand when his kisses continued.

"A'ight. My bad," he said, covering her caressing hand with his own to stop her strokes.

"Too late," she said, freeing his already hard dick to move quickly and straddle him in the darkness.

"Jaime," he moaned as she massaged his dick with both her hands.

His hips thrust up.

The light came on and his hand was still extended from when he turned it on.

"I'll make sure you get up," she promised, working the tip as she released a drizzle of spit to coat him.

He cried out.

With her eyes steady on him, she bit her bottom lips as she rose onto her knees to guide her core down onto him. She gasped and whimpered at the feel of him filling her. She leaned down to suck his mouth into hers, pressing her hands to the side of his face as she began to move her buttocks and send her tightness up and down his inches.

He sucked her tongue and extended his arms to fill his hands with her buttocks.

She broke their kiss to look at him, getting lost in their heat and his eyes.

"I love you, Jaime," he whispered to her as they moved their hips in unison. Slowly.

And it was there in his eyes causing her heart to swell. "I love you, Luc, don't ever believe I don't love you," she whispered, speaking her truth before she kissed him deeply.

Together they worked for their climax and their cries mingled in the air around them as they clung to each other.

Almost desperately.

The next morning, Jaime and Luc left their condo and walked down the tiled hall together to the elevator. She smiled as he held his phone with one hand and covered his mouth with the other to yawn. "You good?" she asked, reaching up to swipe a small piece of lint from the red V-neck lightweight silk sweater he wore.

"I'm still getting that head tonight or nah?" he asked.

She arched a brow and smoothed her waist-length ebony

weave behind her ear. "I took care of you last night," she reminded him as the clear doors slid open.

"Damn sure did," Luc confirmed.

They shared a glance with smiles in their eyes before looking forward as he pressed the button for the lobby as the door closed.

Both of their phones rang.

"Jaime Pine," she said.

"Luc Sinclair," he said.

"The Tuckers had to reschedule the walkthrough from this morning to late this afternoon," Katie said.

Jaime checked her watch. "Okay, Katie. Thanks. Does the team know?" she asked as the elevator slowed to a stop and the doors opened.

She glanced at the video vixen with long colorful nails, her surgery-enhanced body on display as she stepped on the lift in gravity-defying neon heels. She arched a brow and stiffened her neck at the appreciative glance the woman gave Luc.

"Hi there," she said.

Jaime turned to face Luc. He was busy talking to Kendell and didn't notice the woman. She smiled up at him. His face became confused. "Hold on, Kendell," he said, before lowering the phone. "What's up, baby?"

"Nothing," Jaime said, choosing to be mature even though she wanted to childishly wiggle her weighted down engagement finger in the woman's face.

Luc pressed a kiss to her brow before raising the phone and walking to the corner of the elevator. "I'm leaving now. Is the car downstairs yet?" he asked.

His step out of the gap between the two women left them to eye each other.

Jaime gave her a look that said "Sorry."

The woman nodded in understanding and gave her a thumbs up.

The elevator slid to a stop at the lobby and Jaime watched the woman's exaggerated walk away before stepping off before Luc. "If I fall asleep during the panel discussion it is your fault," he said as they strode together across the lobby.

"She's pretty," Jaime said.

"Who?" Luc asked, sliding his phone into the pocket of the red slacks he wore.

She hitched her chin forward toward where the woman from the elevator was walking ahead of them.

"Miss Too Much?" he balked. "Too bad she doesn't know it."

"I think she knows it," Jaime disagreed.

The uniformed doormen greeted them both with a nod as he held the door open for them to step out on the street.

Luc shook his head. "If she did, she would realize she doesn't need all that," he said.

"*Or*...she dresses to make herself happy," Jaime said, surprised by the need to defend her. Men and their assumptions and judgments of women were tiresome.

They both looked as she climbed behind the wheel of a red Bentley.

"Really, I don't give a fuck," Luc said, looking down at her.

"You sure, Luc?" she asked.

"I'm fucking positive," he assured her.

She wasn't sure she believed him.

He walked over to his waiting car as the sounds of New York echoed around them. "Have a good day," he said. "I'll be back around eight."

Jaime gave him a little finger wave as he climbed into the back of the car with Kendell waiting for him. She turned on her heel as she watched the vehicle ease into traffic. For the first time, perhaps ever, she found herself doubting the freedom Luc took as an executive in the music industry. He came and went without question from her. Was she a fool to trust him so blindly?

The way he trusts me?

To let her own infidelity lead her to not trust him was...

Hypocrisy.

She felt nauseous but wasn't sure if it was the morning sickness she had thus far avoided or just being sick of her own bullshit.

Chapter 10

One week later

Graham leaned against the counter separating the waiting area from the tattoo area of Inked by Lola. He watched as one of his best friends finished up a rose tattoo on the nape of a customer who sat backward on a chair. He liked watching her work. Lola took her art just as seriously as he treasured his own.

When he first met the edgy beauty to get his first tattoo, he had been young, wild, and led by the head below his belt wanting to fuck her. She and her girlfriend, Kezia, had made sure he understood that dick was not their preference. Over the years they had become essential in his life. Kezia, now a hairstylist for celebrities with natural hair, kept his beloved locs healthy for over fifteen years and although he hadn't gotten a tattoo in years, hanging out at Lola's shop when he was in town was considered necessary. They taught him to be a better stripper when he first started, encouraged him to finally eat pussy—something he refused in his foolish youth—and were his biggest supporters about taking his art career seriously a few years ago.

Graham eyed the painting he did of them in a loving embrace that graced the rear wall of the colorfully decorated salon. It was through their suggestions to their celebrity clienteles that his prominence rose quickly. And when they wed a couple of years ago, he served as their best person at the small wedding ceremony held at their favorite restaurant.

He loved his lesbian friends and considered them family.

"Where you headed today?" Lola asked him in her raspy and soft voice as her client rose to examine her tattoo with a small mirror in her hand and the large mirror on the wall behind where she stood.

He gave her a smile that felt sheepish.

Lola grinned, deepening the small diamond piercings in her dimples. "Never mind. That's a Jaime look," she said, raising her hands to push her waist-length dark blonde dreads back from her face.

"Yoooooooo. It's mad perfect," her client said with her thick New York accent as she handed Lola the mirror. "I'm so glad my friend put me on to you."

"Thank you, love," Lola said, applying protective cream and a plastic barrier over the tattoo.

As she took the woman's credit card for payment, Graham checked his time. He was supposed to meet Jaime at the Empire State Building and then grab a quick lunch with her at a street vendor—something he hadn't done in years. "I gotta jet," he said, rising to his full height.

The customer gave him an appreciative look and lick of her lips as she passed him on her way through the waiting area and out the door.

"Women still throwing pussy at you left and right?" Lola asked as she drummed her long black nails against the countertop. "You still ducking or what?"

Graham faked a basketball move like he was trying to shake off a defender to get a clear shot at the basket.

They laughed.

"You sure about starting things back up with Jaime?" Lola asked, ever protective over him and his heart.

He nodded. "I love her," he declared.

"I know that," Lola said as she nodded. "Is it enough? Is she over the past?"

He thought about it and all the frustration her jealousy and suspicions had brought their relationship in the past. "I can't blame her though. That's the thing. I fucking get it, you know? And we not really back together anyway, so it's cool."

"Okay," Lola said with obvious reluctance. "Don't keep her waiting then."

He gave her a dimpled smile that he knew was a charmer. "Tell Kezia I'm sorry I missed her," he said at the door.

"I will," Lola promised with a wink as she motioned to her waiting customer that he was next.

Graham had left his truck at home because it was easier to navigate the hustle and bustle of the city's congested traffic by foot, bike, or public transportation. He walked up the street and then jogged down the subway steps to pay his fare with an app on his phone. Once he stepped off the platform to get on the F train with the throng of New Yorkers, he felt excited at seeing Jaime. To hear her laugh. For her to look at him with those beautiful eyes that hinted at the desire she had for him when their gazes would catch. To feel her touch that could make goosebumps race over his body.

And to fight his desire to sex her until she was sweaty and crying out his name as she clutched the sheets like she was holding on for life.

Graham!

From his seat by a window, Graham looked up when a tall man in his mid-twenties with a fitted cap, sweatpants, long-sleeved T-shirt, and bright red heels set a small radio and small bucket on the floor. The man cued up "Bad Mama Jama" by Carl Carlton. The subways were filled with talented people using the steady flow of commuters to showcase their skills and make money with tips from those willing to give. He watched in amazement as the young man, who announced his name was Domingo, danced, did splits, worked the pole, and solicited crowd participation like he was on stage and not on the F train.

Graham eyed folks. Some avoided him but most enjoyed the show and the diversion from the monotony of their daily commute. When the train pulled to the Thirty-Fourth Street–Herald Square stop he withdrew his wallet and pulled out several hundred-dollar bills. He bent to press them through the slot on the lid of Domingo's bucket.

Domingo's eyes widened as he watched him. "Thank *you!*" he screamed, blowing Graham a huge kiss before he spun and did a split as he exited the train with a chuckle.

He made his way across the people crowding the platform to jog up the stairs to the street. The sun was bright and the early fall winds were a little crisp but refreshing as he made the brief walk to the Empire State Building. He'd been commissioned to do a piece for a collector in Dubai and wanted a firsthand view of the iconic New York location.

And when Graham stood with his hands in the pockets of his lightweight black pea coat, he looked out at the metropolis from his spot on the enclosed observation deck of the 102-story Art Deco building. The 360-degree view of Manhattan was a powerful sight with the noonday sun beaming high above the cluster of towering buildings. The only thing missing at that moment was Alicia Keys singing the chorus to Jay-Z's "Empire State of Mind"...

"In New York," a woman sang off-key.

The moment was too perfectly cliché.

He turned and smiled at Jaime standing there behind him.

"Concrete jungle where dreams are made of," she continued to sing. "There's nothing you can't do."

He bent at the waist to press a welcoming kiss to her cheek as he chuckled. "I was just thinking about that song," he said.

Jaime stepped up to look out at the view. "It's hard not to," she said.

He looked down at her and then at the mustard wrap dress she wore with caramel leather heels. The scent of her perfume reached him. "Beauty should always be celebrated," he said, studying her profile.

She looked up at him.

Such a simple gesture caused his gut to clench as if punched. Being around her made him feel rejuvenated. More alive than ever. The days in between seeing her were not the same. But he knew he was tempting fate.

"I don't know how much longer I can test myself not to have you when I want nothing more than to bury myself deep inside you, Jaime," he admitted.

Her eyes dropped to his mouth.

"Don't," he pled with her as he balled his hands into fists in his pockets to keep from reaching for her and pulling her body to his to kiss and touch. Right there in public. Not caring who watched.

She reached up to stroke his face. He noticed the slight tremble in her hand. He turned his head to kiss her palm. She gasped and took a deep swallow as she closed her eyes. "Graham, I have to tell you the truth, and it won't be easy— but I have to. I *have* to—"

"Jaime."

The hand on his face was withdrawn and Jaime turned her head as she took a step back from him. Graham was confused by the look of shock on her face. "Jaime, what's wrong?" he asked.

"Luc," she gasped.

Luc?

Graham looked over at the man standing in the doorway glaring at Jaime—*his* Jaime—and then back at her as she walked toward him. "Jaime?" he said, frowning.

She paused and looked back at him. Her eyes were filled with alarm but also regret before she looked down as she massaged her temples with her fingertips.

The other man strode over to grip her wrist. "Where is your engagement ring?" he asked her.

"Luc, let me explain," she said.

"You're engaged?" Graham balked.

"And pregnant," Luc added, giving him a hard glare for good measure.

Graham's eyes dipped down to her stomach as he remembered thrusting inside her and filling her with his seed in Grenada. "Is that what you wanted to tell me?" he asked.

"Who the fuck are you, dude?" Luc asked, moving Jaime behind him as he turned to face him.

"Who the fuck are *you*?" Graham said coldly as his anger swiftly rose.

"Her fiancé," Luc emphasized.

Graham laughed, mocking him. "Shit, I can't tell," he said wanting to best him and knowing it was childish.

Luc took a large step.

Graham did as well, ready to end this man questioning him.

"No!" Jaime screamed, coming around Luc's body to stand between them and press a hand to each of their chests.

He looked down at her and saw so many revelations in her eyes. Much more truth than she had told him. Another betrayal. He thought of the time from their past that he laid his love out for her and later discovered that she didn't feel the same.

Who said anything about getting married?

He remembered overhearing those words she said to her friends when they mocked her for trying to have a serious relationship with a former stripper and manwhore. Words that had led to him leaving the party and contemplating the wisdom of even trying to build something serious with Jaime when she made it clear to her friends that she wasn't.

He eyed her.

She was engaged.

She was pregnant.

And he knew from the look in her eyes that he might be the father, but she'd chosen this man—her fiancé— to even know she was pregnant.

Some light inside of him faded but the fire of his anger replaced it.

"You weren't going to tell me that could be my baby, Jaime?" he asked, his tone cold even to his ears.

"I'm sorry," she whispered as her ears filled with tears. "I'm so sorry, Graham."

"What?" Luc roared.

His instinct was to give in to the visceral pain radiating through his chest at the sight of her hurt, but he pushed that aside. "Even now I'm not good enough for you?" he asked, revealing his annoyance, but not his wounded pride.

He gripped her hand and thrust it from his chest before he shook his head and walked off.

"You fucked him, Jaime? Are you fucking kidding me? When? Where?" Luc asked.

Graham heard the same anger he felt in the voice from behind him.

"Grenada," Jaime admitted.

"The trip I *paid* for?" he roared.

Graham paused at that.

"Yo, you wildin' right now, Jaime. Who the fuck *are* you? I don't know you."

Agreed.

Even as his heart pounded and his gut felt twisted from her betrayal, Graham slid his hands into the pocket of his jacket and turned to look at Jaime and her fiancé—the man she chose.

They stood a few feet apart, staring at one another. He was the interloper. He didn't belong.

And the baby?

He frowned deeply.

It could be mine.

Jaime glanced past her angry fiancé at him. "Forgive me," she mouthed, as a tear raced down her cheek.

He turned and strode away across the black tiled floor to reach the elevator. A small crowd was behind him and he felt them sneak glances in his direction as the metal doors opened and the elevator's liftman opened the gate. He moved to the rear of the elevator and turned to see Luc walk away from Jaime as she reached out for his arm.

He was glad when the doors slid closed to free him from their drama, but he wasn't as lucky with his anger. Nor his pain. He clenched and unclenched his jaw.

No, no, no.

The elevator slid to a stop as he remembered how quickly her hot passion had turned to panic in Granada. With quick strides, he made his way across the towering Art Deco lobby.

"Let me down. Let me down. Letmedown. Letmedown," she'd said as she pushed to put distance between them.

He reached the doors to exit and stepped out onto West Thirty-Fourth Street. Even with the blares of cars horns, the rumbles of buses, and the shrill echoes of police sirens filling the air, he heard nothing but Jaime's words that day: *"I have to go."*

It reverberated. Mocking him.

"I have to go. I have to go. I have to go."

"Man, fuck her," Graham muttered as he took long strides up the street. He wished he'd ridden his bicycle instead of catching the train because right then he could use the distraction of navigating traffic to keep his mind off possibly having a child with a woman he...

His steps faltered.

What?

Graham didn't know what he was supposed to feel for Jaime, but his heart betrayed him because hate for her did not exist. Still, he wanted his feelings for her to be gone, not claimed.

I might have a kid? With Jaime—who is not my Jaime. Who is engaged to be married to another man? And pregnant by either him or me.

"Shit," he swore, wishing like hell he had never laid eyes on Jaime Pine again.

Rewind . . .

"I love you, Luc, don't ever believe I don't love you."

It was those words that Jaime whispered to Luc before she kissed him deeply that bred suspicion. It wouldn't leave him. To him, it had been an odd way to proclaim love.

The night she came home brimming with lust after the art show had already sent his "Spidey Senses" into overdrive and now his instincts told him he was right.

Something was off.

In the past, relationships hadn't been his thing. He used to keep numerous beautiful women on speed dial to savor his lifestyle and they had always taken great care in showing him just how much they appreciated the time behind the velvet rope.

And then he met Jaime, and everything changed. His wants. His desires. His relationship goals.

He'd never thought when he finally settled down that he would be the kind of man to check on his woman. Snoop. Invade. Never.

Until that morning.

From his office in Midtown, he looked through hours of footage in their condo and watched the woman he loved for any sign of what his gut was telling him was trouble in paradise. And then there she was in color scrolling through her phone and alternating between smiles, sighs, and tears before she made a call and told someone she would meet them at noon at the Empire State Building.

He'd barely been able to focus on his meeting as he wondered just who that someone was.

Finally, he knew to have peace of mind he would take off down the slippery slope and go check on the activities of the woman he loved. His fiancé. The mother of his unborn child.

His stomach felt twisted like a pretzel as he rode the elevator up to the observation deck on the 102nd floor. The doors opened. This twist unraveled to be replaced with something similar to a kick. He frowned at Jaime—*his* Jaime—with her hand pressed to the face of another man as she looked up at him with her emotions etched in her face and her eyes.

The man turned his head to kiss her palm.

A gesture he had done many times himself.

The fuck.

Luc felt as if the world as he knew it crumbled into a thousand pieces at that moment. There was no denying there was something between Jaime and this man. A connection. That was clear even without him hearing what they said to one another. The steps he took to stand in the doorway felt heavy as shit. "Jaime," he said in disbelief, hating that he hoped there was a better explanation than what he clearly saw.

She dropped her hand and stepped back as she looked over at him.

In shock.

In guilt.

In conflict.

Damn.

"Luc," she gasped, as she walked over to him.

"Jaime," the stranger said, his voice deep and confused.

She stopped and looked back at him.

That tore at his chest like the scratch of a bear's paw.

She looked down at her feet and brought her hands up to massage her temples.

His eyes widened at her bare hand. Another vicious lash. He walked over to her and grabbed her wrist. "Where's your engagement ring?" he asked, stuck somewhere between anger and hurt.

"Luc, let me explain," she said.

Explain what? That you're cheating on me?

"You're engaged?" the stranger asked.

Luc glared at him wanting to smash his fist into his face. "And pregnant," he emphasized.

"Is that what you wanted to tell me?" the stranger asked as he stared at Jaime's stomach.

Wait? What?

His heart raced and dread began to sink into his bones.

"Man, who the fuck are you, dude?" he asked with a cold snap as he put Jaime behind his back.

I don't know him. Does he know me?

"Who the fuck are you?" the stranger asked.

No, he doesn't.

"Her fiancé," Luc said.

So you the side dick.

Side dick. My woman got another man. This got to be a fucking nightmare.

The stranger laughed at him. "I can't tell."

This motherfucker . . .

Luc took a step to fulfill his desire to knock him the fuck out for violating. He kept his eyes on him, ready to fight, and not caring that the man had a few inches on his tall height. *Fuck it. Do work.*

"No!" Jaime yelled, pressing her hand to his chest.

He shook his head as he looked down at her hand on the chest of the other man as well.

Another hot and searing lash.

"You weren't going to tell me that could be my baby, Jaime?"

The final blow.

"I'm sorry. I'm so sorry, Graham."

Her tears meant nothing to him as it settled in that not only was she unfaithful but the child she carried—the one they were preparing for—might not be his.

"What?" Luc roared.

He felt ignored as they stared at one another.

"Even now I'm not good enough for you?" Graham asked, his voice cold before he removed her touch from his chest and walked past them to leave the observation deck.

She stepped over to watch him leave and he saw in her eyes that she wanted to go behind him.

Fuck that.

"You fucked him, Jaime? Are you fucking kidding me? When? Where?" Luc asked, stepping in front of her to block her view of him.

She shook her head as if to deny his request, but then answered. "Grenada," she said as more tears welled in her eyes.

He felt a coldness overtake him that could rival the frigid

chill of a blizzard. "The trip I paid for?" he yelled, not caring of the eyes they drew with their drama on full display.

She nodded and closed her eyes.

"Yo, you wildin' right now, Jaime. Who the fuck *are* you? I don't know you," he surmised as his anger twisted his lips.

She looked up at him. He cared nothing about the pain and regret he saw in the brown depths. The façade was gone.

Take a bow, Jaime.

He looked past her to the skyscrapers surrounding them. He wondered so many things but had had his fill for the day. He looked down at her. She was looking beyond him. He didn't need to turn, knowing her lover was her aim. He shook his head. "Stay the fuck away from me, Jaime," he said, letting the coldness he felt seep into his tone.

"Let me explain, Luc," she said, reaching for his arm.

He snatched from her grasp. "Explain what? What the fuck could you possibly say?"

"He's my ex," she said.

"And?" he balked.

"We had something—"

His hand slashed the air. "Nah, y'all *got* something," he spat.

"You don't understand, Luc," she said.

"And I no longer give a fuck," he said. "You took everything we had this last year and some change and pissed on it."

"I'm sorry," she whispered.

"For what?" he asked.

"Hurting you," Jaime admitted. "I didn't handle this right and for that, I apologize. I truly apologize for not dealing with my feelings in the right way."

That stung the wounds already left open and exposed by her betrayal.

"Your feelings for him?" he asked with a sarcastic smile.

She licked her lips and locked eyes with him. "For loving both of you," she admitted as she held up her hands as if useless in her choices.

"I need to be away from you, and I need you to stay *the fuck* away from me," he said. "Find out which one of us is the father and let me know. Other than that. This shit right here—us—is done, Jaime. I need somebody I can build with. Not somebody stabbing me in the back."

"I haven't slept with him since Grenada," she offered.

He eyed her in contempt. "You think that matters?" he asked, with a scornful shake of his head.

"Yes," she affirmed. "Seeing him was about closure, not starting something new."

"And what was fucking him in Grenada about?" he asked snidely.

"Seeing him there was a surprise, Luc."

He eyed her with contempt. "Good to know I paid for you to get fucked."

"It wasn't just about sex, Luc," she said, her eyes showing her conflict.

Love.

For loving both of you.

He looked down at her hand. "Is he the reason you never would set a wedding date?" he asked.

She shook her head, but again, her eyes betrayed her, the same way she deceived him.

"I never thought you would be this kind of—"

"Kind of what? Bitch? Whore? Slut?" she asked. "Don't call me out my name, Luc."

He released a full belly laugh before he turned and walked away.

His steps weren't long enough and fast enough to put distance between them. The desire was so urgent that he took the stairs and ate a dozen or more flights up easily before he regretted the decision. "Shit," Luc swore, placing his hands on his hips as he paused on the landing to take in gulps of air.

Grimacing at his fury and indignation at her betrayal, Luc whirled to pound the side of his fist against the gray wall.

Later that night . . .

Jaime lay on the middle of the bed of her hotel suite on Fifth Avenue nearly curled into a ball. Her tears were spent, and her body was weak. She risked it all and lost.

She eyed her engagement ring sitting on the bedside table beside her phone.

Her truth was that she had not been ready to marry Luc.
And I should have been honest about that.

Her truth also was that she had deep and profound feelings for both. She was equally disturbed that neither would answer her calls. So, she stopped trying.

For now, she welcomed the solace.

After more than an hour on the deck looking out the glass at the Manhattan skyline, she had made her way to the nearest hotel. As soon as she reached her suite she had run to the bed and collapsed onto it under the weight of her guilt, shame, and heartache. She ignored all phone calls and kept replaying the scenes from atop the Empire State Building. There was no right to be found about her actions.

She knew that.
But I love them both.
She knew that as well.
I can't have them both.
Even though they both fed a different hunger and desire in her, she knew that, too.
And now I have neither one.

Jaime sighed as she rolled over onto her back and pressed her hands to her belly. "*We* have neither one," she said. "Not in the way we would have. Forgive me for that. But I promise all that I am, all that I have, and all that I will be ever be, is about you from now on."

And it was the picture of her pressing her face to the sweet neck of her newborn baby that finally gave her the peace she sought.

Chapter 11

Virginia Osten-Pine's long and drawn-out sigh into the phone said more than words ever could.

Jaime held the phone away from her face as she stepped onto the elevator of Luc's building, still looking like she did yesterday although night had come and gone. A call to her realtor revealed a perfect rental in Tribeca that would not be available for another two weeks. She had a choice of paying over six grand to stay in her hotel suite for that time, accept Renee's offer—and risk hearing about her foolishness in involving herself with Graham again—or go home to her parents, where her mother only knew the wedding was off but nothing more of the sordid details. She chose the latter.

God help my last nerve. May she not jump on it too much.

She placed the phone on speaker as she massaged her nape. "Mother, we can talk about all of this when I get there. Okay?" she said.

"Does this mean you're going to raise the baby alone?" Virginia asked in a loud whisper that seemed to hiss like a snake.

Maybe if I pay extra I can get the condo sooner.

"Call Luc and fix it, Jaime!" Virginia urged.

Maybe Renee's anti-Graham campaign won't be so bad.

But she wasn't up for any Graham slander.

"Mother, I have to go. I'm meeting the movers at Luc's" she said, as the lift stopped on the sixtieth floor of his building and she exited to make her way down the hall.

Jaime entered the condo, confident Luc was gone, and she would have the time and space to pack her things. She closed the door and leaned against it as she looked around. Everything was spotless as ever.

Bzzzzzz. Bzzzzzz. Bzzzzzz.

She looked down at her phone in her hand. A text. *Luc.*

She ignored the message and called his number. It barely rang once before he sent the call to his automated voice mail message. She checked the text.

LUC: What part of stay the fuck away from me did I not make clear?!?!

"I'm just here to get my things, Luc," she called out knowing he was watching her via the video surveillance. She understood. Yesterday had been a shit show that caused *everything* to change. *Absolutely everything.*

But in the aftermath, after a good cry which led to an even better night of sleep, Jaime was beginning to welcome the distance. She needed the time to think because the business of juggling two loves had kept her from focusing on her reality. A living, breathing baby would emerge from her body in seven months.

I'm going to be a mom—a mama, not a mother.

After skipping a shower but changing into jeans and a sheer long-sleeved white tee, she was in her closet, gathering her jewelry into a designer travel case when the movers arrived. For the next couple of hours, she supervised them boxing her clothes, shoes, and accessories.

She gave the house a final walk-through to make sure she hadn't left any of her items behind. As it became clear the only thing left was her, she bit her bottom lip and blinked to prevent tears. Yesterday, this had been her home. Today, she was no longer welcomed here.

Bzzzzzz. Bzzzzzz. Bzzzzzz.

She picked up her phone from the top of the island in the now empty closet. A text.

LUC: Leave the key and the ring.

That stung like alcohol poured into an open wound, but she worked the house key off the ring and then slid the engagement ring off her finger as she left the closet to walk over the room. She held up both items to the surveillance camera to wiggle at him before she set both on his bedside table.

"Luc," she said, walking over to the black glass bubble in the corner. "You didn't deserve the way I've treated you these last few months. I apologize for hurting you," she said truthfully.

She held her phone a little tighter in her hand thinking it would vibrate.

It didn't.

With a few soft nods of understanding, she looked at his spectacular view of the city one last time before she turned. Her line of vision landed on the sketch. *How could I forget it?*

She set her keys and phone on the end of the bed before kicking off her navy Converse sneakers to climb up onto the bed and take it down.

"This is one helluva mess I've gotten us into, huh?" she asked the representation of herself.

The eyes seemed to say: "Sorry, girl."

"Anything else?"

She stepped off the bed and nodded at the burly mover in a black coveralls who stood in the doorway. "Just box this for me and that's it," she said, handing him the frame before she quickly slid on her sneakers and picked up her things.

"This is dope," he said about the sketch before turning to walk away.

"Yes, it is."

She had to bite her lips to keep from saying that her ex—the well-known painter Graham Walker—did it. The last thing she needed was for Luc to overhear that.

Wait. Now I have a new ex. What a fucking mess.

Jaime padlocked the rear door the movers used to reach the service elevators before she left the condo via the front door, making sure it was also securely closed behind her. She walked the length of the hall and had just stepped onto the elevator when the vibration came.

Bzzzzzz. Bzzzzzz. Bzzzzzz.

She looked down at her phone.

LUC: The last thing is a paternity test. ASAP.

She cued her phone for a voice message. "Hey, Luc. I will talk with my obstetrician because I assume the safest method will be waiting for the baby to be born," she said. "And I know you may not be as invested as I am anymore, but I won't risk the baby for anything."

Jaime stepped off the elevator on the first underground parking level to quickly make her way to her waiting car. Her phone vibrated again. She waited to check her phone until she was sitting in the driver's seat.

LUC: I was fully invested and happy until yesterday. I want to be fully invested again . . . once I know which of us is the father. But yes the safety of the baby is best.

Bzzzzzz. Bzzzzzz. Bzzzzzz.

LUC: Before yesterday it was our baby and not the baby.

A dig. I deserve that. But I refuse to acknowledge it.

She dropped her phone into the cupholder and pared it to the car's Bluetooth before she reversed out of the parking spot for the last time.

Lately, Jaime was having a lot of regrets.

Instead of reaching her parents, she took the exit on the

turnpike just before the one she normally did to get to their house. She found the closest hotel and checked in. The room left a lot to be desired from her suite on Fifth Avenue, but dealing with the eternal sighs and thinly veiled judgments of her mother would be worse. Much worse.

She decided to give herself through the rest of the week and the weekend before tucking tail and moving back in with her parents for the two weeks. After a trip to Walmart for casual clothes to lie around in, sheets and a comforter for the bed —because she was not trusting possibly laying up in someone's else's dried sex juices, snacks, and microwavable food—and sanitizing wipes to cleans all touchable surfaces, she felt ready for her staycation from hell.

The spray of the water from the shower did feel good against her skin as Jaime tilted her head back to prevent her new cotton bandana and the weave it covered from getting wet. The scent of her vanilla and peaches organic soap rose in the steam and she took a deep inhale of it just as her hands paused over her stomach. There was just the slightest bulge.

In a few more weeks her obstetrician would be able to tell her the sex of the baby via an ultrasound. An appointment she would now be attending alone. "It's just me, myself, and I, that's all I got in the end," she sang of Beyoncé's hit song.

She finished up her shower and wrapped a new plush towel around her body before she used one of the hotel's towels to clean the steam from the large mirror over the sink.

Bzzzzzz. Bzzzzzz. Bzzzzzz.

Jaime looked down at her cell phone on the countertop before she answered. "Hi, Mother," she said, as she wet her toothbrush with hot water.

"Where are you? The moving truck came an hour ago. I had them put most of it in the garage."

Jaime looked at her reflection in the mirror.

I'm ten minutes from your house, in a seventy dollar a night hotel hoping I don't catch crabs or lice.

"Change of plans," she said as she opened the box of toothpaste. "I'll be there Sunday night. Last-minute work came up."

Liar.

"Oh," Virginia said.

Wait for it.

"I never worked while I was pregnant," she said.

And there it is. Judgment was her mother's best friend.

"You were my priority from the moment I knew I was pregnant," she added.

"Unless Daddy got a paper cut or needed a glass of water," Jaime countered dryly.

"That's not humorous."

Jaime smiled as she shrugged her shoulders. "Mother, I have a meeting. Can I call you back?" she said as she squeezed paste onto her toothbrush.

"Please take care of *my* grandbaby," Virginia stressed.

"Of course, Mother. Thank you for the reminder," she said. "*Au revoir, Maman.*"

She made a frustrated face as she jabbed the screen with her finger to end the call. "*Her* grandbaby," she said, pressing her hand to her belly. "Don't worry, Baby, I will protect you from her bullshit."

Bzzzzzz. Bzzzzzz. Bzzzzzz.

She glanced down at the screen as she brushed her teeth. Another text from Luc. She tensed before she bent to rinse her mouth. For the last couple of hours, he was in a Q&A mode. She dried her hands and released a frustrated exhale as she opened the latest of his random message. "What now, Luc?" she said.

LUC: Is he G. Walker who did the sketch of you?!?!?!

"Shit," she swore, dropping the toothbrush into the sink.

Tell him the truth. The same truth I denied him the last three months.

So she did. "Yes, Luc," Jaime said aloud as she typed and then held the phone in her hand as she awaited a response. None came. She started to text him again but paused. Words escaped her. Even an apology seemed pointless.

Bzzzzzz. Bzzzzzz. Bzzzzzz.

LUC: YOU FOUL AF.

She locked eyes with those in her reflection.

Two men. Both betrayed by her design and doing.

A tear raced down her cheek. "I know," she admitted in a whisper.

"What are you going to do?"

Jaime ate from a bag of chips with one hand and used the remote to flip through the cable channels with the other. "I don't know, Renee," she said as the lights of the television flashed across her face in the darkness of the motel room.

"How are you doing? Are you okay?" Renee asked with obvious concern.

"Just wishing everything could be different," she said softly. Truthfully.

"Like what?" Aria asked. "That's the truth you have to face. What would you change? What do you wish it all could look like?"

Jaime didn't know and so she didn't answer.

"Which one do you love?" Aria asked.

"Both," she said.

"Bullshit," Renee swore with swiftness and a suck of air between her teeth.

"Yeah, not true, Jaime," Aria added.

"Why not?" she asked, as she eyed a rerun of *The Golden*

Girls. She dropped the remote and settled back against the wood headboard she had covered with a sheet.

"Do you believe in polygamy now?" Renee asked.

Jaime shook her head. "Of course not," she said.

"Then until you realize you don't love them both you will continue to mourn the loss of both, and it will keep you from moving forward," Renee explained. "To be able to co-parent you have got to get beyond this idea of loving both."

Jaime felt more confused than ever. "If it's not love, what is it?"

"Lust," Aria offered. "Or greed."

"Sins, huh?" Jaime asked.

"Shit, we've all got our sins to bear. I was fucking Jackson out of revenge," Renee confessed. "*And* that was my pride. How dare he want another woman other than me."

"I wish it all was that simple," Jaime said.

"Well, that's one thing you said right, because your situation is complicated as fuck!" Aria exclaimed. "Listen. All jokes aside. I think you fucked up a great thing with a great guy—"

"Thanks," Jaime drawled dryly as she watched Blanche saunter into the kitchen in a flowing silk nightgown and feathered slippers with heels.

"*But,*" Aria stressed. "You have to get the paternity test done before anything else. God willing it's Luc's and y'all can fix this."

"Amen to that," Renee added.

"And if its Graham's?" Jaime asked, hating her friends' insistence on being so against a man they barely knew. "What's y'all vote then?"

"Co-parent and pray," Renee said.

Easy for you to say. I love him.

She pictured a little boy with Graham's eyes and a deep dimpled smile.

"Luc asked for a paternity test," she said. "I thought I had to wait until the baby is born."

"Girl, its 2020 not 1920. They can do it with a blood sample from you and swabs from the two suspects," Aria provided.

"It's a pregnancy, not a crime, Aria."

"You know what I meant."

Jaime eyed the television at Dorothy, Rose, and Blanche sitting at the little round table eating cheesecake in the kitchen. "Do you think we'll be the Golden Girls when we get older?"

"You're *definitely* the Blanche now," Aria inserted.

Renee chuckled.

Blanche was the frisky and promiscuous one who loved men.

Jaime hung up on them.

"That's the truth you have to face. What would you change? What do you wish it all could look like?"

The words of her friend replayed in Jaime's head as she looked out at the bright lights and steady movement of the busy exit at night. Thunder rumbled from in the distance, moments before a light rain began to fall, blurring everything as the water hit against the window.

"Who do you love?"

She closed the curtains and walked back to the bed just as her phone lit up with an incoming call. She had it on silent, wanting no distractions as she struggled once and for all to reckon with her feelings for both men.

Who will I fight for?

She flipped it over to avoid the temptation to answer. She had not heard from Graham. Luc had attempted to call her in the past couple of days, but she was unwilling to face his anger and reprimands, no matter how justifiable. Assuming Graham's annoyance with her matched Luc's, she had decided for the weekend not to speak to either one. She could only assume juggling both men's censure of her would be no easier than juggling both their loves.

"Then until you realize you don't love them both you will continue to mourn the loss of both from your life and it will keep you from moving forward."

And moving forward was key. One thing she did know for sure was more than Luc or Graham, she already loved the child she carried regardless of which man she loved, or which one was the biological father. That she knew.

Four days.

That's how long Jaime gave herself in that hotel room on the New Jersey Turnpike.

That Sunday afternoon, Jaime got dressed and gathered her thoughts, preparing herself for whatever might happen.

Knock-knock.

Her eyes shifted to the door. Her entire body moved into high alert. She exhaled as she reached for the remote and turned off the television before crossing the room to open the door. "Hey," she said, stepping back and waving her hand for Luc to enter.

He barely spared her a glance as he passed her to enter the room. "Not your style," he said as he claimed a seat at the small round table in the corner.

She closed the door. "I'm checking out today and will be at my parents until my rental condo is ready," she explained, moving across the room to sit on the edge of the bed.

He clenched and unclenched his jaw as he gazed out the window at the afternoon sun beaming brightly. "And then you can hang your picture over *your* bed," he said, leveling his eyes on her.

She looked away first. "I'm sorry, Luc—"

"Nah. You said that a dozen damn times, tell me something I don't know," he said with contempt. "Because I'm lost on a lot of shit about you."

He hates me.

"What do you want to know?" she offered.

"Were you going to pass another man's baby off on me?" he asked as his eyes dipped to her belly.

"No, but I didn't know—don't know—which of you is the father and I was intent on you and I making a family together," she explained.

"If you're not lying, you were going to tell him you were pregnant, and he could be the father?" Luc asked, looking down at his watch as a clear deterrent from looking at her.

"Yes," she said with a nod.

"And were you going to tell him another man could be the father, too?"

"Yes," she answered again.

He shook his head and released a sarcastic chuckle. "When were you going to tell me another man might be the father?"

Truth only.

"I wasn't unless the baby wasn't yours," she admitted, looking down at her finger where her engagement ring once sat.

Another caustic laugh as he eyed her with a hard stare. Eyes that once looked at her with love and adoration now were filled with annoyance and contempt.

"Luc, my intent was never to end things with you for Graham. I just wasn't ready to say goodbye to him forever. There was so much between us left unsaid."

"Like?"

I love him.

She ran her teeth over her bottom lip. "We ended things back in 2015 with the hope that we would come back to each other one day, but we just drifted apart. So I freed up my heart—or so I thought—and I moved on."

Luc opened and closed his hand. "You expect me to believe Grenada was the first time you saw him?"

"It was."

"And you fucked this dude—raw—that you hadn't seen or spoken to in years?" he asked with a slight curl to his lip.

"I did," she admitted in a whisper. "And I regretted it as soon as it was over."

"Where?"

She looked over at him. "What?"

"Where did it happen?" he asked, looking out the window.

"You want details?" she asked in surprise.

"Every last one."

"No," Jaime stated firmly.

Experience with her ex-husband had taught her those kinds of details served no purpose but to deepen the pain. *He thinks he wants the truth. He doesn't.*

Memories of her blinding white-hot sex with Graham replayed. His roar when he climaxed echoed. Her cries as her climaxes shook her to her core. *Those details? No, I won't do that to him. I can't.*

It would be like firing a gun at a chest that you thought would only cause a simple entry wound, until turning the body over revealed that every organ inside the body and the back suffered massive damage.

"It serves no purpose to go into every detail," she said, feeling weary as she leaned forward to set her elbows on her thighs and cover her face with her hands.

"Damn, that nasty, huh?" he asked.

She lowered her hands as her body went still as she looked at him in disbelief. It felt too much like when Eric had questioned and berated her about her one-night stand with Pleasure, wanting every sordid detail to then cruelly throw in her face at his sadistic whim.

"Look, I get that you're angry and I get that you feel I owe you anything and everything at this point, but I won't share those intimacies with you. If you require that to continue this conversation, then I understand if you want to end it now."

Luc stared at her in shock. "You're trying to set the rules right now when you were the one who broke them in the first damn place?" he asked with bitter coldness.

She remained silent.

"If I had fucked one of the women always throwing pussy at me—that I'm blocking left and right out of respect for you—then you wouldn't want to know nothing?" he asked.

"What purpose would it serve for me to know where and how you fucked another woman?" she asked.

"Liar."

She sighed.

He rose to stand over her.

Jaime looked up at him.

His hurt flashed in his eyes before he could hide it. "You were mine," he said in a low voice.

She frowned a little at his possessive tone. The urge to question his claim of ownership felt pressing. She understood he was in pain, but she belonged to no one. She wasn't a thing to be owned.

Well, what price did he pay for the title on my life? The ring? The lifestyle? What?

She pressed her hands together, taking a breath to set aside her ego and remember the hurt she caused him. "Luc," she said, reaching for his hand as she rose to her feet before him.

He flinched from her touch.

She dropped her head and her hand. "The very fact that

I admittedly lacked the wherewithal to avoid all of this proves I wasn't ready to be married or to be in a serious relationship," she admitted.

"Have you gone crazy and convinced yourself you have a choice in us being together?" he balked with a frown.

"No, I'm saying I won't fight for it," she declared. "I love you, but I fooled myself into thinking I was ready for everything you have to offer. Everything a woman better than me deserves to have."

He eyed her long and hard. "So you're going to be with your ex?" he accused.

"No," she answered truthfully. "I need to get my shit together and focus on being a mother, not on being someone's wife *or* someone else's long-lost love."

Luc looked confused. "Why does it feel like you're dumping me? The fuck?" he balked. "This some kind of game you playing, because this feels fucked up."

"That I agree we should end things?" she asked.

"I don't give a fuck if you agree," he spouted. "It's over."

Jaime pressed her lips together and said nothing.

He eyed her in disbelief.

"Luc, I'm admitting that I fucked up because *I* am fucked up. Forgive me," she said with desperation as she pressed a hand to her chest. "I already put my desire to be with you or to have him back in my life in any way above what was my best for my child. Because what is best for him or her is to know who his or her father is, and I was willing to lie at first. I was willing to keep that secret."

Luc moved to the window to stare out of it.

Tears welled and she sniffed as she shook her head. "It's a bitter ass pill to swallow that—"

"I'm out of here. I can't do this flip mode bullshit with you, Jaime," he said, walking to the door with long strides.

"It feels grimy as fuck that you looking for sympathy right now. *Real* grimy."

She dropped her head as a tear fell from her face to land on the carpet. She crossed her arms over her chest. Admitting to herself that she showed the same selfishness with her unborn child that her mother showed her was hard, but it wasn't his cross to bear. He had enough on him.

The door to the room closed.

He was gone.

Later that day, Jaime climbed from her car and crossed the sidewalk in Brooklyn to come to the large metal door of the multi-story factory renovated to an apartment building of lofts. She pressed Graham's doorbell. Twice. There was a lengthy wait in between each. She raised her hand to the bell again.

The door opened before she could, and Graham's tall presence filled the entry. His face was stoic. He had a light beard. The clothes he wore were splattered with wet paint she could smell. His feet were bare.

His mood was distant.

"Can I come in?" she asked as her heart pounded like drums.

He shook his head.

Jaime swallowed over a lump and nodded. "I understand you don't have much to say to me," she began as she looked down the length of the cobblestone street. "I don't blame you. I'm here to apologize."

Graham crossed his muscled arms over his chest. His face was still unreadable. But his eyes—those eyes—were on her and she felt nervous under his gaze.

"Forgive me for not revealing I was in a relationship—"

"Engaged," he inserted.

"Yes."

His eyes went down to her left hand before raising back up to her face.

"Forgive me for not immediately telling you that I was pregnant, and the baby could be yours," she said. "I knew for just two weeks—"

"Just, Jaime?" he asked.

She fought the urge to turn and run. "I was going to tell you that day and Luc—"

"Your fiancé," he inserted.

"Yes," she stressed. "My fiancé interrupted that."

Graham wiped his new beard with his hand as he shook his head. "I just want to be clear that what I care about the most is you not telling me about the baby," he said. "You weren't my fiancé. You're not my woman. We weren't even a couple. You cheated on him with me...the same as you cheated on your husband with me years ago."

"Right," she acknowledged. "Look, I really took the time this weekend to evaluate some things and I realize that I've got some work to do on myself, especially before my baby arrives. My focus has to be on becoming a good mother. I'm not ready to be someone's wife *or* open up my heart to all the love I have for you right now. But I should have realized that before I got us all into this."

He looked away from her and bit his bottom lip as if in deep thought.

"Graham," Jaime said, folding her fingers into a fist to keep from reaching to touch him. "I was going to tell you that day. I swear."

"It's pretty fucked up that you even considered not telling me," he said, still looking down the street.

"We both agreed we didn't have a future...and I felt like I could have one with Luc if I kept from him what I did with you in Grenada," Jaime confessed, determined to be truthful with them both. "I did what I thought was best for me, not considering the feelings of Luc or you. And it was selfish of me to not think of my baby first. Yes, before even you or him, I should have made sure my baby had what it needed and that's their father. Even if it meant both of you leaving me alone when I told the truth."

Graham looked upward as he worked his broad shoulders as if to erase some annoyance he felt. "I'm happy to hear you're having some self-awareness," he admitted.

She closed her eyes and released a breath. "I fucked up," she whispered, feeling emotional.

"You did," Graham said, finally locking his eyes on her.

"I'm sorry. I'm so sorry," she said, reaching to cup his firm forearm with her hand.

"You just proved we were right that we could never have anything serious," he told her.

"To be honest, Graham, right now I don't want to try to live up to what anybody wants or needs but my baby," she admitted as she stroked his brown skin with her thumb.

"It could be *our* baby, Jaime," he said, his voice deep.

She smiled. "It could be. Yes," she said. "But right now, I have to get my shit together and focus on being a mommy. To not be to my child what my mother was to me— controlling and manipulative and only caring about what she thought I needed."

Graham looked away again as he nodded in understanding. "Right," he agreed. "I think that's best, Jaime. I'm pissed at you. I'm still dealing with it all and I'm not perfect, *but* I'm proud of you for realizing you got shit to work out."

Jaime squeezed his arm before she stepped back. "I'll be in touch with the details of the paternity test soon," she said, before turning to leave.

"Jaime."

She stopped, but she didn't turn. She couldn't. She

wasn't quite sure she wouldn't beg him to let her stay if she did. She held on to her focus on motherhood and not love or passion.

"I'm hoping it's my baby," Graham said.

Feeling her resolve weaken, she quickly rushed to her car and soon sped away.

Chapter 12

Two weeks later

Luc was hurt. Still.

He hated going home.

He left his car and crossed the parking garage to reach the elevator. With a yawn behind his hand, he leaned against the rear wall as it traveled just one floor to the lobby and stopped. He was surprised. It was late on a weeknight and usually he was able to ride up to his floor without interruption.

Through the glass doors, he eyed Miss Too Much in a lime green bodysuit that left little to the imagination. He pulled out his phone and gave it his attention as she stepped on.

"Hey there," she said, leaning over to press the button for her floor.

"Hey," he said.

The doors closed and the elevator smoothly began to rise.

"I haven't seen your fiancé lately."

Gut punch. He didn't show it. "We're not together," he said.

"Oh. That's too bad."

Luc wasn't in the mood for games. He lowered his phone and looked at her like "Yeah, right."

"What?" she asked innocently as she turned to stand in front of him.

"Don't pretend you care about my relationship," he said.

She shrugged a shoulder. "Okay. I won't," she said, flipping her waist-length dark purple hair behind her shoulder. "I'm feeling you and if you'd get your nose out your phone sometimes, you'd feel me too."

"Really?" he asked.

"Definitely," she assured him as she placed her hand on her hip and posed.

He eyed her from head to toe as the elevator slowed to a stop. "This your floor," he said before turning his attention back to his phone. "You have a good day."

The doors slid open.

She didn't get off.

Luc closed his eyes and shook his head before he looked at her. "What do you want from me? You want to be in a video or just hang out with somebody you think is famous?" he asked. "You got a demo you want to give me? You're looking for someone to fund your lifestyle? What is it?"

She looked perturbed.

"Look, I'll be honest. My head is still pretty much wrapped up in my ex," he admitted. "I would just be using you. And you're not some random dude's cum catcher—"

"Cum catcher!" she snapped.

The elevator doors began to close. He reached out past her to stop it. "I'm not calling you a cum catcher. I'm saying you shouldn't be someone's cum catcher."

"Oh you think you need to tell me not to be a cum catcher?" she asked with attitude.

Luc lightly held her upper arms to guide her back off the elevator. "Let's pretend this conversation never happened," he said, easing back just as the doors once again began to close.

Yo, please don't stop it.

She didn't.

The elevator continued its ascent to his floor and Luc made his way down the hall, wishing he had never ventured into conversation with the woman he had offended by trying to avoid using her. Because all he could offer any woman at that time was meaningless sex. "Fuck love," he muttered as he unlocked the door and entered his condo.

Cloaked by darkness and broken by moonlight, everything was beautiful but haunted. Jaime had removed her physical things but her presence—the imprint of her in the apartment—remained. Reminding him of how he had believed in her and her lies. Mocking him.

And at times making him miss her.

"Shit," he swore as he kicked off his shoes and removed his jacket, leaving them behind in the foyer, before he moved to stretch out on the sofa.

He hadn't slept in their bed since she left.

He turned over onto his back and picked up his phone on the sofa beside him. Long gone was the photo of Jaime from their first date on his screen, but buried in his albums was one he couldn't bring himself to delete. In it, Jaime held the ultrasound from her first doctor's appointment.

Luc wanted to be happy and excited about the baby again.

He wished he could forget the thought of Jaime fucking another man. There was nothing he wanted more than to be in the home with his child helping to raise his child. A family. The same one he never had.

"For loving both of you."

Those words from her mouth when she admitted to having feelings for him and her ex had destroyed him then and still pained him. Walking away from Jaime and her betrayal meant walking away from living in the home with his child.

Might be my child.

He checked the time. It was three in the morning.

"Fuck it," he said, dialing her full number because he had erased her from his contacts.

It rang four times.

"Luc?" Jaime said, her voice raspy with sleep. "What's wrong? Is everything okay?"

Like you give a fuck, he thought, wishing he didn't still give that fuck. But he did.

He sat up on the sofa. "Jaime, what's the update on the paternity test?" he asked.

"Luc, what time is it?" she asked.

"Three."

"Studio session?" she asked, sounding amused.

"Yeah," he replied, turning his head to look out the window at the night sky.

The line went silent.

"Jaime—"

"How are you, Luc?" she asked.

"Like you give a fuck," he shot at her, unable to deny himself.

More silence.

"Can you ever forgive me?" she asked, filling the quiet.

"Nah," he answered quickly, saying it more than he felt it. "The paternity test?"

"Right," she said, clearing her throat. "My next appointment is in two weeks. I think they do it by blood tests—"

"Me, you, and your ex," he inserted.

A pause.

"Yes," she eventually said. "At my next appointment, I'll speak to the doctor about making the arrangements for testing."

There was so much he was tempted to say. Questions. Reprimands. Maybe even reconciliation.

He swallowed them all down. He needed to know if he was going to be a father or not. Right now, that's all that mattered, and everything banked on that. For his child, he would do anything. Even fight to forgive his or her mother.

"Text me the details when you have them," Luc said before ending the call and tossing his phone onto the coffee table.

Hell on earth took on a whole new meaning for Jaime.

The accommodations were lush. Food was readily available to feed her growing cravings. The skills of Margaret, the housekeeper and cook, was above par. Even the view from her window down at the pool and garden was sublime. Suburban life had its privileges.

But this bit of suburbia included her mother's mouth and controlling nature.

Jaime drove her vehicle onto the drive of her parents' three-story brick colonial home. She couldn't bring herself to climb from her vehicle and enter. "Fuck this shit," she muttered as she called her realtor.

It rang just once.

"Jaime. How are you?" Reynold asked in his big and booming voice.

"Ready to move. Update, please," she said bluntly, cutting to the chase and skipping the niceties. *Spare me the bullshit.*

"Okay. So they aren't finished with the repairs to the apartment—"

Jaime pounded her fist on the wheel. "How much more?" she asked.

"A week. That's firm," he added before she could ask.

"Seven days or five business?" she asked.

"Seven."

"Okay. I love the apartment. The lease is just for a year. It will make my commute better because the Jersey Turnpike is killing me," she reasoned.

"Unless you want to reconsider buying. You made a great profit off your house," he reminded her.

And I put half into a trust for Eric's daughter when she reaches adulthood.

"I'm still not sure just where I want to settle down again," she admitted. "House or condo? Jersey suburbs or NYC? Cash or Finance? No, I'll rent for now."

"Are you ready to sign the lease now?" he asked.

"Yes," she agreed as she picked up her briefcase and tote bag before leaving her car.

"Then come into my office tomorrow...and maybe we can have dinner to celebrate," Reynold suggested.

Jaime pictured him. Tall, wide, and solid, his smile was at the ready, and his laughter was infectious. In his looks, he reminded her of Gerald Levert, the late and great R&B singer. They worked together often because he hired her to stage many of his rental and sales properties. He had previously made his attraction for her known. She had previously declined his request with politeness. "I'm pregnant," she said, ready to end his chase once and for all.

"Oh," he said, sounding both stunned and disappointed.

"Close your mouth, Reynold," she said to him in a singsong fashion. "See you tomorrow."

She ended the call with a chuckle, feeling in a better mood because her days at the house that Virginia Osten-Pine built were dwindling. She'd already purchased new furniture that was stored in her design warehouse. She was ready to take joy in living in Tribeca and preparing for the arrival of her child.

She entered the house through the side door leading into the spacious chef's kitchen. With a yawn, she wished Luc had not chosen the wee hours of the morning for a chat on paternity. She was exhausted.

Margaret looked over her shoulder, pausing in cleaning the stainless Viking stove. "You missed dinner," the middle-aged woman said in mock reprimand. "And your mother was not happy about it."

She's not happy about very much . . .

Jaime set her things on one of the dozen stools surrounding the island. "Where's everyone?" she asked.

"Your mother had a church board meeting, and your father is in his office," Margaret said, removing a plate to sit in front of Jaime at the island. Utensils rolled into a linen napkin followed. "He doesn't want to be disturbed."

Jaime kicked off her heels—something that would give her mother a conniption—and sat down on one of the stools to enjoy the meal of smothered chicken, mashed potatoes, and sautéed baby corn. She took a deep inhale, trying to quickly deal with the nausea she always felt just before she ate. "Hopefully, Baby will let me keep this down," she said before saying grace and then taking a bite.

"When do you find out what you're having?" Margaret asked as she pulled on her black overcoat over her uniform.

"In two weeks," Jaime said.

"Team Girl," Margaret said with a wink before leaving to head home.

Bzzzzzz. Bzzzzzz. Bzzzzzz.

Jaime set her fork down on her plate and picked up her phone from atop her things on the stool beside her. She answered the FaceTime call. "Hello, ladies," she said, already knowing both Renee and Aria were on the line.

She was right. She leaned her phone against her glass of fresh-squeezed lemonade.

They were in costumes and Jaime chuckled as she resumed eating her food. "The annual Richmond Hill Halloween party?" she asked.

"We're headed to the clubhouse in a little bit," Renee said, dressed as Supergirl complete with a long wavy wig. "We wanted to check on you."

"What did Margaret cook tonight?" Aria asked as she leaned in closer to the phone in her Wonder Woman garb.

"Smothered chicken," Jaime said before taking another bite.

"You sure you don't want to come to have fun?" Renee asked as she held up a black latex catsuit on a hanger. "We rented you a costume, too."

"Rented?" Jaime drawled with a hard look. "Me and my little belly will pass."

"You're hardly showing, Jaime," Aria said.

True. Still . . .

"Kingston is Batman."

Jaime chuckled. "Who knew y'all loved comics so much," she said.

"I love being sexy more," Aria said. "Kingston chased me around the house before we left—"

"Hey!"

"Hello, Kingston," Jaime said at his holler of protest at Aria telling their bedroom business.

They swung the phone in his direction, and she laughed at seeing Batman—mask and all—sitting near the fireplace in Renee's house. "Mind your cape don't float into that fire, Kingston," she teased.

"Exactly," he drawled in obvious annoyance.

Kingston was not here for it. Jaime agreed. "Thanks for the invite but I'm good. I had a long day. I just want to climb into my bed for some rest."

The phone swung back.

"Guess who else is here," Renee said with her eyes dancing with glee.

The phone swung again. Superman was sitting across the

leather ottoman from Kingston. Jaime choked on her food. Chocolate Angel from Grenada.

Damn, Renee's pussy talk is a bad motherfucker.

Jaime waved and forced her confusion not to show across her face. "Hello there—"

"Sanders," Renee supplied.

He waved in return.

"I have *so* many questions," Jaime said.

He chuckled.

The phone swung again.

"He surprised me today," Renee said. "It's gonna be one *helluva* night."

Jaime wiggled her eyebrows.

"At least we won't hear it this time," Aria said, lifting a glass of white wine in a toast to *that*.

"Wait. What?" Kingston said in the background.

Jaime laughed. "Okay. I miss y'all," she admitted.

"We miss you too," her friends said in unison with playful pouts.

"I gotta go. Sleep is calling. Y'all have fun," she said, rising to scrape the few remnants on her plate into the trash. "Bath and bed for me."

"Bye!" they all said.

She quickly washed her dishes before grabbing her things and leaving the kitchen. She eyed her father's closed office door as she neared the steps to the second floor. "I'll just peep my head in," she said, wanting to see the face of her jovial and good-natured father.

Unlike her mother, Judge Franklin Pine was nothing but easiness, understanding, forgiveness, and indulgence—unless her mother pressured him to be otherwise.

She cracked the door.

"Frankie, I miss you so much."

Jaime frowned and paused with just a sliver of the door

open at the sound of a woman's voice. *Frankie? Who the fuck is Frankie?*

"We'll see each other tomorrow, Nance," her father said.

Jaime's mouth fell open and her eyes rounded. *Nance? Who the fuck is Nance?*

"If it wasn't for you supposed to be golfing on Wednesdays, I would never see you," the voice whined.

Jaime's heart pounded as she leaned in to press an eye to the crack. She could just make out her father lounging in his office chair looking at his phone during his own FaceTime call without a care in the world. *Slick ass.*

"You know I'm retired now, Nance," he said. "It's hard to get out as much."

"Yes, but it's been fifteen years of this sneaking—"

Fifteen years!

She eased the door closed and then turned to press her back to it as she closed her eyes, feeling the weight of her father's façade as a husband, father, and honorable judge fade. At that moment, everything she ever felt or thought of her father—her Daddy—died. The hurt was immense, and her tears came swiftly.

"Jaime? What's wrong?"

She looked at her mother closing the front door and observing her. She forced a smile as she used a trembling hand to wipe away the wet trail of a tear. "Nothing," she lied, walking away from the closed door that had opened such disappointment inside her for her father.

Virginia eyed her and then the door as she set her tote and keys on the table in the foyer. A look crossed her face for the briefest moment. "How are you feeling today?" she asked.

Tell her.

As much as Jaime judged her mother, she could not deny that Virginia Osten-Pine was loyal to many faults to her

father. More than he was being, in that very moment, in the
house he shared with her. His happiness was her goal. Her
life's work.

"A little tired, but I'm going up to bed," she said, her
voice soft as she just couldn't find the will to fight the deep
and profound sadness she felt for her mother.

Tell her.

Virginia walked over and extended her hand with a
sweet smile.

Jaime felt like a child as she took it and squeezed it tight
as her mother pressed their hands to her bosom of the plaid
tweed coat she wore with a silk white tee and jeans with
heels and her ever-present pearls—this time Chanel. They
climbed the stairs together.

"When I was pregnant with you, I slept all the time,"
Virginia said.

Tell her.

"Did you have morning sickness?" Jaime asked, never
willing to discuss her pregnancy with her mother before.

"Just nausea at the smell of food. I hardly ever threw up,"
Virginia said as they reached the landing that was large
enough to be a bedroom itself.

"Me too," she said in wonder.

Virginia smiled as she opened the door to Jaime's room
and pushed it open. Her mother released her hand and
walked in ahead of her after turning on the dome-shaped
Swarovski chandelier in the center of the tray ceiling. "All I
thought of was giving you a better life than I ever had. That's
all a mother can do," Virginia said as she picked up a pale
pink vintage stuffed teddy bear.

Tell her.

But it will destroy her.

The same way I destroyed Luc.

No. Worse.

Jaime set her things on the bed as she eyed her mother softly straightening the bear's tutu. "Did you have any cravings?" she asked as she kicked off her shoes.

Virginia set the bear back on the shadow box shelves. "Not really," she said, touching a photo of Jaime at eight doing a pirouette at one of a thousand dance recitals from her childhood.

Tell her.

Jaime turned her back as she thought of her father—her hero—downstairs making plans with his mistress of fifteen years. She felt a deep hurt as if his offense were against her as well.

But I'm grown and out in the world making my own offenses . . .

She bit her lips to keep any tears from falling.

"Jaime."

She rushed into her bathroom and ran the water to rinse her face. She shook her head, feeling as if her silence made her complicit in her father's dirty deeds. Her heart broke for her mother. It was shattered.

"Shit," she swore in a whisper into the sink as the water ran. "Damn, Daddy. Why?"

"Because he's a flawed man," Virginia answered.

Jaime stood up straight so swiftly that she felt dizzy. She reached to grip the edge of the sink to steady herself as she eyed her mother leaning in the doorway with a contrite face. "You know," she said.

"About Nance?" Virginia said, coming over to take one of the hand towels rolled and stacked on the corner of the marble sink. "Yes."

Jaime couldn't hide her shock—or her confusion—as her mother guided her chin up with a soft hand and used the towel to pat her face dry. "She was his court clerk," Virginia explained with eyes that brightened with unshed tears. "Now he pretends to love golfing to get at his little slut. Your father doesn't have the coordination to properly swing at a small ball."

Jaime grabbed her hand. "Does he know you know?" she asked, curious about this dynamic of her parents' marriage.

"Of course not," she said, crossing the room to place the towel in the hamper that was hidden in the wall. "I made the mistake of visiting his chambers and her demeanor—the over-the-top niceties—was enough to make me suspicious."

Virginia left the bathroom and picked up a framed picture she insisted was kept on the bedside table since Jaime was small. It was her parents. Not her choice.

"How did you know that I knew?" Jaime asked as she leaned in the doorway, eyeing her mother continuing to stare at the photo.

"On your face was the same disappointment I felt to discover the man I love feels I am not enough woman for him," Virginia said, stroking the photo with her thumb—perhaps feeling regrets.

"I thought you had the perfect marriage, Mama," Jaime said. Trying to reconcile what she believed with what was true.

Virginia turned to face her and did a curtsy of thanks for her performance.

"Why?" Jaime asked.

"At that time, your father and I had been married for more than two decades," her mother said, looking down at her sizable wedding rings. "You were already grown and out of the house. Being his wife and your mother was all I knew. I wondered what did I do wrong. What did I miss? How could I fix it?"

Nothing, Jaime thought, reminded, of Luc's perfection and how none of it mattered when she longed to be with Graham.

"I chose my life—the one I carved out for myself,"

Virginia said as tears wet the jewelry. "The one I carefully prepared just the way I *thought* I wanted it."

"Didn't it hurt?" Jaime asked.

Virginia looked up at her and there in her eyes that Jaime had inherited was the rawness of her agony. "It destroyed me," she confessed before she recovered smoothly, had a small laugh, and plastered her smile in place. Perfectly.

"Any regrets?" Jaime asked.

"Enough to build a house if they were bricks."

Jaime felt disturbed that for her mother the heartbreak of her husband's infidelity was a price she was willing to pay for her lifestyle and to save face. A trait she inherited that showed up in her marriage to Eric. And then, in a way, with Luc.

"Does he know you know?" Virginia asked.

"No," Jaime said with a shake of her head. "I overheard him on the phone with...with..."

Virginia shook her head, offering her reprieve from saying the name of her husband's mistress.

His Jessa Bell.

"I just shut the door," she admitted. "I was so..."

"Disappointed," mother and daughter said in unison as they looked at one another.

Jaime left the doorway of the bathroom to sit down on the side of the bed. She looked at the photo of her parents. "I should have burst in the room and read his ass for filth," she whispered with anger.

"No."

Jaime looked up at her mother in surprise. "Why not? Why won't you say something? Call him out. Make him stop. Trust me, discovery is a hell of a thing to end shit down in the dark," she said, thinking of her debacle on the observation deck of the Empire State Building.

"Letting him know at this point that I was aware of his affair all this time and allowed it—am complicit in it—may cause too great a shift in my marriage for me to bear," Virginia explained. "I prefer the charade and, at times, I am amused at watching him think he's getting away with something."

Jaime fell silent. She felt weary and it was more than just her fatigue.

Virginia reached to stroke her chin before she turned to leave the room. "Say nothing. Let me handle this in my own way," she said, pausing in the doorway.

"Mama—"

Virginia turned as she smoothed her updo, wiped the tracks of her tears, notched her chin higher, and settled her hand on her hip. Perfectly posed and poised. The façade back in place.

"Okay," Jaime agreed.

And then Virginia turned again to leave the room.

Long after she bathed and climbed into bed, naked and raw with emotion, Jaime thought of her mother's unhappiness. The price she paid. More than ever, she was resolved to have happiness. To seek and find her pleasure in life.

I will not sacrifice that to make anyone *happy again. Had I just been truthful with Luc, Graham, and myself . . .*

It was time to choose and accept nothing but the truth. Always.

"Graham. Fight for me. For us. Please."

He tensed at the sound of Jaime's voice near his ear. He shivered as he turned his head to capture her mouth with his own as he grabbed her body to pull her atop his. She was nude and the feel of her softness against the hard contour of his body caused his dick to match the rest of his form.

She licked hotly at his lips before she sat up with her hands hoisting her full breasts up with her taut brown nipples poking through her fingers as she circled her hips slowly. "You can't turn me loose. Stop fighting it, Graham."

He pressed his hand to her chest to lower her upper body to the bed as she spread her legs wide atop his. He raised her hips and she settled each of her soft and thick thighs on a shoulder. "I love eating you," he whispered against her pussy before sucking each of her plump lips into his mouth.

Jaime teased her nipples as her hips seemed to arch with a life all their own at the feel of his intimate kisses. "Yes," she sighed.

Graham sucked her clit into his mouth unhurriedly. Back and forth. In and out. So slowly. He had to fight to take his time and keep the pace as his dick hardened beneath her quivering buttocks. He wanted to savor and not just feast. Not yet. Self-control was everything.

He licked the plump and throbbing bud with the tip of his flickering tongue.

The back of her feet tapped his back as she circled her hips against his mouth and released an impassioned cry.

He moaned—deeply—as he eased his tongue inside her. Deeply.

Jaime's cries seemed to be a mix of pleasure and torture. It fueled him. With a drizzle of his spit, he wet her before he sucked her clit again. Deliberately slow. His dick ached to be inside her. He fought it and it felt like going to actual war would be easier. Feeling almost crazed with his desire, he slid his thumb across her soft buttocks to ease inside her rear.

"You like that?" he whispered against her flesh, already knowing the answer, as he eyed her roll her body like a snake and bring her core against his mouth.

"Yes," she admitted in a hot little whisper as she freed her breasts to extend her arms above her head on the bed.

Graham finger fucked her rear as he stroked inside her tight and wet core with his hungry tongue.

She gasped as if she was devoid of breath and her hands clutched the sheets into fists as she quivered from her head to her toes.

He felt it. He savored it. He knew he pleasured her even while his hardness ached as he denied himself the joy of easing her body down until her pussy snugly fit on his dick. With a deep moan and grunt of pleasure, he drew her plump and pulsing clit into his mouth. It was slick and hot against his tongue.

"Damn," he swore before taking the bud into his mouth again.

Relentlessly, he sucked her as he watched the satisfaction play out on her face as he pushed her over the edge, into an explosive climax he felt hit his tongue. Her body jerked so roughly with the bursts that he had to lock his arms around her hips to keep her from running from her pleasure . . .

Graham awakened with a start and sat up straight in the hotel bed with his hardness tenting the sheet over his naked body. He looked around the dimly lit room for what had pulled him from one hell of a dream.

Brrrrrnnnggg.

The phone.

"Damn," he swore, reaching for it on the bed of his suite in Accra, Ghana.

His heart hammered. "Jaime?" he said, looking at her number.

Coming straight out of a dream about her that was disturbed by a call from her shook him. He couldn't deny that as he answered the phone. "Hello," he said, checking the time.

It was a little after two in the morning in Accra. Making it a little after ten at night on the east coast.

"Graham, I'm sorry to call so late," she began.

He lay back on the bed as his heart betrayed him as it pounded so very wildly at the sound of her voice. "What's up?" he asked, hearing the thickness of sleep in his voice.

"My next doctor's appointment is in two weeks and I

will be sure to set up everything for the paternity test then,"
she said. "It's time we all know the truth."

"Agreed," he said. "I'm out of the country but I should
be back by then."

"Okay. Good," she said. "How are you?"

Hurt.

"Good," he lied, looking down at his unrelenting
erection. "How are you?"

"Good," she said.

He doubted that was true. "Jaime—"

"Yes, Graham?"

He brought his knees up and set his arm atop one as he
massaged his eyes. "Never mind," he said, pushing aside
words of forgiveness.

They weren't fully true. Not yet.

Maybe not ever.

"Graham—"

He shook his head. "Don't," he requested, denying her
the chance to weaken him or find a crack to exploit. "Night."

A brief silence.

"Goodnight, Graham," she soon said.

He ended the call and tossed the phone across the bed to
land near the foot before he flopped back down onto the
bed. His erection remained. The sound of her voice had
sustained it. "Shit," he swore, reaching beneath the sheet to
grip the thick base as it slightly curved to the right.

He hissed at the feel of his hand. Memories of eating
her—in and out of his dream—were vivid, making him
hungry for her. His celibacy did nothing to curb his cravings.
Famine made a feast mouthwatering. He stretched his legs as
he flung the sheet away to stroke his inches slowly with a tight
grip that built that sweet anticipation of an explosive nut.

He needed it. Craved it. Worked for it.

With his precum, he slickened the strokes of his hand as

he thrust his hips up to jack his dick. With a close of his eyes, she was there with him. Naked. Wet. Ready.

"Jaime," he moaned as he pictured her. Watching him. Wanting him.

He imagined her coming up between his open legs to lower her head and take his hot tip into her mouth.

"Jaaaaiiiimeeeeee," he cried out with a hiss, picking up the speed of his hand and tightening his grip as he felt his climax build and erupt from his dick. His hard inches jolted with each squirt sending his cum landing wherever it may. He grunted and shivered as he fought the sensitivity of his hot dick to lengthen his nut.

"Jaime," he moaned again. He stroked the last of his nut from his dick as her image faded, with her giving him one last imaginary lick of his cum.

"Shit," he swore.

Jaime Pine had him all the way fucked up and he knew it.

Chapter 13

One month later

Jaime parked her car in the parking lot of the collection lab. She eyed the glass mirrored building, reluctant to leave the warmth of her vehicle to battle the brutal cold on the East Coast. It had to be done. They all were separately scheduled to submit samples—blood from her and a cheek swab from each of the men.

A strong wind blew that appeared to be frosted. The skies were gray, and her temperature gauge said it was forty-five degrees. Not the worst that the season would bring, by far, but enough to make her hesitate to be in it. She gathered her faux fur around her and slid on fur-lined leather gloves before she finally grabbed her monogrammed tote from the passenger seat and left the car. Her strides in thigh high leather boots were long and rapid. Her head was ducked to avoid the chill from hitting her face.

The glass door was held for her as she quickly entered the building with a visible shiver. "Thank you," she said.

"No problem."

She whirled at his voice and didn't hide her surprise at

seeing her ex standing there as the door swung closed by itself behind him. "Graham," she said, loving the fur-lined full-length leather trench he wore with a bulky turtleneck sweater, denims, and black Timberland boots.

I am in love with this man. Still.

He leaned down to give her a welcoming side hug. "How are you?" he asked in a warm voice that made her forget the crisp chill outdoors.

She inhaled his warm and spicy scented cologne and fought the desire to clutch his body close and weave her fingers through his dreads. "I asked for different appointment times for us all," she said as she reluctantly took a step back from his allure.

"It's cool. I had to change my appointment time because I have to fly back to Ghana this afternoon," he explained, sliding his hands into the pockets of his coat.

His eyes were on her and caused her nerves to be wrecked with far too much ease.

"I better go," Jaime said, pointing her thumb back toward the registration desk.

Graham gave her a single nod with his lips pressed as if keeping himself from saying more.

She turned and walked to the counter to sign in as the young woman behind the glass slid it open. "Jaime Pine," she said as she removed her billfold from her tote. "I have a ten o'clock appointment and I preregistered online. It said I needed to bring identification."

"Yes, I already pulled up all your info. You also prepaid."

"Yes," she said handing the woman her driver's license.

"Let me make a copy of this for your records."

Jaime nodded, trying not to feel such embarrassment to have to get a paternity test to know who fathered her baby. Her smile was forced when the young woman returned with her ID.

"If you're ready, they are."

"I'm ready."

A door opened and another woman in colorful scrubs waved her over. "Jaime Pine?" she asked with a welcoming smile.

"Yes."

The process went quickly and for that Jaime was thankful. She exited through the door that she learned led to the other side of the outer office. She slid on her coat and lifted the edges of her bobbed hair over the collar before she closed and then tied it with the leather belt.

"How'd it go?"

Jaime turned in surprise to find Graham sitting there. "It was okay. Not bad," she said with a shrug as she picked up her tote from where she sat it on a waiting room chair. "Necessary."

"I know you hate needles," he said.

She eyed him as he rose to his full towering height. "You can find it in you to give a fuck about me after what I did?" she asked.

"I'm just realizing there's not very much you can do to make me completely not give a fuck," he admitted, using the leather gloves he held to lightly tap the top of her head.

She felt emotional and looked down to prevent him from seeing tears well.

She failed.

"Hey, hey, hey," he said. "No tears."

"It's the baby and my hormones. I'm so emotional lately," she explained.

"And your lips are plumper," he observed.

"I know!" she wailed with a playful wince. "And my neck is darker than the rest of me. Like what the fuck kind of transformation I am going through?"

"Motherhood," Graham reminded her.

"Right, but he owes me big time when he's an adult," she quipped.

"He?" Graham asked.

She tilted her head to the side at the softness of his voice. It revealed so much. "Yes. It's a boy."

A boy with Graham's eyes and dimpled smile.

That thought warmed her.

Graham's eyes dared to show excitement. "I wish this all was different. I want to be happy. I want to make plans. Hope. Dream," he said. "And I can't, Jaime. Not yet anyway."

"I'm sorry," she said, meaning every bit of it.

"For being pregnant? Never," Graham said as he slid on his gloves. "Can you imagine the story we'll tell our kid about running into each other after years—and giving in to a one-time indulgence we both had reasons to fight—and we create him? It's kind of amazing."

Yes, it is.

Energy shimmied over her entire body. "Without all the details of course," she said, trying to lighten the mood.

Graham chuckled. "Of course," he agreed as they walked to the door together. He held it open for her again.

"Thanks," she said as she passed him to exit.

"Where's your car?" he asked.

Jaime pointed to it. "I'm pretty close," she said as the sounds of cars whizzing past on the nearby interstate echoed around them.

She unlocked the car with her fob before he opened the door for her to ease onto the smooth leather of the driver's seat. "The results should be back in a week," she said as she started the car.

"Jaime."

She looked up at him as she removed her gloves. "Yes, Graham?" she asked, hoping he would say this time what he denied himself when he was in Accra weeks ago.

"Real shit. Wouldn't it be something?" he asked.

Her heart swelled with love for him at the hope she saw in his eyes. "Absolutely *something*," she agreed softly.

Graham tapped the edge of the door before he closed it and stepped back.

Long after she pulled off and headed to her Manhattan offices to meet Renee and Aria for lunch, she was reminded of the heavy price of unhappiness.

Jaime pushed her salad around on her plate as she pretended to listen to whatever Aria and Renee were discussing as they ate the takeout in the conference room of her office. But her thoughts were on Graham.

Why was she letting her head deny what her heart knew so very well? *I love him.*

She could convince herself of many things, but even in the face of the man she had committed to one day marry, she could not deny her love for Graham. *I need him.*

And at that moment in Grenada where the choice was to keep her pledge of fidelity to Luc or have that moment with Graham, she had risked it all to have it. *I want him.*

"Ladies, I have news," Aria said as she patted her afro. "We're moving!"

Jaime looked to her in surprise. "Newark?" she asked.

Aria nodded excitedly. "Well, we compromised on just where in Newark, but I don't care. I want to go home!" she said, doing body rolls as she snapped her fingers.

Renee looked from Jaime to Aria. "Jaime, you knew about this before me?" she asked.

It was then Jaime focused on her food and took a bite of her hearty salad.

"Well damn, Aria," Renee said.

"I mentioned it in passing because I didn't think I could convince Kingston to move," she explained. "But I have, so we are. It means living in just as beautiful a house for less money which means less work, which equals more dick."

Jaime laughed.

"And then there was one," Renee said. "When did Richmond Hills become the big bad boogeyman?"

"Hmmm. Let's see. The year was 2010. A woman soon proven to be a hidden enemy sends a mocking message to her three friends about which of their husbands was her lover and they all lived in a subdivision named Richmond Hills," Jaime said in her best Mary Alice voice-over from the TV show *Desperate Housewives*.

"Okay. True," Renee admitted as she dropped her fork onto the plastic container holding her salad. "I'm gonna miss y'all."

"Renee, we're not leaving any time soon. We have to sell the Richmond Hills house and find one in Newark that we love," Aria reminded her, reaching across the Lucite table to squeeze her hand.

"It's just feeling the loss of so much lately. My whole focus has been my career and my kids," Renee said, leaning back in the chair as she pushed her food away.

"Don't forget Fudge," Aria said with eyes filled with mirth.

Jaime laughed.

Renee shot Aria a stare usually directed at her children when they were small and misbehaving.

"Sorry," she mouthed.

Renee waved her fingers to dismiss it. "It's fine. Do you know Jackson had the nerve to come to my house late one night with a bottle of wine and probably a blue pill hidden away somewhere on him?" she said with an incredulous face. "I told him if he didn't get his ass and his limp dick off my porch that I would show his wife video footage of him sniffing around my door."

"Uhm, okay. Now I know you're serious. You are done-done with Jackson," Aria said.

Renee pointed at her in affirmation of her being right. "I

assume he is *done-done* with me 'cause I haven't heard from him since."

"What about your second ex-husband?" Jaime asked out of curiosity.

Renee sucked her teeth. "Fuck his thin–dick–having ass, too. Shit. Hell with 'em both."

Aria pressed her hands to her face. "Thin! Oh my!" she exclaimed, feigning being mortified.

Jaime laughed.

Renee smiled as she raised her bottle of peach-flavored Perrier. "May their current wives delight in their dicks more than I did," she toasted. "Being in love has a way of making an imperfect dick just fine."

Aria and Jaime raised their bottles of mineral water as well.

They all laughed as they finished their lunches.

"Can you imagine the story we'll tell our kid about running into each other after years—and giving in to a one-time indulgence we both had reasons to fight—and we create him? It's kind of amazing."

Jaime dropped her fork and rose from the table. She stood at the window to look out at the city as she recalled the rest of her conversation with Graham.

"Real shit. Wouldn't it be something?" Graham had said.

"Absolutely something," she had agreed softly.

"Jaime. What's on your mind?" Aria asked, interrupting the recollection that made her insides warm.

She focused her eyes on her reflection in the window. "Graham," she admitted, seeing the truth of her feelings in her eyes. "I saw him at the DNA lab when I went today and..."

"And what?" Renee asked sharply.

She looked back over her shoulder just as her friends shared a look.

Jaime rolled her eyes. "What?" she asked, but then she

held up a hand. "You know what? It doesn't even matter what you're thinking. I don't care. I love him. I love Graham Walker. I am in love with Graham Walker. I have always loved Graham Walker. I will always love Graham Walker...and I really don't give a fuck whether y'all understand it or not. It's my heart. My pussy. My business."

"You're going throw a chance to fix this with Luc for him?" Renee asked, shoving her lunch away again. "Luc's perfect."

Aria shook her head to show her disagreement with Jaime's declarations.

"That's the thing. He is perfect...on paper," she said, turning to walk back over to the table. "But it all was surface. Good sex. Sure. Fun times. Yes. But when it comes to going deep? Wanting more. Asking for more. *Seeing* more. That's Graham. Deep and meaningful," she stressed.

"That's all the ploys and bullshit he learned to woo women out of their panties and their money," Renee retorted.

Jaime laughed with sarcasm. "I never once voiced an objection when you fucked a total stranger all night long," she said, starting to tick her issues off on each of her fingers. "I didn't say shit when he skipped his young and happy ass to the States to fuck you some more. Not one word. Hell, I don't know. Is he still here? I never asked. Guess why? It's none of my damn business. Huh? Right?"

Aria held out her hand. "Jaime—"

"No, when Kingston had y'all asses deep in debt up to his balls did I say one damn contrary word about him? Did I say leave him? Did I say he doesn't know what the fuck he is doing because a doctor he may be, but a businessman he is not? Did I once tell you he gonna have your ass round here like Gertie off of *Good Times* eating dog food as meatloaf? Hell no. I. Did. Not!"

"Seems like you had that on the tip of your tongue for a minute," Aria said with coldness.

Jaime applauded. Slowly and mockingly. "Did I once let it trip off my tongue though? No. I supported my friend and her choices. Both of you."

And they both had the decency to look properly chastised.

"We only want what's best for you," Renee explained.

Jaime's hand slashed the air as her friend parroted the same bullshit line her mother used over the years to justify her controlling behavior. "No! You want what you think is best for me and that is *not* the same," she stressed.

"You choose Graham over *Luc*?" Renee asked.

Jaime pursed her lips and released a long, drawn-out breath as she reclaimed her seat and leaned back against it. "And if we go by past behaviors should any man choose me over another woman when I cheated on my husband and then my fiancé?"

"That's real as fuck, Jaime," Aria admitted.

"Yes, it is," she agreed. "That night at that party at your house, Aria, when y'all asked if I was serious about Graham and I said marriage wasn't an option. I lied because I didn't want my friends to judge me. I was ashamed of his history. I denied how good he made me feel out of the bedroom. At that moment I chose y'all over him. Just dumb. The days of people telling me who, when, and how to love are over."

Jaime took a steadying breath. "And let me add this," she said, eyeing them both. "Even if my happily-ever-after is not Graham because we're both too scared our pasts just won't let our love for each other be great, then it's unequivocally not Luc...or I wouldn't have cheated on him. Not if I was deeply *in* love with him. I wouldn't have risked it all if I was *in* love with Luc. There would have been no room for anyone else. And that may not be what being in love looks like for other people but that's what it looks like for *me*."

Her eyes felt strained as she struggled not to cry. "He's a

good man. But he is not my man," she admitted, accepting
the truth hidden there inside her the entire time.

Shit.

Jaime held up her hand when they both rose to come to
her as she failed at holding back her tears. "He doesn't *see*
me," she whispered with wet cheeks, thinking of his anger
when she tried to own up to her issues in that hotel room on
the New Jersey Turnpike. "It's all surface. All neat and
perfect and no deeper than a fucking bowl of water."

"What do you mean he doesn't see you?" Renee asked.
"He's always doing things for you like when he surprised
you with the trip or he took you racecar driving in Vegas."

Jaime laughed a little. "Because one night, years ago,
Graham helped me to remember that as a child I dreamed of
racing cars," she explained, having a soft smile at the
memory. "Graham sees me—flaws and all—and can still
wish the best for me. Be concerned for me—like waiting
around to check on me because he knows I'm scared of
needles. Even after knowing I even *thought* about denying
him his child."

Overwhelmed with emotions and regrets of pain caused,
she closed her eyes and silently wept. "He wants me to be
better. Not gifts, diamonds, and trips, but whether I am
being the best person I can and how I can be better. And cares
if I am truly happy at my core and if not, how can I be. And
that is *absolutely* something."

The women all fell silent as Jaime used napkins to pat the
wetness from her face and settle herself as she felt emboldened by her impassioned description of just what Graham
Walker's love looked like.

"And Sanders is not still here. Thank you very much,"
Renee said, breaking the quiet.

Jaime looked over at her to find her smiling. She laughed.

"And I am *not* Gertie!" Aria added.

"I was trying to make a point, y'all," she said, with an apology in her eyes as they began to clear up their food.

She was thankful they all were able to laugh together.

Renee grabbed one of Jaime's hands and Aria the other.

"It was just time to be honest with myself and y'all about my feelings," she said, for her own ears and theirs. "I wouldn't admit the truth of what I wanted because deep down I knew it was even more disrespect against Luc."

"But if you're not honest about what you want then you're disrespecting yourself," Renee finished.

Jaime nodded.

"We got you," Aria promised as she pressed a hand to Jaime's slightly round belly.

"You don't make it easy, Jaime, but yes, we got you," Renee said, splaying her hand on her belly as well.

The baby kicked.

Everyone jumped in surprise.

"Did y'all feel that?" Jaime asked, turning her head left and then right to eye them.

"Yeah, my godson's got one hell of a kick," Renee said. "Football?"

"Or a dancer," Jaime asserted. "Whatever he wants."

"Your godson?" Aria asked.

"Okay, our godson." Renee compromised.

"Don't I have a say?" Jaime asked.

"No," they answered in unison.

Late that night, Jaime dropped her stylus on her tablet. She was doing consulting for owners of a new build construction on the layout of their home from scratch. She took a sip of ice water as she sat atop a pillow on the floor in front of the fire. Feeling a little stiffness, she unbent her legs and wiggled her toes in front of the heat as she stretched her arms above her head.

She loved her apartment and needed the solace after a day of hustle and bustle at the office and being in and out of design showrooms to give life to her visions for three separate projects. There was a lot she wanted to get done before the baby was due next year in April. She looked down the hall at the closed door. Inside, she was beginning to get his nursery together.

"I just hope the doctor knows what she's talking about," she mused aloud as she swiped through the tablet to open the mock-up plan of the nursery that was charcoal gray and varying shades of blues.

"Gotta make it fly as fuck for Mama's boy," she said, even though her prenatal app said the baby couldn't hear her voice for two more months.

She set the glass on the oversized wooden tray atop the low-slung quilted ottoman before she lay back on the ivory shredded leather rug and lowered the waistband of her rose-gold leggings to splay her hands against her rounded belly. "Twenty-four weeks to go," she said to him.

Jaime sat up and reached for one of the baby books stacked neatly on the tray.

Bzzzzzz. Bzzzzzz. Bzzzzzz.

She reached for her phone, surprised at the caller. "Hey, Luc," she said as she rose from the floor with her finger marking her place in the pages of the book.

"I got your check."

"I thought I owed you that," she said of the check she wrote to cover the entire trip to Grenada.

"Hell, more than that."

"Name your price then, Luc," she said as she sat down on the sofa.

"I'm not talking about money."

Jaime adjusted her rose-gold athletic bra. "I know," she said.

"Sending this check was a slap in the face."

"That wasn't my intention. I finished a big job and had some extra money and I felt owed you that after everything that happened," she explained. "The baby is kicking like crazy. Renee said he will probably be a football player," Jaime said.

"He?"

Jaime felt déjà vu.

"Yes, it's a boy."

Silence.

"Luc?" she asked to make sure he was still there.

"I went for the test," he said.

"I know," she said, feeling such remorse for the position she put them all in. "The results should be back in a week."

"And then what?" he asked.

"And then I try to fix the mess I made with the father and co-parent," she said truthfully.

"Co-parent?" Luc said with scorn. "It's not what I want."

Jaime gazed into the fire as she stroked her chin. "Would you fight me for custody?" she asked, feeling alarmed.

Luc was far wealthier and more powerful than she was. *Just how angry is he?*

"I'm not a monster, Jaime."

Relief flooded her as she pressed a protective hand to her belly. She was rewarded with another kick.

Mama's boy.

"*If* the baby is mine, we should get back together and raise him under one roof," Luc said. "I can't be a visitor in my child's life, Jaime."

"And if he's not your child?" she asked.

"Then we keep going our separate ways."

"So you're suggesting we stay together for the child and nothing else?" she asked, with her brows furrowed.

"You want me to raise another man's child?" Luc balked.

"No, definitely not, but I'm not getting married and pretending to be happy—not even for my child, Luc," she said, unable to do anything but speak her truth.

She thought of her mother's dilemma and shook her head as she turned her lips downward.

"Pretending? So now you were unhappy, Jaime?" he asked.

"No."

I didn't know I wanted and needed more.

"After everything that's happened, we both would be now," she insisted.

"Why?"

"*Why?*" she mimicked. "Luc, you can't go a moment without throwing verbal jabs and digs at me. You think I want my child to grow up knowing his father hates me?"

It had been six weeks since he caught her with Graham and his anger with her was still palpable.

"By the time the baby is here—*if* it's mine—I would—"

"What? Forgive me?" she interrupted.

"I can forgive. I will never forget."

Jaime's eyes went to a photo of her mother—sans her father—that she recently had enlarged and framed to sit on one of the shelves that flanked her fireplace. She thought of her pain at discovering her friend and her husband carrying on right under her nose. And then the venom Eric had shown her behind closed doors with his words and demeaning sex acts as he punished her for cheating on him. "No, you never forget," she agreed.

"It's different for a man, Jaime. The thought of another man with your woman is—"

"No different than the pain and disrespect a woman feels when her man is with another woman, Luc," Jaime said, rising to her feet. "I'm not feeding into this 'it's a man thing' bullshit. Pain doesn't recognize gender."

"You wouldn't understand."

She agreed and didn't try to understand. "Where are you?" she asked, picturing him lying on the sofa with his ankles crossed and his arm behind his head.

"At home."

"On the sofa?" she asked.

"I haven't slept in that bed since you left."

"I never violated our bed."

"But you fucked me on it under his picture of you. Same difference as far as I'm concerned."

Jaime winced. "I should have been honest with you about it after I saw it hung in the house."

"I guess it was funny to you, huh?"

"Never," she said honestly.

In the silence that followed he eventually released a heavy breath before he spoke again. "So you're saying even if I'm willing to try to fix this for our kid—*if* he's mine—"

"You don't have to keep prefacing everything with 'if he's mine,' Luc," she said, trying her best to swallow her irritation.

"Just don't want you thinking I'm raising another man's seed."

She rolled her eyes to the ten-foot ceilings. "Trust me, you've made it clear as fuck," she assured him.

A doorbell sounded in his background.

"You have a guest. Maybe its Miss Too Much," she said.

"Maybe it is," he agreed. "Let me hit you back."

Beep-beep-beep.

The call ended. Jaime tapped the corner of the phone lightly against her chin as she thought of Luc with another woman. She hadn't considered he was already back on the prowl. Serving up the same special treatment he gave her— good dick, good tongue, and good money.

I didn't cheat for a lack of good sex.

She pictured him with someone else. Eating her with the same skill. Fucking her with the same diligence. Making her cum with ease.

She waited for countless seconds for jealousy or anger. *Nothing.*

If Luc was ready to fill the spot she destroyed then he had every right to the same happiness she was claiming for herself.

Luc dropped his phone on the chair and stood up to walk over to the door in his black basketball shorts and ankle socks to open it. "Miss Too Much," he said, taking in her hair, now in shades of pink and up in a top knot with the cropped sweatshirt and shorts she wore with fuzzy slippers.

"Ronnie," she offered. "But I am too much, and I like it."

"How can I help you?" he asked.

"I wanted to give you a chance to apologize for calling me a cum catcher," she said.

"No. I said I didn't want to treat you like a cum catcher," he corrected her.

"You are the type of man that categorizes women on sight," she said, easing past him to enter his apartment. "I really thought about this and I think someone—namely me, because I got my own money—should buy you a clue."

Luc turned to watch her walk around his apartment. "I'm good," he assured her as he closed the door.

"Not if you think the woman in Fashion Nova is a cum catcher and the one in Gucci is not," she said, reaching in the front pocket of her sweatshirt to remove a blunt and lighter. "You smoke?"

"Nah," he said, leaning against the wall as he watched her. Miss Too Much lit her blunt.

"No smoking in here. I hate the smell of that shit," he said with a nod to the sliding doors where the winter winds visibly swirled outside.

"Cool," she said taking one long draw before she bent in front of the fireplace to put out the blunt against the metal grate.

His eyes dipped to her peach-shaped buttocks.

She looked back over her shoulder and caught his eyes on hers. With a soft laugh, she did a little twerk before rising. "So, like I was saying. I wear tight clothes. Long nails. Neon colors. I have fun. I hang out with my friends. I like trips and shopping sprees," she said, directing a two-inch, pointy, rhinestone-encrusted nail at him.

"Yes, but what else do you like?" he asked from his spot on the wall.

"Being honest with who I am and what I want," she continued, climbing onto his sofa on her knees as she faced him across the room. "Listening to City Girls...or reading Cornel West. Taking Tequila shots or running my online cosmetic business that I'm currently trying to get on the shelves of the big brand stores. Fucking or fighting. Whatever. I'm complex. Most women are. Open your mind, Luc Sinclair, or you gone wind up in your big, beautiful apartment lonely and getting over another ex...after another ex... after another ex."

Luc pushed off the wall to come over and stand behind the sofa. He looked down at her. "Ok so let's be clear. You want me to fuck you, right? Am I wrong about that?" he asked.

Ronnie reached to run her hands down his tattoo-covered chest before gripping the rim of his shorts to jerk down and expose his dick. "No, you're not wrong. You fly as fuck. I like your style and I especially love you got your own bread and I don't have to worry about a Negro tryna find a come-up," she said as she looked up at him as she pursed her lips and blew a cool stream of air against it.

It stirred.

"Or I might want to chill out and watch CNN while we talk politics," she said, dipping her head to suck one of his balls into her mouth.

His hips thrust forward like he had no control over them.

Luc had always played by the rules in relationships. Always been the good dude. The gentleman. The caregiver and provider. The protector. And he went all-in with Jaime. All the way the fuck in. And he was rewarded with a broken heart and feeling like a fool.

A motherfucking fool.

As Miss Too Much began to suck his dick, he thought of the countless women he turned down over the years being Mr. Good Dude. *Fuck that. I am who she made me. A savage. Another woman won't get the chance to destroy me again.*

"What if all I want is to fuck you?" he asked as he buried his fingers in her hair and pumped her head as she sucked him to hardness.

No fuck that. Don't ask for shit.

"All I want is to fuck you," he corrected, as he tilted his head to the side to watch her cheeks hollow as she sucked him with deep moans.

You good, Babe? What you need, Babe? What can I do for you, Babe? Let me fly you and your friends to Grenada, Babe. Here, take my heart and stomp on it with your heels, Babe. Fuck all of that. No woman would ever get that from him again. Fuck all them.

Miss Too Much took all of him into her mouth until she gagged. He held her head in place as he pumped his hips and grimaced as he fucked the back of her throat. "That's right. Suck my dick," he said as he bit the side of his tongue.

That Luc Sinclair was gone.

He hissed and then flung his head back with a roar as his

cum filled her mouth. She leaned back to jerk the rest of his nut out of him as his cum shot against her face. On her eye. The corner of her mouth. Her hair. Chin. "Catch my fucking cum."

Fuck it.
Fuck her.
And fuck love.

Chapter 14

Knock-knock-knock.

From her kitchen, Jaime looked over at the front door as she tapped the serving spoon against the side of the seafood stew she'd prepared. She set the utensil on the ceramic spoon rest atop the marble countertop. She was nervous as she smoothed her hands over the black knot-front maxi dress she wore as she made her way around the massive island to cross the living room and reach the foyer.

With a deep inhale and exhale she raised the pewter latch and opened the front door. "Thanks for coming," she said, looking up at him with a nervous smile.

"No problem," Graham said as he began to remove his gloves and coat. "They're calling for snow late tonight."

"I won't keep you long," she promised as she took his coat from him to hang in the hidden hall closet.

"My truck and I can handle it," he promised her.

I believe him.

"What smells so good?" he asked.

You.

"I made a stew with lobster, shrimp, and lump crab meat with garlic biscuits and fresh-squeezed fruit juice," she said, leading him into the kitchen.

"Well damn," Graham said, going to the sink to wash his hands.

Behind him, she eyed his tall, muscled physique in the V-neck sweater and denims he wore. Graham's body was pure steel, honed by exercise and good eating. He moved with strength. Power.

She swallowed hard as she licked the corners of her mouth. *Sexy motherfucker.*

He looked back over his shoulder at her.

She forced a smile as she raised her eyes from the sight of his tight buttocks.

He had the nerve to look bashful as he turned to lean back against the edge of the counter as he crossed his muscled arms over his chest. "I'm here, Jaime. The question is why?" he asked.

I love you, but I can't say it because I may be carrying another man's child. Or it could be a little boy with your eyes and smile.

"I thought we should do something we really haven't done these last few months since we—"

Fucked.

"Reconnected," she said instead.

Graham looked brooding. "Our past?" he asked.

"Our past," she confirmed.

"Seventeen years," he said, eyeing her with intensity. "There's a lot to unpack."

She nodded. "Then the sooner we start the better," she said as she leaned forward against the island that separated them. She envisioned crawling across it to fling herself at him and had to shake her head a little to free the tempting thought. *Lord, he's so sexy. But he's also smart. And creative. And deep. And forgiving.*

Graham gave her a smile that exposed his charming dimples. "Then let's get at it," he said.

On the floor or my bed?

Wait, not sex. He means talking.

"Let me fix our plates," she said. "You go to the dining room."

"Dining room?" Graham balked. "Very formal."

Ding-dong.

Jaime frowned at the intrusion as Graham walked into the adjoining room. "Who is that?" she asked herself.

"Don't tell me you invited old boy, too," Graham said.

"Definitely not," she assured him as she made her way to the foyer again to check the door viewer to see her parents there. "What the fuck?"

She turned and pressed her back to the door. Graham and her parents. *What ironic karma pit of hell is this?*

He came to the edge of the kitchen to lean against the counter. "What's wrong?" he asked.

"My parents are doing a drop-in," she said with a weak smile that trembled more than her suddenly nervous stomach.

"What you wanna do?" he asked.

"Disappear," she admitted.

He chuckled. "I know the last time I encountered your mother it was not ideal," he said.

"You think?" she asked, remembering a decade ago when he walked out of the bedroom naked and holding his dick while she and her mother were in the living room of her rental townhome.

"But I might be the father of their grandchild," he reminded her. "Maybe it's time to get to try to go beyond it, Jaime. Face the past and all that."

Ding-dong.

"Right," she said, pushing off the door. "At least you're dressed this time."

"Maybe she forgot," Graham said as he turned to walk back into the kitchen.

"I doubt that," Jaime stressed as she turned.

His chuckles reached her as she opened the door.

"Surprise!" Virginia said, giving her daughter's cheek a

brief kiss before she breezed past Jaime to enter the apartment in a blur of pearls, tweed, and fur.

Jaime eyed her burly father. "Dad," she said, air-kissing his cheek as he hugged her with one arm.

"How are you, Jaime?" he asked.

Pissed at you.

She saw her mother's eyes on her and forced a stiff smile. "Fine," she said, her tone short. "What are you two doing in New York?"

"Your father had dinner with friends not far from here and I insisted on attending with him," Virginia said with a wink at Jaime that was awkward and obvious. "Funny thing, they never showed up. Had a flat tire or something your Dad said."

Was his wife finally putting a leash on her husband in her own little way? *Good.*

"How's golfing, Dad?" Jaime asked.

Franklin Pine looked flustered. "I've given it up," he said.

Oh shit!

"Yes, I told your father that we needed to spend more time together. Right, dear?" Virginia said.

"Right, dear," he droned.

Another wink from her mother behind her father's back.

Oh, Virginia was on his ass and he didn't even know it.

Graham stepped into the living room.

Virginia's shocked inhale of breath was deep and low and long. And funny. But Jaime dared not laugh.

"What's wrong, dear?" Franklin asked.

"Mother. Dad. This is Graham Walker—"

"Why is it every time I drop by my daughter's home unexpectedly, I run into *you*?" Virginia asked, losing her normal composure. "At least you're dressed *this* time."

Franklin's jowls quivered as his eyes widened in understanding as he glared at Graham. When Jaime had needed their help financially in the days after she left Eric, his mother had filled him in on the incident at the townhouse and he ordered her to stay away from the then-unknown man if she wanted his assistance.

"Hello, Mr. Pine. Nice to see you again, Mrs. Pine," Graham said, extending his hand to first her father and then her mother. Neither accepted it. "I apologize for what happened that day. Please forgive me."

"Manners," she pointed out as Graham left his hand extended.

Franklin's back stiffened in indignation as he gritted his teeth and took the hand offered to him. "You understand our confusion with seeing you here after all these years, while my daughter is pregnant, and not long ago she was engaged to another man," Franklin said.

"I understand that," he said, smiling at him before now offering his hand to her mother again.

Graham is fucking with them.

Virginia offered him no more than two of her fingers to grasp before she withdrew her hand. "We only stopped by since we in town," she said, her haughtiness on high. "And we don't want to interrupt."

Jaime stepped in their path to the door. "Actually, you should meet Graham because he might be the father of your grandson," she said, rushing the words with none of her concerns of yesteryears on how her parents would be disappointed in her.

"Might?" Franklin said, his round face masked with confusion.

Virginia nodded in understanding. "Is he the reason the engagement with Luc ended?" she asked.

"No, he's not. That was my doing—or rather undoing, Mother," Jaime said, eyeing her. "I need to be honest with you both because I can't imagine anything worse than living a lie. Right?"

Virginia's gaze on her was unwavering.

Jaime turned to her father. "Right, Dad?" she asked. "You never would want to live a lie and have everything someone thought of you destroyed by the truth. Isn't that what justice is all about? Truth? Integrity? Being honest with who you are. Flaws and all. So that you can live in the light of truth and grow so that you don't wilt in the darkness of your secrets and lies."

Franklin eyed her strangely.

Virginia stepped in between them. "We'll be going," she said, leaning in close to kiss Jaime's cheek. "Please don't."

Jaime nodded in agreement with what her mother implored.

Graham came to stand behind her and warmly pressed his hands to her shoulders. She welcomed the support, not knowing how he knew that at that moment she needed it.

Her father's gaze on her was questioning as he kissed her cheek as well before turning to open the door and leave. "Jaime, we'll talk soon," he said over his shoulder.

Virginia left as well, pulling the door closed behind them.

Jaime took a step to lock the door and then rest her head against the cool metal.

"What was that between you and your father?" Graham asked.

She smiled. He was always so observing. So aware. He missed nothing. Sought knowledge of everything, big and small. She turned and walked back over to pat his chest as she passed him on her way to the kitchen. "Hopefully, his awakening," she said.

Graham took a sip of the punch as he eyed Jaime across the dining room table. He cleared his throat. "Think your parents will ever forgive me?" he asked as she set a steaming bowl of stew in front of him before ladling herself a bowl from the large tureen on the table between them.

"I think they have their own business to be focused on," she said dryly.

He chuckled as he eyed her, loving the way pregnancy was rounding her face and plumping her lips. "I was childish back then. There were better ways to scare you off once I realized I was falling for one of my clients," he said.

"*Or* you could have accepted your feelings for me," she said.

He thought back to that time over a decade ago. "I wasn't ready. I was young. Wild. I had been through a lot at that point. Was settled down more than I had ever been," he said, thinking of the wealthy married woman, Smyth, who had kept him in a luxurious Upper East Side lifestyle that allowed him to attend college. Her caveat? The fidelity her husband wouldn't provide. Having Jaime back in his life during those months after she first left her husband and moved into that townhouse had been hard to resist. Smyth ended things because of it.

"You scared me," Graham confessed.

They joined eyes.

"Everything with you was different. Better. Sex. Conversation. Laughter," Graham admitted. "I was too young and dumb to understand that it wasn't a bad thing to care for a woman. To desire her. Want her. Need her. You. To need *you*, Jaime. What I felt for you scared the shit out of me and I did dumb shit to force you to end it because I didn't have the strength to walk away from you. If you called, I was coming. In hindsight? I loved you. You were the first woman I ever loved, Jaime Pine. The *only* woman I have ever loved."

She looked slightly stunned.

"That's my truth," he said raising his glass in a toast to her.

★ ★ ★

Jaime looked on as Graham knelt before the grand fireplace to light the log inside it as snow began to fall outside. As the fire grew, the blaze of yellow, red, and orange flames cast its light upon his profile, seeming to transform his caramel complexion into bronze.

"I owe you an apology, Graham," she said from her spot in the corner of her oversized sectional sofa.

He looked back over his broad shoulder at her. "For?" he asked, closing the grate before he rose to his full six-foot-nine height.

"Letting what my friends thought of you make me deny to them how much you meant to me back then," she said.

"The party at your friend's house," he said as a look shadowed across his face.

She remembered searching for him at Aria's and Kingston's party until a step out onto the porch proved he and his car were gone. She walked to her house nearby to discover he wasn't there. Two days after not hearing from him she went to his penthouse apartment and walked straight into his kidnapping.

"I should have stood up for you," she said with regret.

He crossed the leather area rug to sit on the other end of the couch, seeming to dwarf it. "Those six months we were together—really together—was dope, until that moment I overhead you tell them no one was talking marriage. It tore me up. It made me feel like shit. Like I still was just that dude you were using for sex—this time without paying for it."

The crackle of the fire filled the silence that followed.

"Forgive me?" she finally asked.

He looked down with his brows wrinkled. His long lashes seemed to whisper against the top of his high cheekbones. "That plate is pretty full," he mused, glancing up at her with a slight twinkle in his beautiful eyes.

"And I'm going to keep feeding it to you until you eat it," she said, pointing her finger at him.

He stared off into the fire. "We'll see," he said, sounding unsure.

Out the window, he saw the snow began to fall in earnest but felt no rush to leave. Things were being said that needed to be said between them. He looked over to where she stood beside him staring out at the street being transformed to pure white. "Why couldn't you trust me?" he asked, taking a sip of the hot chocolate she'd made for them.

"Really, Graham?" she said dryly into her cup.

"No, really," he said, his eyes searching her profile. "Those six months—"

"Before the rooftop," she said.

He remembered that day and had come back to it so many times over the years. "Yes," he said.

She turned to face him as she leaned against the wall. "Walking away was tough. Well, agreeing to walk away. You were the one who wanted the break," she reminded him.

"You were the one who wouldn't let us have a future," he countered.

"Running into women who shared your body—"

"Who you thought shared my body," he inserted with a shake of his head. "You accused me of everybody. Any woman that blinked at me twice. Any woman that stared a little too long. Any woman that spoke. It was ridiculous, Jaime."

She took a sip of her chocolate so deep that a dot of melted marshmallow was on her nose. "It was," she confessed.

Graham chuckled.

"What?" she asked in confusion.

He lightly raised her head to bend down and kiss the froth from the top of her nose. "Marshmallow," he said against her mouth.

He felt her shiver as they stared at one another. Deeply.

His eyes moved about her face, taking in everything, including the reflection of the falling snowflakes in the brown depths of her own. They landed on her mouth and she opened her lips a bit. Temptation overtook him as he dipped his head to kiss her. Softly at first. And then with his tongue probing hers. Stroking it before he suckled the tip.

His dick awakened as she kissed him back with a soft and easy moan from the back of her throat. As he placed his free hand to her back and pulled her closer, he felt the roundness of her belly. He ended the kiss with a step back. It wasn't her pregnancy that deterred him. It was remembering that the child inside might not be his.

And it stung when he wanted nothing more than her son to be *theirs*.

"It's getting late," Jaime said as Graham handed her another rinsed plate to load into the dishwasher.

"You ready for me to go?" he asked.

Never.

"Nope," she said instead. "You ready to go?"

"Not yet."

Not ever? Maybe?

"Why were you in Ghana a while back?" she asked, as she watched him scrape the rest of the stew into a plastic bowl.

"Just traveling. No work," Graham said.

She eyed his profile. "You can take the rest of the stew with you," she offered.

He smiled, dimples and all. "I will take you up on that. I

get tired of cooking for myself all the time," he said as he snapped the lid on the container.

"I have a question, Graham."

He looked over at her. "Fire away."

It was tough because she wasn't sure she wanted to hear the answer. "If we didn't run into each other in Grenada were you ever going to call?" she asked as she removed a clean dish towel from the folded stack in the drawer by her.

He accepted it and dried his hands. "Honestly, I don't know. Had I thought of you? Damn near every day. Did I wish things could be different between us? Always. But I was just so sure we would never be happy, no matter how much we tried because of our history—my history," he said, pressing his hand to his chest as he turned to look down at her.

"And my cheating on my husband with you," Jaime added before busying herself closing and starting the appliance.

"Hey," he called to her softly.

She looked up, hoping her disappointment didn't show.

"My love for you was never in question. It still isn't," Graham told her with conviction. "It's believing that sometimes even love isn't enough. So I let you be, because I thought I would never measure up to what you felt you needed."

She remembered the years she waited for him to reach out. "I needed you," she admitted, closing her eyes, and forcing a smile as she felt weepy. "For all those years I thought: Wow. He came to me. He said he loved me. He said he wanted to try something real with me. He wanted more than sex. He wanted me. He convinced me he loved me. And then I never heard from you again. I thought you were across the country or remarried or had relapsed back into drugs. Or you no longer thought you loved me. I thought a thousand different things and all of them led me not to call you, but I never imagined you were right in Bedford, New York. Single. Doing fine. Living fine... *without*...me."

Graham took a large step to pull her into his arms. "I wasn't living fine," he said. "I was surviving. Missing you. Wishing things could've been different then and still wishing it now," he said as he rubbed circles onto her back. "Forgive me for not reaching out and at least explaining why we wouldn't work?"

Jaime closed her eyes against his chest and felt weak from his closeness. Still. Six years after the rooftop and seventeen years after first seeing him dance, his very presence was electrifying.

She smiled as she shrugged one shoulder. "We'll see," she said, mimicking him.

"Ha, ha, ha," he said as his chuckle echoed inside his chest and she pressed her face closer against it to enjoy the rumble.

Donny Hathaway's soulful voice singing "Song for You" filled the room as they swayed together in front of the fireplace. With his head lightly resting atop hers, he held her body and eyed the sketch he gifted her on the mantel. Graham could almost forget her actions that were wedged between. Almost.

For a few moments, he closed his eyes as Donny sang of a deep, resounding, soulful love that may require some forgiveness. He allowed himself to forget her deception and just drink in being in the moment with this flawed woman he loved, who risked her entire happiness to be with him. Again.

"We are all alone and I was singing this song to you," he mouthed.

★ ★ ★

Jaime walked around the nursery with its shades of grays and blues, touching items as she looked forward to one day laying eyes on her child. For her, the room was her greatest work. There was nothing but love in every detail.

The dark gray crib was flanked by gray velvet curtains with a tiny blue pinstripe. Sheer blue curtains would allow in light while the heavier curtains would shield the baby from cold during the winter seasons. The polished wood floors were covered with a large and plush gray area rug and on the largest wall was an animated mural of animals in shades of blues, grays, and bright white against the pale gray wallpaper. Wooden shelves lined with toys. Frames ready for the dozens of pictures she would take. A small working section in the corner for the nights she worked while she watched over her baby.

All of it with the baby's safety and comfort in mind. "Are you excited about being a mom?"

She glanced over at where he leaned in the doorway with his hands in his pockets as he watched her. "More than anything," she admitted as she picked up the blue version of the same teddy bear she had as a child. It took her weeks and quite a bit of money to purchase the item that was now a vintage collectible. "I started off fucking up, *but* I am determined to do better, have better, do more, and be more for him."

Jaime stood before a charcoal gray slider with thin blue pinstripes and a large matching blue pillow that she wanted to monogram. She bit her lip to keep from asking Graham what he would name him, knowing that was cruel. They had to be done with hurting each other. If not for the child they may share, then to rectify their long history.

"I'm glad we're trying to mend things. I know it doesn't mean we'll get back together. I'm clear on that, but I would never want you to be my enemy, and I hope that you want the same," she said. "For twelve out of the last seventeen years of my life, you were in it in some way. And if I count the days you were in my thoughts and my heart for the last five, then those years count too, Graham."

His eyes were on her steadily.

"Seventeen years is a long time, whether we knew what we felt or not. Whether we knew what to do with it or not. Whether it looked wrong or not," Jaime said passionately, her eyes bright with tears. "Forgive me, Graham. Forgive me. *Please.*"

"Jaime," he said with a shake of his head. He directed his gaze down at the floor as if looking at her was too much.

"Graham," she implored with emotion.

"I might have a child on the way, and you weren't going to tell me," he yelled before he took a step back and released a harsh breath.

Jaime gasped and covered her face with her hands at his release of unbridled anger at her.

"I'm tired of you making me feel like I ain't good enough. Like you never can choose me," he said, tempering his words. "First it was your friends and what they think of me. Then it was your fiancé and what you imagined happy looked like for you...*with him.* But that's the shit. You keep choosing men you end up cheating on...*with me.* Always second string for you. Cool. But with me possibly being a father you *still* don't choose me, Jaime. I still don't measure up to the father of your child?"

Her insides felt as if they died with his words. What was she to say when faced with the truth? What could she say when "forgive me" was worn out and overused? What could she do but accept that she was dealt a hand and played the wrong card?

★　★　★

Graham lay on the couch with the darkness of Jaime's living room broken up by the lit embers of the fireplace. The weather had taken a turn into a blizzard, visibility was low, and the streets were not year cleared of the inches of heavy snowfall. He wanted to let their emotional scene in the nursery fuel his journey back to Brooklyn but accepted that maybe it was not safe to make the trek home just yet.

With his hand behind his head, he looked at his sketch of her again and was unable to take his eyes off of it or to shake the awareness that in every stroke was his love and longing for her. It was why he sent it to her and out of his life, hoping he would be freed of her as well.

He'd been wrong.

It truly was a raw and beautiful piece of artwork. Worthy of one of his exhibits but not meant for public consumption. It exposed more about him than perhaps any other piece he'd ever done.

I love her.

We love each other.

He forced his gaze from the sketch, wishing he could find the sleep that Jaime had in her bedroom. He tossed back the throw she gave him and sat up on the sofa. He looked around the room. His eyes landed on a flash of red on the built-in shelves. Curious, he rose and walked over to find a small toy car in front of a photo of her behind the wheel of a racecar.

She did it!

He smiled remembering how he helped her to pull that childhood memory from wherever she had placed it during her adulthood. He liked that she had not forgotten the dreams of her childhood. He liked it a lot, knowing he played a role in it.

He placed the car back on the shelf and made his way to the half-bath in the hall. He turned the light on and relieved himself with a long sigh. After he washed his hands, he cut the light and closed the door behind him. Down the hall, Jaime's door was closed. He turned and walked to it.

Her tears were muffled but he heard them. Was affected by them. He knew the words they had exchanged bothered her. The fire of his anger had singed her emotionally. The betrayal he felt had been his truth, but it didn't lessen the effect on her or his innate desire to shelter and protect her and the baby—even from his own words and actions. He turned the knob and opened the door.

The sounds of her cries increased with that move. She was on her side in the middle of the king-sized bed that seemed more pillows than anything. Her body was racked with tears.

Damn.

He felt a sharpness radiate across his chest and squeeze his heart as he crossed the hardwood floors. "Jaime," he said before he neared her.

She dug her face deeper into the mound of pillows as she swiped away her tears with the side of her hand. "Something wrong?" she asked, her voice shaky.

Graham climbed on the bed and crossed it on his knees to reach her. "Stop crying, Jaime. Think of the baby," he soothed her as he spooned his body to hers and pressed kisses to the back of her head. "It's okay. I don't hate you, I promise. I told you that no matter what happens between us I will always love you and I meant it."

And he did.

She nodded and snuggled back against him. He held her into the wee hours of the morning until her soft snores came. Soon he joined her.

That next morning Jaime awakened to find Graham gone from her bed. For a second, she wondered if she had dreamed about him, but the scent of him still clung to her pillow and sheets. She flung the covers back to cross the room and look out the window. Some of the streets were already cleared and the winter sun beamed brightly.

She turned to find Graham and noticed the tray on the suede bench at the foot of her bed. On it was fresh fruit, yogurt, a bagel, and a glass of juice. She picked up the folded piece of paper to find a small sketch of her sleeping. Inside he wrote:

> *Headed home. It's safe. Don't worry. Thank you for the talk last night. We needed it.*
> *Graham*

Not: Love, Graham. Still, she cherished it. He must have gone to the store because none of the items had been in her fridge. The act was more of a show of love than words could ever be. And the small sketch was adorable.

She took a sip of the juice. It was icy cold although it was free of ice.

He couldn't have left that long ago.

"Graham!" she gasped, taking off out of her bedroom and down the hall that seemed longer than usual. She reached the front door and lifted the latch before she jerked it open.

He was striding down the middle of the hall.

"Graham," she called, thankful it was empty of her neighbors.

He turned and her heart skipped as if she hadn't just spent the last twelve hours with him.

"I didn't want to wake you," he explained.

Jaime remained in the doorway, fearful she would lock herself out of her apartment in her emerald green slip. In her rush, she'd forgotten the matching robe.

"Did you love him? Luc?" Graham asked, surprising her and revealing that it was the first thought on his mind.

"Not the way I loved you," she admitted with every bit of her heart. Truthfully.

Please believe me.

Graham's eyes became distant. He raised his glove to wave goodbye as he turned to walk down the hall.

"Graham," she called from the doorway once more.

Again, he stopped and turned.

"I need you to know that what happened between us in Grenada was not just sex," she said. "Sex is just the physical side of it. That was love. Even in my anger for you, I couldn't deny myself. That was love. I didn't realize it then, but I know it now. I hope you believe that."

Graham nodded. "I do. I'm just glad you finally know it," he said before he turned and walked away.

Chapter 15

Jaime's thoughts were still on the night she shared with Graham for the rest of the day. She felt hopeful that they could fill the gap between them. She was determined to fight to show him that she regretted her choices. And she allowed herself to dream that after the baby was born—regardless of paternity—that she and Graham could build something together.

Maybe. Maybe not.

Still, she was optimistic.

Bzzzzzz.

Jaime leaned forward to press the intercom. "Yes, Katie," she said, crossing her ankles in the tight satin pencil skirt she paired with a matching button-up shirt that she had worn untucked to make room for the baby.

"Ms. Virginia Osten-Pine is here to see you."

Another drop-in?

"Send her in," Jaime said removing her compact to check her appearance. She thought twice about it and snapped it closed to drop back in her leopard-print tote without using it.

I'm pregnant. Had a long emotional night. And it has been a busy morning of work. Who gives a shit if I'm not picture-perfect?

Jaime rose as her mother entered the office. She came around the desk to meet her with a brief hug and kiss on her cheek. "You really are getting around these days, Mother," she said as she moved to reclaim her seat behind the desk.

"And how are you not scared of those high heels in your condition?" Virginia said before setting her tote on the edge of Jaime's desk and taking one of the seats positioned before her spacious desk.

"I could dance in heels, Mother. I'm fine," she said, picking up her phone to check for incoming emails.

"I want you to know I recognize when you do that," Virginia said.

Jaime set the phone face down to look over at her. "Do what?"

Virginia studied her nails nonchalantly. "Switch up between Mama and Mother depending on what I say," she said.

Jaime pretended to focus on her computer. "I do that?" she asked with feigned ignorance.

Her mother chuckled. "I know my child just like one day you will know yours," she advised.

"Care to share what you are doing out and about in the city alone?" Jaime asked.

"I owe you an apology and I wanted to do it in person."

Jaime's eyes widened as she leaned to the left past her twenty-seven-inch desktop computer to look at her mother. "Say what now?" she asked.

"That young man—"

"Graham," Jaime provided.

Virginia nodded as she smoothed her silvery strands back into the low chignon style she wore that day. "Seeing Graham reminded me that I was so angry at you that I called you some horrible names after I first learned that you cheated on Eric," she began.

Slut. Whore.

"I remember," Jaime said, still pained at the words shot at her like daggers.

"Now that the truth about your father's...dalliance...is out, I can admit I was still hurting about what he was doing to me. My anger at him was behind the anger I felt at you," Virginia confessed.

Jaime leaned back in her chair and eyed her mother with incredulity.

"I said to you the things I wanted to say to him, and I was wrong, Jaime," she said, twisting her precious diamond rings around on her slender finger before she reached for her purse and withdrew a folded monogrammed handkerchief—a relic in current times—to dab at her tears.

Jaime pushed back in her chair to come around the desk and pull her mother's body to her side.

"Don't ruin my hair, Jaime," Virginia said around her sniffles.

Jaime stiffened. Some old habits were hard to break. "Of course, Mother," she said as she patted her shoulder instead.

It was Virginia's turn to go rigid. "I am who I am, Jaime," she said. "And that's all I've known for sixty years."

"I'm learning that it's never too late to change," Jaime said, determined to change her own patterns to choose her happiness and speak the truth on what she wanted without hurting someone else in the process.

Although Luc's Instagram stories were proving to be quite adventurous, with a bevy of beauties always at his side, Jaime knew it was all a mask for the hurt she caused. And then with the same sinful deed, she wrecked Graham as well. "You just decide to change. Get up every day and focus on not messing up in the same way again no matter how many times you've done it before," she said, thinking of both men.

The one she loved and the one she was in love with.

"You seemed to have inherited that from your father," Virginia said, sliding in one of her beloved critiques.

Jaime sighed. "Thanks for the apology and the judgment, Mother," she said as she moved over to the small fridge to remove two bottles of mineral water.

"What judgment? Your father is a cheater and you've done it twice—that I know of—"

Bzzzzzz. Bzzzzzz. Bzzzzzz.

Jaime handed a bottle to her mother before she reached to pick up her cell phone. "Jaime Pine," she said as she leaned against the edge of her desk and crossed one ankle over the other.

Virginia frowned in distaste as she eyed the drink. "Straight out of the bottle. I refuse," she said, setting it on the desk.

"Hey, Hamilton. What's up?" she asked her youngest design consultant.

"Madison says we left behind the custom name art," he said.

Jaime pinched her forehead. "Y'all are at the Cobble Hill redesign. Right? So that would have been a delivery from RMW," she said, thinking of the metal fabrication company they used for such projects.

"Yes."

"Let me have someone check the warehouse and I'll call you back," Jaime said, setting the phone down and then moving around the desk to press the intercom.

She frowned a bit to see her mother watching her so intently. So curiously. "Katie, can you have someone see if there is a delivery box from RMW downstairs?" she asked as her mother opened her tote to remove her eyeglass case as she came around to the rear of the desk as well.

"Hold on, let me check the inventory list first," Katie said.

"Mother, what are you doing?" Jaime asked as she sat behind her desk.

"Seeing you on top of things around here," Virginia said with her back arched as she clutched the edge of her desk to roll the chair forward.

"Okay, Jaime. It was logged into inventory. Matter of fact you signed for it two weeks ago, so it arrived," Katie assured her.

"Then I need someone to check downstairs," she said succinctly.

Virginia leaned back in the chair and crossed one leg over the other, looking pleased with herself as she eyed Jaime.

"Remember you have a team in Cobble Hill, another in Harlem, and the delivery guys are on lunch before that big haul to the beach house in Montauk, Jaime. I don't think anyone else is here but me and you," Katie said.

"Okay, I'll check," Jaime said, before ending the call.

"You have three teams working under you?" Virginia asked over the rim of the red tortoise eyeglasses she now wore.

"Yes, Mother," she said as she searched under the paperwork and house plans on her desk for her set of work keys.

"You've come a long way, huh?" Virginia said, looking around as if for the first time.

"Yes, Mother," Jaime said, with her phone and keys in hand. "Stay here. Touch nothing. We'll go to a late lunch after I get a messenger to take this package—once I find it."

Jaime left her office and quickly strode down the hall. "Be right back," she told Katie.

As she punched the button for the elevator, Jaime was rethinking the workload she took on as of late. She was in full grind mode, using it to distract her from thoughts and regrets of her actions with both Graham and Luc. But it was wearing on her. As soon as she stepped on, she leaned back against the rear wall and closed her eyes. She was just into her second trimester and the boost of energy she was supposed to feel had yet to appear.

Bzzzzzz. Bzzzzzz. Bzzzzzz.

Jaime didn't bother to look at the phone yet. The service

in the elevator was abysmal. Instead, she thought back to dancing with Graham as Donny Hathaway's music serenaded them. She hummed "A Song for You," remembering her head pressed to Graham's chest as his heart pounded with such force and speed. Just like her own.

On the basement level, she stepped off and checked the missed call before calling Hamilton back. "Did y'all find it?" she asked even as she continued long strides down the brightly lit wide path flanked by gated storage units.

"Yes, someone put the box on the passenger seat," he said.

Jaime stopped, feeling relief. "Put me on speaker, please, Hamilton," she said, with one hand on her hip as she tilted her foot up in her heels.

"Go ahead, Jaime," he said.

"Listen. This is a crazy time for me, and everybody knows it. I need my teams—each team and each person on every team—to be on their shit and to stay on their shit. Before a call is made to me, you check everywhere. Anywhere. Even in the craziest of places so that my pregnant ass is not in a fucking basement about to search through crates. Take that extra step and look for something you think is not there, because I'm sorry but thinking to check the inside of the delivery truck's cab is not a Hail Mary. It's a missed pass. Does everyone understand me?"

Affirmations from every team member flooded the phone in unison.

"Good," she said before ending the call.

Jaime eyed her two side-by-side units, landing on a chair wrapped with padding. She remembered a custom blue velvet armchair a client had changed their minds about. *It would be perfect for the baby's room*, she thought, wishing she could be sure this was the chair she was thinking of.

She opened the first unit and flicked the switch up to further illuminate the space as she eyed the furniture pieces, artwork, and accessories she collected over the years. "Let's see," she said, setting her keys atop a wooden crate that came to her hip before she began to unwrap the chair.

Jaime pulled on the knotted rope and felt resistance. "Shit," she swore with furrowed brows. She pressed her thighs against the chair to shift it to the left in case a knot was wedged between the chair and the crate beside it. It shifted. She pulled again and her body propelled back and slammed against a tall crate, rocking it. She looked up just as another small box tilted forward and dropped down onto her head.

Jaime cried out at the sharp pain as she fell forward onto the corner of the crate. She gasped in horror as her world spun, sending her crashing to the floor beneath her. "No," she moaned as she felt a wave of nausea and sharp pain across her lower back and stomach as she felt unconsciousness was near.

"Please, God, no," she cried as she fought for the strength to rise and failed.

She winced at the insistent pain radiating across her belly and wailed. With blurred vision, she looked up at the edge of her phone on top of the crate. "Help me," she whispered, fading into darkness as wetness escaped her.

An ear-piercing scream stirred her as she felt her head raised slightly and placed on something.

"Oh Lord, my baby. Oh, my poor baby. Oh, Lord. Oh, Lord. Oh, Lord. Hold on. Help is coming. I'm here," Virginia said to her as she stroked her hair back from her sweaty face.

"Mama," Jaime whispered. "My baby, Mama."

"I'm here. Help is coming," Virginia whispered as she pressed kisses to her brow.

Jaime's eyes closed as tears wet her face before she moaned at the spasms attacking her body. She heard the whispers of her mother's prayers for a moment just before she slipped back into the darkness.

★ ★ ★

Luc stared out the window of the jet trying to fight the fatigue he felt. Flights back and forth between New York and Los Angeles, a showcase he set up for his artists last night, plus an early morning fuck with an eager woman he met last night had him worn out.

"Can I get you something...to drink, Mr. Sinclair?"

He released a yawn as he looked up at the flight attendant. A blonde beauty with a curvaceous body pressing against her uniform stood by his chair with an invitation in her crystal blue eyes. She made an offer to assist him, but he was clear that was asking something of him. He took a moment to consider following her to the rear of the plane to fuck her from behind as he twisted her tresses in his fist. "No, I'm good for now. Thanks," Luc said, unable to muster the energy to get up and attack the pussy the way he'd discovered she liked.

Her disappointment filled her eyes before she smiled and walked away. He did lean over and look back to watch the sway of her buttocks in her pencil skirt.

"What's up with you lately, Luc?"

He cleared his throat at the soft and raspy voice questioning him before he turned to eye Zhuri sitting across from him. Her pink 'fro was in its full glory and her oversized shades covered her eyes as she folded her petite body in her seat beneath a blanket. "Not a thing," Luc finally answered as he shifted forward in his seat.

His assistant, Kendell, was eyeing him as well.

"Happiness ain't between thick thighs," Zhuri sang. "If you think so...you'll be...disappointed by that *lie*."

Luc eyed her as she raised her shades above her brows to give him a hard look.

Kendell chuckled.

Luc glared at him.

His smile faded.

"Bull*shit!*" Blaze called from behind him.

Luc raised a fist in the air in solidarity to the protest of her opinion. Life was lovely. Now that he opened the door to the endless possibilities of pussy, he was never alone, and his condom-covered dick stayed wet. And sometimes—most times—he barely thought about Jaime at all.

"You wildin'," she said.

"I'm *single*," he stressed.

"Heartbreak is some bullshit whether it happens to you or you cause it in someone else," she said, bugging out her eyes before she dropped her shades.

"Fuck love," he said.

"Of self, though?" she asked. "Sharing your body ain't self-love, bro."

"Take a nap, Oprah," he drawled.

"Sure will. With peace, positive energy, and self-love for days," she said, pulling her cover over her head.

She'll be the fuck alright.

He checked the time on his diamond watch. They would be landing in New York soon. "Is the video ready?" he asked Kendell.

"Yessir," his assistant said, handing him the laptop to view the footage of the showcase last night.

Luc put in his AirPods before he opened the device. He squinted when Zhuri walked on stage to applause and bowed before she took a seat at the piano. He had seen the performance live but not with the close-up view the video offered. He nodded at the emotions so clearly displayed on her face as she sang. Heartache. Joy. Passion. Sadness. She hit a high note and he felt the goosebumps that let him *know* she would be a star. Music was in his blood. Part of his DNA. It excited him more than the mouth or pussy of any woman could.

More than Jaime ever could.

He stiffened at that thought, curious of its origin.

"Luc."

His eyes looked over to Kendell holding his phone in his hand. The look on his face sent a cold chill over his body. "What?" he asked, as his heart began to pick up its pace with fear.

"Jaime's in surgery to save the baby," Kendell said.

His hands gripped the armrest of his chair. From the corner of his eye, he saw Zhuri's blanket lower. He looked at her. She took off her shades. Again, her feelings were easily readable on her face. This time it was fear and compassion.

"Luc. They want to talk to you."

He stood and took his phone from Kendell as he made his way to the rear of the plane. "Excuse me," he said to the flight attendant. He couldn't remember her name. He could barely remember any of their names. All of them just tools to help him forget her.

Jaime.

He raised the phone to his ear as he looked out the window of the jet to the clouds it sped through. "Yes," he said.

"Luc, it's not good. They're not sure if Jaime or the baby will pull through," Renee said.

Again, a chill raced over him.

"Which hospital?" he asked.

"We're at NYU," she said. "Listen. We're going to call Graham, too. I'm sorry but you know the situation with the baby. So we thought we should tell both of you."

The feeling of a sharp slash across his chest was not as intense but it was there. Still.

"Luc, you there?" she asked.

"Renee, I'm on a plane coming back from LA. Can you keep me updated?" he said.

Now she was silent.

"Look, are you coming?"

That was Aria.

He closed his eyes. He didn't want to be sitting in a

waiting room with the man she cheated on him with awaiting news of a baby he didn't know was his.

But what if it is?

And what if it isn't?

"Luc, look, you know where we are. The choice is yours."

Beep. Beep. Beep.

Luc lowered the phone and released a heavy breath.

Graham felt uneasy. He couldn't explain it or shake it.

He stepped back from the large canvas panel with his paintbrush in his gloved hand and old school R&B slow jams playing through his on-ear headphones. He eyed the piece he was doing of a mother holding her newborn son transitioning through to a grown man now protecting his mother. He bent his head to the side and studied it, before taking a step forward to add contouring to the muscles of the man. Since he arrived home from Jaime's apartment that morning, he had begun sketching the idea out. All day long he had been consumed with it. Lost in it. It was far from complete. There was no rush.

Graham set the square wooden palette that held his mixture of oils down on a nearby stool. His eyes kept going to the work in progress as he cleaned his brushes. He was already making plans for the layering of colors he probably wouldn't get to for days. He worked his shoulders as he dried his hands before he removed the sleeveless overalls he wore. Nude, he crossed the wide divide to the line of barnwood wardrobes against the wall. He paused with a soft grunt as that unease returned.

Maybe I'm coming down with something. Or it's anxiety.

He grabbed his running gear and quickly dressed, stopping at the door to yank on his Northface bomber jacket, skull cap, and gloves. Running pumped him up and then calmed him down. With Biggie thumping in his ears and the chilly wind attacking his face, Graham ran to Brooklyn Bridge Park's waterfront to enjoy the view of the bridge with the late afternoon sun still brilliantly bright amongst the frost of winter. Biggie's "Juicy" played and he slowed down from a full sprint to a jog with the change in tempo.

"You never thought hip-hop would take it this far," he rapped along with his all-time favorite MC.

His phone rang, interrupting the music. He slowed to a stop to pull it from the inside pocket of his coat and smiled at the old school photo of him and his parents when he was five years old. "Ma Dukes," he said.

"Hey, Graham," Cara said. "You running? You sound like a pervert breathing hard in your momma's ears, son."

He chuckled. "Yes, on the run. No, on the perversion," he answered her. "I'm headed home now. Where's Pops?"

"I'm here, son," Tylar said.

"I'm on speaker?" he asked, carefully eyeing a pit bull that was walking his owner more than the owner was walking him. "You supposed to give somebody a heads up before you put 'em on speaker."

"Boy, please, you ain't saying nothing no one wants to hear," Cara said.

He could imagine her waving her hand dismissively.

"Actually, son, there is something your mother and I wanted to talk to you about," Tylar said. "Did you get the test results yet?"

He looked off at the bridge across the East River in the distance, thinking of all the emotions that had plagued him as he stood in the doorway of the nursery in Jaime's apartment last night. Everything from joy to pain, but ultimately landing on hope.

"Not for a few more days I think," Graham said, looking down as he kicked a pile of snow. "I'm ready."

"We know you are, son, and so are we," Tylar said.

During dinner with his parents one night after an SA meeting, he had been unable to keep the possibility of a grandchild from them when they talked about looking forward to it one day. Graham didn't regret that decision, even though they could face disappointment when the results finally came in.

"And Jaime? How's that going?" Cara asked.

Graham scowled. He didn't know if it was from the cold whipping against his body without him moving and generating heat or the thought of Jaime and how he couldn't completely forgive her for not telling him about the baby.

"You keep choosing men you end up cheating on... with me. Always second string for you. Cool. But with me possibly being a father you still don't choose me, Jaime. I still don't measure up?"

"We talked. Things are better, not best," Graham said, leaving it at that.

"Son?" Tylar called, his voice sounding closer than it had before.

"Yeah, Pops," he said, beginning to walk home.

"I will never be the one to ask you to be anyone's fool," his father began. "But I also have been blessed with so much forgiveness in my life that I have to encourage you to give that same blessing to someone you love."

His mother had forgiven his father plenty. Graham had learned his past treatment of women from watching his father run through them with the same regard given to tissues—something to be used and then discarded.

"I hear you, Pops," he said.

"Okay, here's your mother."

There was a slight rustling during the transfer of the phone. "Graham, let me add, if that whore personified can change—"

"Hey!" his father hollered out in the distance.

"Anyone can," Cara finished calmly.

He laughed just as he received another incoming call.

"Hold on, Ma," he said, not recognizing the number. He answered the call. "Hello."

"Graham Walker, please," a female voice said.

"Speaking."

"Graham this is Aria Livewell, Jaime's friend."

He frowned. Deeply. "What's wrong?" he asked as he came to a stop, his body going tense with alarm.

"She fell at work today—"

Graham's dropped his head and locked his knees to reinforce them.

"She's in surgery at NYU Tisch Hospital."

He looked up to confirm his location to decide if it was quicker to go home for his truck or just hop on a train. "I'm on the way," he said.

"Graham, you know the situation. We told Luc, too."

"I don't care about none of that," he balked. "I'm on the way."

"Okay. See you when you get here."

He switched back to his parents on the other line. "Ma, I gotta go. Jaime fell and she's in surgery," he said, checking for oncoming traffic before he crossed the street.

"Oh no, Graham!" Cara wailed.

"What hospital, son?"

"NYU Tisch."

"Keep us updated," Tylar said.

He ended the call and took off at a full sprint with his phone still tightly gripped in his hand. Graham made it home in record time and was thankful no overzealous cop decided to stop during his run and question him for suspicious behavior that wasn't at all suspicious. Behind the wheel of his truck, he made his way across the Brooklyn Bridge to eventually hop onto the FDR. His heartbeat never slowed, and his hand gripped the wheel like a vise as he drove with speed, reaching the hospital in record time. Barely taking the moment to throw his truck into park, Graham dashed from the vehicle and raced into the hospital.

After getting instructions to the surgical waiting area, he quickly made his way there, trying hard not to run through the halls. He passed an open doorway.

"Graham!"

He stopped and turned to see Jaime's mother in the doorway. His eyes dropped to take in the blood on her skirt and he knew then that Jaime's condition—and that of the baby—was even worse than he imagined.

"We're all in here," Virginia said, looking as frightened as he felt.

"Thanks," he said, retracing his steps to follow her into the room.

She reclaimed her seat next to her husband, who gave Graham a nod of welcome. Aria waved. Her head was on the shoulder of a man he assumed to be her husband. Her eyes and his shoulder were wet with her tears. Renee's eyes were shielded by shades, but Graham didn't doubt they were as swollen and reddened as her friend's.

"Grab a seat and try to send positive energy like we are, Graham," she offered.

He nodded as he claimed a seat in the corner by one of the windows looking out at the city streets. The blue of the sky deepened as late afternoon transitioned into the early evening.

The air of the waiting room was silent and tense as the minutes ticked by into another hour and then another. He contemplated a world where Jaime didn't even exist and felt utterly helpless and hopeless. He thought of losing the baby before he got to claim him and adore him, and he wanted to weep.

"Excuse us, everyone. Hello."

He looked over at his parents standing in the doorway

and although he never considered asking them to come—and was a grown, self-reliant, strong man—he was glad to see them.

"We're Graham's parents," Tylar said, moving around the room to shake the hand of everyone as Cara gave them weak smiles as she rushed to her son.

She sat beside him and instantly gathered his larger hand into hers. He held it tighter as his father stood beside him with his back pressed to the window as he placed his hand on his son's shoulder, offering silent comfort.

"Oh, Graham," she sighed, resting her head on his shoulder. "My poor Graham."

"We're here son. We got you," Tylar said.

Thank God.

His eyes kept going to the blood on Virginia's skirt. Jaime's blood. *So much blood.*

"From her head," Virginia said, her face desolate.

His eyes shifted up to find she was looking at him.

"Jaime went to the basement to look for something and she took so long," Virginia said in a haunted whisper. She stared down at the floor with dazed eyes as if replaying the scene in her mind. "I went down to look for her because we were going to lunch. And I wanted to see what she was doing down there. To tell her I was proud that she was so independent and could take care of herself in a way I never dreamed of for her. In a way I never did for myself. In a way that she never would have to accept anything from anyone for the sake of security. I never thought I would find her on the floor like that."

She gasped and released a wretched cry as she bent over and covered her face with her hands. They were stained with some blood as well. Her husband hugged her as he bent to whisper comfort into her ear.

The closed door on the side wall opened and a woman

fully donned in scrubs stepped into the waiting room. "Jaime Pine," she said.

Everyone stood.

"We're her parents," Franklin said.

"We're all here for Jaime," her mother added. "Feel free to talk."

"I'm Dr. Usher," she said. "The surgery is complete, and Jaime is in recovery. The accident caused both a head trauma and an abruption in the placenta. There was severe blood loss during surgery and unfortunately, I'm sorry to tell you all that she miscarried."

The women all released cries of disappointment. The men provided comfort, with Aria's husband sliding an arm around both his wife and her friend.

Graham dropped down to his seat, thankful that Jaime's life had been spared, but tortured for the lost life of the baby. He covered his face with his hands, remembering Jaime walking around the nursery with so much joy about being a mother and him holding so much inner hope that she carried his son.

His disappointment was piercing.

His pain profound.

"When can we see her?" Franklin asked.

"She'll be in recovery for a good bit, but the nurses will let you know as soon as she is in a private room," the doctor said. "We're going to keep her here under observation."

Just this morning he had awakened in her bed with her body snuggled close to his, and it took everything in him to get up and leave before he pleaded with her to let him stay. Then, all that mattered was the grudge he carried for her not telling him about the baby.

A boy. And now he's gone before he even got a chance. Damn.

"Would you all like to pray for Jaime...and the baby?" Cara asked.

He ignored his mother.

"Graham?" she implored softy.

He looked up and everyone was in a ring with their hands clasped. There was an opening in the circle between his parents and both of their hands were extended toward him. There was a time his anger with God, his mother, and the church where he was violated would make prayer a nonviable option for him. And in even in that moment, the little bit of faith he held onto was wavering, but he rose and took each of their hands to close the prayer circle because although the baby was gone, Jaime was not, and for that he was beyond thankful.

This is what numb truly feels like.

Since she awakened and was told of her miscarriage, Jaime shifted from visceral pain to cold numbness with bouts of tears randomly in the mix. And although she understood everyone wanted to visit her, she truly wished they all left her alone to her grief. Platitudes were the worst.

"He's with God."

"He's in a better place."

"Pray for understanding."

"I feel for you."

"We're here for you."

"Anything you need."

I need my baby.

"Jaime."

She turned her head toward the window and closed her eyes as a tear silently ran down her cheek. Her parents were downstairs eating dinner in the café. Kingston, Aria, and Renee had left with promises to return the next day. Luc was a no-show. She met Graham's parents for the first time before they too took their leave. Hours later, Graham remained by her side.

Jaime couldn't bear to look at him because she just *knew* that her son was his and he would have grown up to look just like his father. "Just go, Graham. Please," she whispered. "I can't look at you right now."

"Please, Jaime," he said, his voice deep and serious.

I created my own karma. I thought I could have everything I wanted. I went in that storage room. I killed my baby.

She shook her head and released a cry that echoed against the ceilings and walls.

His hand enclosed one of hers and the scent of his cologne intensified as she felt him bend over her body. "Jaime, please don't turn away from me. Please. I love you so much," he whispered near her ear.

She made the mistake of turning her head on the pillow. His eyes were resting right next to hers with tears of his own. Those beautiful brown eyes with long lashes. Her heart broke all over again. "Ever since...I found out...the baby was a...boy," she wailed in between moans of agony as her tears came in earnest. "All I could think...is I hope...he has ...your eyes and your dimples. Oh God, help me."

She closed her eyes, and her body shook with tears as she clutched the sheets into the fist of her free hand and gave in to the endless waves of pain, disappointment, and regret. "Graham, please go. Please," she begged.

"Graham, give her time," her father said, his voice gentle but firm.

He hadn't even realized her parents had quietly reentered the room. He could only imagine how they felt seeing his presence upset her even more. He didn't want to make things worse for her.

And with that he released her hand, and the scent of his cologne eventually faded away.

★   ★   ★

Luc lay in the middle of his bed looking up at the ceiling with the arm and leg of Miss Too Much draped over his body. His thoughts were on Jaime and her baby. It was still hard to believe the difference between before the day he discovered she was cheating on him and now. He looked up at the empty spot over the bed where the art of her lover had hung above them. Anger still caused tension to radiate across his shoulders.

Easing from under Miss Too Much, Luc sat on the side of the bed and picked up his phone from the nightstand. *No missed calls from Renee or Aria.*

Rising to his feet he strode around the bed to leave the room. He pulled up Renee's number and called her. It rang endlessly before going to voice mail. He ended that connection and found Aria's number to call instead.

It rang just once.

"What, Luc?" Aria snapped. "What could you *possibly* want?"

He clenched his jaw as he leaned against the same wall he leaned on the day he decided he wanted Jaime Pine in his life. "I wanted to check on her," he said.

"The best way to do that would've been to drag your ass to the hospital like Graham did," she said.

"Man, fuck *him*," he snapped, his voice cold.

"You know what? I was on some fuck Graham shit for years, but today he showed the fuck up so now I'm on fuck you," she said.

"Aria, just answer him and hang up. It's over," Kingston said to her in the background.

"No, he's gone get this heat. He called *my* mother-fucking phone," Aria snapped. "Now lie and say you weren't in New York when your artist, Blaze—who was on your plane when you went live while boarding—was on his Insta-gram story back in the city, Luc. How did he get back to New York if you didn't?"

"Look, I didn't call for all of that, Aria. I made a choice…
just like she did back in Grenada," he said, knowing he
sounded spiteful when in fact he was hurt.

"Motherfucker!" Aria exclaimed.

"Okay, give me the phone," Kingston said as she
continued to call Luc everything but a child of God.

"Man, triple fuck him!" she lobbed.

"Listen, Luc, it's Kingston. Jaime came through surgery,
but she lost the baby," he said calmly.

"Do you care?" Aria railed in the background. "*If* it was
your child."

Her words mocked those he had said to Jaime more
times than he could count.

"Thanks, Kingston," he said before ending the call.

Still, leaning against the wall he could see Jaime that first
day walking around the living room as she made notes on
her tablet. As he watched her and wanted her.

*"I believe you are the woman for any and every job, Jaime
Pine."*

For a little over a year, he believed that. He'd been
wrong and his heart paid the cost.

In the vision, she looked over at him and gave him one
final wave before the image faded. As he turned and walked
back to his bedroom, he said goodbye to Jaime Pine for the
last time.

Graham stood in his loft staring at the painting. He had
been planning to title it "Mother, Mother" when he was
done and gift it to Jaime once the baby was born. The
thought of her inconsolable grief shook him to his core, and
he closed his eyes, finally allowing his own tears of grief and
remorse to glide down his cheeks in privacy.

*"Ever since… I found out… the baby was a… boy. All I
could think… is I hope… he has… your eyes and dimples."*

His gut told him that was his son. His boy. His seed.

He released deep breaths through pursed lips that inflated his cheeks as he fought to control his torment. He failed and gave in to sinking beneath the depths of his grief until he flung his head back and released a cry. Fueled by his hurt for Jaime. Deepened by his despair for her.

And himself.

With his vision blurred by his tears, Graham took long strides across the loft and dug his fingers into the canvas to rip it with force. Again. And again. And again. With fury and brute force.

Until it was as torn and shredded as he felt.

Chapter 16

One month later

Jaime awakened with her pillow clutched to her body. The curtains of her bedroom windows were open, and she looked out at the snowfall in front of the streetlight. She released a heavy sigh. Perhaps her millionth in the last month. Since her release from the hospital, her bedroom had become her haven. Sleep was her savior.

If not for the daily visits of her mother and friends she wouldn't have risen to wash, taken her pain medications, or even played with the food they forced her to eat. Her business was in the hands of Madison and Katie. Her body was in the hands of her doctor. Her spirit felt lost and bereft.

She allowed herself the time to grieve but she wasn't done. Not by a long shot. But she was making headway. Small step by small step.

She rose from the bed in a long cotton gown with tiny rosettes, not even remembering being helped into it. She mustered a feeble smile; sure, it was her mother's doing. She owned nothing like it. The smile faded as she gingerly pressed a hand to her belly. With a sharp intake of breath, she closed her eyes. Life would never be the same.

Barefoot, she padded across the room to the bathroom. As she relieved herself, she was thankful the bleeding had stopped. It had been a reminder of her loss. "Shit," she swore as she rose, feeling the aches of her body from being in her bed for nearly all of the last month.

As she washed her hands, she eyed her reflection and saw a version of herself that was unfamiliar. She dragged her fingers through her tresses and felt tangles. Her hair was wild. Her face was pale. Her eyes were swollen and reddish from constant tears.

Who cares, she thought, turning from the reflection and leaving the bathroom.

Jaime flipped the switch on the wall outside the bathroom to turn on the lamps positioned about the room, now offering pockets of light. Atop the bench at the foot of her bed, slightly covered by a cotton robe that matched her gown, she noticed a tray holding mail. Lots of it.

She sat on the end of the bench and flung the robe away to pick up the first of the stacks. Christmas cards. Bills. Advertisements. Medical bills. At those, she sucked air between her teeth and ignored them. She wasn't ready to see what it would cost her to be saved while she lost her child.

My baby.

She looked into the unlit fireplace opposite her bed as her loss weighed down her shoulders. "Damn," she whispered.

The doctor said she would be able to have another child one day. That was of no help because she wanted the one she lost. He could never be replaced. *Or forgotten.*

"Never," she swore in a whisper before she forced herself to continue through the mail.

She paused at the logo of the diagnostic center that performed the paternity test. Her hand closed, balling the envelope into her fist. Did it matter anymore which man fathered a child that would never be born into the world? Luc hadn't cared enough to come to the hospital. Graham had disappeared in the weeks after it.

Perhaps both were happy it's over. Pain radiated at that.

"Jaime, please don't turn away from me. Please. I love you so much."

No. She didn't believe that about Graham. Not at all. *But where is he? I asked for time, not a total disappearing act.*

They all were supposed to be sent the test results and by now they knew the truth even if she did not. She smoothed the envelope, flattening the wrinkles as she furrowed her brows with a wince. She set the envelope on the end of the bed, trying her best to ignore it and the truth it contained as she continued through the mail.

Her eyes kept going back to it.

It would not be ignored. She rose from the bench and grabbed the envelope as she left her bedroom to walk down the hall to the nursery. She pressed a hand to the wood and let her forehead rest down upon it as she tightly gripped the doorknob before turning it and pushing the door open. She reached in to turn on the ceiling light, to bathe the room with light as she stood rooted in the doorway.

It felt like punishment to even be there—standing there—looking at a room that would forever remain empty. She felt like crumbling and had to lean against the doorjamb for support. She didn't know how long she stayed there, clutching the frame, and fighting for strength before she finally took a step inside the room. She walked to the lounge chair and picked up the pillow she'd hoped to have mono-grammed before she turned and dropped down onto the seat, pressing her face against the smooth velvet. "Jaymie," she whispered, having given her son her name since she hadn't known the father to give him his.

Forgive me, son.

Her tears wet the pillow and told the story of her loss. When she folded her hand into a fist again the rustle of the envelope echoed in the silence. She pushed the pillow between her body and the chair as her fingers tore into temptation. She hungered to know just which man should have been there to share in her grief.

She gasped as she dropped her hand and sent the paper floating gently to the area rug atop the hardwood floors. She bent her legs to surround with her arms as she settled her chin on her knees and stared down at the truth. "Damn," she whispered, reckoning with the results.

Jaime was stunned.

Craving a drink, she eventually left the nursery and made her way to the kitchen. In the fridge was a half-finished bottle of red wine. She uncorked it and took a deep drink of it straight from the bottle. And then another.

The front door swung open and Jaime dropped the bottle to the floor with a crash as she reached for a knife from the block on the counter. "Who is it?" she yelled, brandishing the weapon.

Graham stepped inside the apartment holding bags and closed the door with a nudge from his foot. "It's me," he said, eyeing the knife she still held with a death grip.

Jaime eyed him with a mix of confusion, surprise, and anger. "What are you doing here?" she snapped.

"Hoping you put the knife down before you hurt yourself," he said, coming into the kitchen to set the bags on the marble.

"You just pop up after a month and with a key to my damn house no less," she said.

Graham removed his leather coat, hat, and gloves and set them on the island. "Still thinking the worst of me, huh?" he asked, his voice and eyes serious. "When will that get old, Jaime?"

She relaxed her stance and her grip on the knife as she eyed him calmly unpack groceries. "Wait? Huh?" she said as she scratched her head with her free hand. "Where'd you get a key?"

"It's yours," he said as he placed milk and juice in the fridge. "I've been using it all month while you were escaping from the world in your bedroom."

She stiffened at that. It felt like a Virginia Osten–Pine level backhand judgment. "I was grieving my baby," she snapped.

"*Our* baby," he corrected her.

They stared at one another.

"*Can you imagine the story we'll tell our kid about running into each other after years—and giving in to a one-time indulgence we both had reasons to fight—and we create him. It's kind of amazing.*"

"I grieved him too, Jaime…before I even knew he was mine," Graham said with his eyes still brimming with his sadness.

"*Jaime, please don't turn away from me. Please.*"

She believed him.

"I been staying here, sleeping on the sofa," he explained. "Mostly making sure you were okay at night once everyone else went home."

"Graham," she said, taking a step toward him that landed down on a shard of glass.

"Ow!" she cried out, lifting the foot to keep from pressing more of the glass into it.

He came around the island, his boot crushing the glass beneath it, as he grabbed her waist and set her on the island. "Hold still," he demanded as he bent to eye the piece of glass still embedded in her foot. "It's pretty deep but I don't think you'll need stitches."

She watched him closely as he removed the glass and

then pressed a towel to the wound before he strode away to return with the first aid kit from her bathroom, proving his familiarity with her apartment. "Graham," she said.

"Huh?" he asked intensely focused on cleaning the cut while he held her ankle in his hand.

"Look at me," she said, not caring about her foot or the constant throbbing of her injury.

He did.

"We did something absolutely amazing," she said, still stunned at that fact.

His eyes warmed and she knew he remembered their conversation that day outside the lab. He nodded. "Yes, we did," he agreed.

"Then why did God take him?" she asked in a whisper.

Graham shrugged one broad shoulder as he pressed a gauze pad to her foot before he began wrapping it with his tape. "It wasn't his time," he finally said, releasing her bandaged foot to look at her. "I asked my mother the same thing and she promises that God forgives all and doesn't punish. That's not how He works. It wasn't his time, but he was here long enough for us to love him and remember our hope for him for the rest of our lives."

I needed to hear that.

"Okay," she said, feeling emotional but not as helpless as she had.

"Stay there until I get this up," he said, moving to the cabinet under the oversized farmhouse sink to remove the brush and dustpan set.

"Why didn't anyone tell me you were here all this time?" she asked as he bent his strong and muscled body to clean up her mess.

He paused.

She saw it.

"Looking at me seemed to make you feel worse," he

said. "But I still wanted to be near you, Jaime. I needed to be near you and hoped you would realize you needed me, too."

Graham rose to his full height. "But you didn't," he said before turning to empty the wine and glass into the trash.

Jaime eyed him. "I lost a child."

"Yes, I hate that you went through that. If there was anything I could've done to prevent it I would have," he said, impassioned. "I lost a child too, Jaime."

I killed him.

"Don't worry about it. I'm glad to see you up," he said before picking her up to set her down on her foot. "Does it hurt to press down on it?"

"A little bit, but I can walk on it," she said.

"Good," he said.

She looked up at him. He returned the stare as she reached up to press her hand to the side of his face, stroking his cheek with her thumb. "I felt guilty for it all," she admitted. "I didn't have to go in the storage unit. I didn't have to try and move that heavy chair and...and..."

Graham gathered her body close to his. She brought both hands up to grab the shirt on his back as she buried her face against his hard chest and sought her strength from him. "Shit," he swore before he swung her up in his arms and carried her out of the kitchen and down the hall to her bedroom.

She raised her head from his shoulder. "I want to go back in the nursery," she said, eyeing the gray and blue room.

Jaymie's nursery.

Graham set her down on her feet and followed her as she limped into the room.

She looked around. "I want to pack it up," she said, looking back at him.

He looked unsure. "Are you ready for that?"

She eyed the crib. "Yes," she said. "I want you and me to

do it. Just us. A final goodbye to our son that we can do together."

Graham stepped up beside her.

"Okay?" she asked as she looked up at him.

He nodded.

"Let's cover the furniture with sheets and pack everything else in an empty storage bin I have in the hall closet," she said. "We can donate it."

"What if you have another child?" Graham asked.

"Doesn't matter. That child won't be Jaymie and these were *his* things," she stressed, finding some strength in respecting his memory no matter how brief his existence.

Graham left the room and soon returned with sheets and the container. "Can I say a prayer first?" he said.

She eyed him in surprise, knowing his struggle with his relationship with God. "Yes, please."

He reached for each of her hands and stroked them with his thumb as he lowered his head. "Dear Lord. I am praying for the spirit of our son, Jaymie Walker—"

Jaime stiffened in shock. Because the pregnancy was still early in gestation, a death certificate was not required, but Jaime had still wanted to name him for herself. She never thought about the surname. But it was right. She bit her bottom lip and nodded in approval as she lowered her head again.

"May he be surrounded by the ancestors that have gone on before us. May his soul be at peace. At rest. And out of pain. Father God, help his mother and me, and all who loved and hoped to meet him one day, feel solace as we continue to grieve his loss. For these things, I pray in Jesus's name. Amen."

"Amen," Jaime agreed.

Slowly they began to fold and pack away the things that Jaime purchased for him. Together they covered the crib, chair, and lamp with sheets to protect them from dust. "I may donate them too," she said.

"It's up to you," Graham said. "You purchased everything."

She watched as he picked up the container.

"I can take this wherever you want it to go," he offered.

"Thanks," she said, pausing to allow herself a final look before she left the room.

She smiled a bit to see Graham had paused to do the same. Together they walked down the hall. She finished putting up the groceries he purchased as he set the container by the door.

"I was going to grill some salmon and make a salad," he said as he entered the room. "Want some?"

"Not really," she said, having no appetite.

He looked at her. "How about I make you some and put it away in case you change your mind," he offered.

She shrugged one shoulder before she nodded.

Graham reached for a new bottle of wine and poured her half a glass before he got busy cooking them dinner. Saying nothing, Jaime sipped her drink and eyed him over the rim before she left the kitchen to walk around the apartment. Nothing had changed.

Except me.

Jaime looked across the living room at Graham before she made her way back toward the kitchen. "What have I missed?" she asked, as she leaned against the wall.

He glanced back at her over his shoulder as he seasoned the fish. "Not much, believe it or not," he said. "The ladies will all be glad to see you up and about. We were worried you might need..."

She frowned a little as his words trailed off. "Need what?" she asked.

He focused on preparing the food.

"Need what, Graham," she asked again.

Wiping his hands on a dishtowel he turned to look across the island at her. "I was going to ask my therapist, Dr. Templeton, to come over and have a talk with you," he said.

Jaime looked down into her glass.

"Would you like to talk to him?" Graham asked gingerly.

She cut her eyes up at him. "No. Not yet," she said. "I took the time I needed—as much as I wanted—to grieve. Let me get back to work and life and see how it goes. But thank you," she stressed.

He nodded his approval as he turned back to his food preparation.

"How are you, Graham?" she asked before another sip that was beginning to warm her belly.

His movements paused. "Better now," he said without turning.

"Have you been painting?"

Again, he visibly paused. "Some, but not like normal. Whenever the ladies come over, I go home to try and get some work done," he said as he wrapped the marinated salmon in plastic before setting it in the fridge.

Normal isn't normal anymore.

"I should be okay if you need to get back to your loft," she offered, even though she did not want him to go.

He smiled and the dimples appeared. "You kicking me out?" he joked.

"Never," she said seriously. "But I know you miss your art."

Graham looked like he wanted to say something. "I'm gonna take a shower while the salmon marinates," he said.

"What were you about to say?" she asked, feeling sure that it was some other thought he kept from her.

"I was offered an artist-in-residence position at a museum," he said, unable to contain his happiness about that.

She smiled and walked over to slide her arms around his waist to squeeze him tightly. "Congratulations, Graham," she said, happy for him even as she couldn't escape wondering if their son would have inherited his talent.

Along with his eyes and those dimples.

"Thanks," he said, pressing a kiss to the top of her head.

"Which museum? When do you start? For how long? Any pieces you have in mind to create for them?" she asked, lowering her arms to take a step back from him.

"The museum is in Paris, Jaime," he said, watching her carefully.

She instantly turned her back to him to keep from showing him her disappointment. "Paris," she said, forcing joviality into her tone that sounded awkward. "Paris should be amazing."

"Jaime," he said.

He took a step forward. She knew that from her senses shifting into high alert before he even landed his large hands on her shoulders to gently turn her to face him again. She lowered her eyes. He used a finger to her chin to raise her head. She closed her eyes.

"Jaime," he said again, his tone admonishing.

He was leaving again, and she had no right to ask him to stay. They weren't in a relationship. Neither promised the other a future even as they declared love for each other.

I have no right to ask him not to go.

"Look at me, Jaime," he demanded.

She opened her eyes and instantly got lost in his.

Please don't go.

The look in his eyes changed and she saw his regret. "I love you, Jaime," he said.

She shook her head and jerked it away from his touch.

Stop saying that and you're leaving. So why say it? Why keep me honed into you and you're leaving me? Again.

But she didn't say it. She didn't have the will to argue.

She couldn't find the fuck to give to debate his decisions for his life. They had reconnected after so many years and now it was time for that to come to an end.

It's over.

"When do you leave?" she asked.

"Not until you are better," Graham said.

She looked at him, immediately believing he was sacrificing his career and his happiness to ensure that she was safe and okay. Her anger dissipated. She released a heavy breath and gave him a smile tinged with sadness. "Is your inability to forgive me the motivation for you to leave the country?" she asked, unable to help herself.

"No," he answered her quickly and emphatically. "The position was offered to me. I didn't seek it out."

"Of course it was. You're brilliant, Graham," she said in a soft voice. "I'm so proud of everything you've overcome. Everything you have accomplished. The man that you are and the even greater one that you're becoming."

There was much more she wanted to say. To reveal. To plead.

Graham, please don't go.

But she refrained. It felt selfish to even ask him to refuse such an opportunity. She had already selfishly given in to her wants and desires without thought to others or the consequences.

And she could see how badly he wanted the position.

"Tell me more about it," she asked, as she forced herself to show him nothing but pride of him and joy for him.

"The museum wants me to curate an exhibit honoring Blacks in Parisian history. We're crafting the list of subjects, but I definitely want to include Joseph Bologne, Chevalier de Saint-Georges," Graham said as he led her to the living room to settle onto the couch.

Jaime listened to him describing the eighteenth-century conductor of a symphony orchestra who was the son of an enslaved Black woman. He revealed he had already begun to research more about the man some considered the "Black Mozart," and his enthusiasm was infectious. The joining of history and his art was ideal for him. The well-respected museum offering him the position without his provocation was groundbreaking. Even when he spoke of his plans for the next year that he lived in Paris, she didn't let the panic she felt show. She was grateful for the warmth offered by the lit fireplace even as she felt cold at the thought of never seeing him again.

Her eyes dropped to his mouth.

Kiss me.

His hands.

Touch me.

The imprint of his dick against his pants.

Fuck me.

And the spot behind his chest where his heart pumped life into his body and held love for her—that she knew.

Forgive me.

"When do you leave?" she asked again.

Graham rubbed his hands over his mouth as he looked into the blaze inside the fireplace.

She saw his struggle between wanting to be there for her and wanting to claim this major accomplishment—a feat for a young Black man who overcame so much in his life. She knew what he needed to hear. She took a breath and freed him, knowing missing him again would be her cage.

"I'm better," Jaime said.

Graham looked over at her. His eyes searched her face.

"I'm better," she repeated, reaching to cover his large hand with one of her own. He picked it up and kissed the back of her hand. She shivered from the feel of his lips against her skin. Her heart broke, but she allowed a small smile to form on her lips.

He stared at her. His desire for her was undeniable in his

eyes, but she knew his determination to not indulge in sex frivolously. When she rose and withdrew her hands from his, she helped him to deny his longing once more—and admitted that even one last tryst with Graham would do nothing to ease the heartache to come.

"Let's talk about more over dinner," she said. "I'm going to put on some clothes for the first time in a month."

He rose as well. He started to reach for her, but closed his hand into a fist instead, denying them both. "The food should be ready in twenty minutes," he said.

"Be right back," she promised, turning and walking out of the living room as quickly as she could without revealing how badly she needed to not be so close to Graham.

In her bedroom, she gladly closed the door and then leaned back against it as she closed her eyes and fought like hell not to let sadness overtake her life again.

Life goes on. Even after losing your child . . . or the love of your life.

She crossed the room to reach her bathroom and was soon standing nude beneath the spray of the shower. Her hand slid across her belly and she recoiled at the feel of the slightly raised edges of her scar. She looked down at her belly. By now it would have been heavy with their baby. Since her release from the hospital, she had avoided that reminder of her surgery. Of her loss.

Jaime released a shaky breath and pressed her soap-covered hand against her womb. She thought of the moments she and Graham shared to say goodbye to him as his parents. It had been necessary, and her grief was no longer as searing.

She relaxed her body and continued her shower, not feeling thankful that her sorrow was easing but at peace that it was the next step in her healing. In time, she hoped she would begin to feel the same acceptance for Graham being gone from her life. *Hopefully sooner than later.*

Jaime dressed in an ivory oversized boyfriend sweater that came to her knees and slipped off one shoulder. She left her bedroom and walked down the hall. When she came to the second bathroom, she could hear the shower and paused. Thoughts of Graham naked as the water hit the hard contours of his body caused her to lean her head against the door as she pressed her hand to the wood.

All her rationale of needing space and wanting to respect his celibacy was harder to accept at that moment. Not with just a door and a few steps between her and Graham. She dropped her hand to the knob and gripped it tightly.

Fighting temptation.

Let it go. Let him go.

She turned and pressed her back to the door just as it opened and left her to fall backward onto the floor with a shriek as the steam escaped in swirls.

"Jaime?" Graham asked in concern, squatting down.

She opened her eyes and gasped. The towel around his waist gaped open, exposing his dick dangling between his open thighs.

And *that* was too hard to deny.

Quickly, she turned over onto her side and raised her head to take his inches into her mouth with a shuddering groan.

"Oh, shit!" Graham exclaimed as he dropped to his knees and thrust his hips forward as she eagerly sucked him to hardness.

Jaime dragged her tongue from the thick base, along the pulsing vein running along the length of his dick and then to the tip to circle and then suck deeply as he weaved his fingers through her hair to grip.

"Jaime," he said, looking down at her with his eyes filled with his desire—almost wild with it—as he stroked inside her mouth.

She shifted her head this way and that as she adjusted to the slight curve of it to take in as much of him as she could.

"Careful," he warned, his voice thick with his satisfaction.

She loved the feel of it against her tongue—the softness of his skin covering such hardness—but freed his dick as she moved to kneel in front of him. He shifted his hand to grip his dick as he watched her pull her sweater over her head to fling it away, leaving her in nothing but yellow lace panties.

Graham placed his free hand on the side of her face as he lowered his own to suck her lips with a deep moan that seemed to be filled with hunger, his love for her, and his anguish at being unable to deny himself.

And perhaps at allowing himself the treat of their passion as a final goodbye.

Jaime broke their kiss to tilt her head back and close her eyes as she fought for her tears not to fall. He kissed her neck as she snaked her arms around his waist to press against his muscled back and bring their upper bodies together. The feel of his smooth chest hair tickling her taut nipples sent goosebumps over her entire body.

"Stand up," he ordered.

She placed her hands on each of his broad shoulders as she rose before him. Graham eyed her body, and the heated look in his eyes warmed her core as he leaned forward to press his face against the plump vee, bringing his hands up the back of her calves.

She shivered.

Up to the back of her thighs.

She slightly gasped.

He eased his hands under the yellow lace to gather her buttocks into his hands as he bit the mound through her panties.

Her knees buckled and she cried out.

Slowly he removed her panties. He came around her

body and rose from his knees, retracing its path with his tongue from her ankles, calves, thighs, and then buttocks. He took a deep bite of each cheek before kissing them and rising to lick every inch of her spine. He felt her shiver against his tongue.

"Graham," she sighed at the feel of his hands on her breasts as his fingers skillfully teased her nipples.

Against her back, she felt his heart pounding. The hard length of his dick was cupped by the cheeks of her buttocks. Against her neck, he blew streams of cool air before sucking her nape and stoking her desire to have him inside her.

Giving in to the desire to see him, she turned and pushed him back against the bathroom door before rising on her toes as she gripped his shoulder. He settled his hands on her hips as she looked up into his eyes. "You are one beautiful man, Graham Walker," she said softly as she raised a hand to stroke his face as she spoke from her heart.

It was a face she could stare at for the rest of her life.

Wake up to. Kiss upon. Make smile. Fill with pleasure.

Fight to have in her life.

Fight for him.

She shook away the selfish thought and focused on her pleasure—the kind of satisfaction only Graham could provide. A blend of electric passion and peace that left her shaken. With a look down at his dick hard against the thick towel, she loosened the cotton cloth from around his waist and freed his inches to take in her hand. Grip. Stroke. Tease the tip. Feel the pulse of its vein against her palm. Forever.

Fight for him.

Swiftly, he lowered their bodies to the floor inside the open doorway. She gave in to her emotions and let her tears silently race from under her lids as she used her legs and arms to cling to him.

Fight.

Graham kissed away her tears.

"What's wrong?" he asked against her ear.

Him setting aside his pleasure to check on hers evoked such despair at the thought of not having his love—his all— in her life. Looking up into his eyes, with more tears filling her own, she was overcome, and the stirrings of her soul could not be denied.

Fight for him. Like I didn't before on that rooftop five years ago.

"We have to make this work. We have to, Graham. We have to figure it out," she whispered to him fervently. "We have to try like we didn't try before—"

Graham's body went stiff and the tip of his dick throbbed against her core like a pounding heartbeat. His eyes searched hers.

She found hope there inside his pause. His silence emboldened her.

"I love you with a deepness that I can't explain, and I want to give it to you just as deeply and just as strongly, Graham," she implored. "We can have this for the rest of our lives together. We can promise it. We forgive the past. We can *fight* for a future."

Graham closed his eyes and lowered his head to rest on the floor beside hers as he took deep breaths.

Fight for us, Graham.

He rose quickly and stepped over her to stand in the hall. His erection made a shadow against the floor.

Jaime sat up and turned her body to face him as she looked up at the man she loved. "Tell me you don't love me," she said, feeling her face shift with her conviction. "Tell me you didn't want me to be the mother of your child. Tell me you can walk away and never see me again. I dare you to tell me *any* of that."

Graham slid his body down the wall into a squatting position as he eyed her fiercely, his face twisted with his battle to forgive and forget or continue his own fight to let everything they meant to each other fade.

She leaned her head to the side against the door. His eyes shifted to take in the move.

"What is it with us and doors?" he asked.

"Symbolic of closure?" she asked with the hint of a smile.

They stared at one another before their eyes searched the other's face. "Seems like we say goodbye a lot over the years," he said.

We don't have to. Not anymore.

Fight for it, Graham.

"No, this time it's *au revoir*, remember?" she said.

Again, he stared at her and she refused to lower her eyes or shield the love she had for him from its depths.

"I promised myself I would not have sex again unless it was with a woman I was in a relationship with," he said.

I want your love not just your sex.

"Graham, I choose you," she said. "You are the man I choose to spend the rest of my life loving through it all. I choose you to love me in a way no other man ever could or ever would. I choose to forgive our past and focus on who we are today. I choose to prove to you that I will never betray you or make you feel less than ever again. I choose to support your journey to Paris and travel there to visit you to support you as you face this immense challenge in your career. I choose to one day bear your child. I choose to be there in your life as we age, and your dreads grow silver with every passing year. I choose you, Graham Walker."

Again, he looked down the length of the hall from his squatting position with his erection now eased.

Fight.

"Graham, don't let me and what I did, or our past, fuck this up," she implored with no shame at her pleadings as she watched him lower his muscled legs to stretch out before him.

"I broke that promise in Grenada, Jaime," he continued,

glancing away down the long length of her hallway before looking back at her with those eyes she loved.

Feeling frightened at his next words, she looked away from him and down at the floor.

"I won't break it again," he said.

She nodded, understanding his conviction even as her disappointment stung like crazy.

At the feel of his hands wrapping around her ankles, her eyes widened. And when he tugged to yank her toward him across the smooth polished hardwood floors she gasped.

"So, it's a good thing you're my woman," he said, reaching to grab her waist and lift her onto his lap. "Right?"

This is worth fighting for.

She released a breath filled with her relief and happiness. "Right," she said softly.

Graham raised his hands to her back to bring her forward. "My heart, my mind, and my soul choose you," he spoke against her mouth before kissing her. Deeply.

Jaime was thrilled by the strokes of his tongue against her own as she gripped his strong arms as she felt his dick harden and snake upward against her stomach. The smooth hairs of his chest teased her nipples to hardness, and she shifted forward on his lap to press her clit against the hard base of his dick.

"Fuck me," she demanded softly, wanting to feel the inches inside of her. Deeply.

He wrapped an arm around her waist and turned their bodies so that he was above her. She spread her legs and raised her head to kiss him as he arched his hips and entered with a hard thrust. With a gasp against his mouth, she closed her eyes and released a shuddering moan at the hard feel of him filling her. Desperately. Her heart was as full of love for him as her pussy was brimming with his dick.

His thrust was deep and hard as she dug her fingers into his buttocks, pushing him deeper inside her as he buried his face against her neck and suckled her racing pulse. Each forward motion of his hips ended with a clench of his cheeks and a grunt that seemed to vibrate against his chest.

"Yes!" she gasped with each deep dive of his dick inside of her as he raised and lowered his hips as if driven by madness.

Each thrust propelled their bodies across the floor as he fucked her down the hallway.

She enjoyed the ride. The feel of his hardness. The sweat of his body. The slam of his balls against her. The heat of the precum he released inside, slickening his thrusts.

And when their heads bumped against the wall, having left the original spot of their sex behind them, he continued his wicked onslaught. He slid his hands beneath her bottom and raised her hips as he quickened his pace and rode them both to a thunderous climax, their rough cries mingling in the heated air above them and echoing against the halls.

The Postlude

Eighteen months later

Jaime looked to Aria and then Renee where they all stood outside the ornate gates of the Richmond Hills subdivision. She wondered what was in their minds as they stood there in silence and eyed the gate, stone wall, and security booth used to keep them secured from the rest of the town. In truth, she was joyful that this would be her last time being anywhere near it. For her, the place meant nothing but sadness and destruction.

Those things were no longer a part of her life.

Thank God.

First, Aria and Kingston sold their Richmond Hills home for a new one in the Vailsburg section of Newark a few months back. Today, Renee had just completed the loading of a moving truck for her move to a two-bedroom condo closer to her work in New York.

Our days at Richmond Hill were over.

"It's time," Renee finally said with a nod, still tanned from her summer in Grenada.

Aria nodded in agreement. "Farewell, Richmond Hill," she said, kissing two fingers before throwing up a deuce.

Bzzzzzz. Bzzzzzz. Bzzzzzz.

Jaime smiled as she pulled her phone from the back pocket of the jeans she wore to help her friend pack. A Google alert. Outside of herself, there were only two people she checked on.

She smiled a bit as she read the wedding announcement. Over the last six months, she had been relieved to see that Luc's wild ways documented via social media had been replaced by posts of him with just one woman—his artist, Zhuri, whose Grammy-winning debut album had gone platinum. She worried he would never recover and had only kept up with him with the hope he would outgrow his heartbreak. *He deserves love. Good for them.*

She deleted the Google alert on Luc, finally feeling free to do so.

"Jaime, your ride is here," Aria said.

She tucked her phone back in her pocket as she turned to see Graham's pickup truck. He lowered the window to wave at them. Renee and Aria did the same while she gave him a loving smile, amazed at the last year and a half they spent together. Not even the distance between New York and Paris had defeated their love. FaceTime and long weekend visits had been the cure for what could have been a disaster. *It is anything but that.*

"I'm heading out. Thank you both so much for your help," Renee said, already moving toward where her and Aria's vehicles were parked, where the stone line curved leading into the subdivision. "Let's do lunch next week. I'm dying for some seafood."

"Cool with me," Aria said, also headed to her SUV.

Jaime gave the gate to Richmond Hills one final look before crossing the distance to the truck. Graham had already left the driver's seat and came around the hood to open the door for her. Like always, he looked sexy as fuck without even trying, leading her to use the height of the chrome running board to lick at his mouth as she pressed her hands to his face.

"Hello, Mr. Walker," she said against his lips in between kisses.

"At your pleasure, Mrs. Walker," he returned with a smile.

She grunted in pleasure at the sound of it as she dipped the tips of her thumbs into his dimples. After seven months since their intimate wedding at the nineteenth century *Chapelle Expiatoire* in Paris, she was still getting used to being Mrs. Graham Pine-Walker. The romantic ceremony, attended by just a dozen close friends and family, had been followed by them all taking a sightseeing tour of the historical landmarks of the city aboard a private cruise down the Seine with delicious food and dancing to a live band long into the night.

Graham dipped his head to press a kiss to her neck. "You're sweaty," he said.

She nodded. "I worked very hard and deserve a treat," she said.

Graham raised his head to look down at his wife. "Like?"

"The works," she said without hesitation.

"But that means I get treated as well," he reminded her.

"Exactly," she said. Softly.

His eyes darkened with his desire and mimicked her own. "Let's go," he said, watching her ease onto the passenger seat before closing the door.

At the familiar soft coos and bubbly giggles, Jaime whirled on her seat and smiled at the chubby brown face of their eight-month-old son, Graham Walker, Jr., strapped securely in his car seat. He extended his arms to reach for her with his hands opening and closing into fists as if he wished he could grab her.

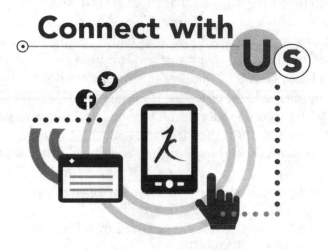

She smiled and her eyes reflected the love she had for him. Their son with Graham's eyes and dimpled smile. At times she thought of Jaymie. Wished he too had survived to exist in the world. But she was still learning to be content that everything happened just as God intended it to be.

"Hello, G-baby," she said, using her nickname for him.

He released a bubble and then giggled when it burst.

At the start of the engine, she realized Graham had long since climbed into the driver's seat. "I thought we were picking him up from my parents' together," she said, turning forward to secure her seat belt. "But this is better."

Graham smiled. "Good, let's get home, put him down for a nap and then we can shower and—"

"Treat each other?" she finished, reaching to massage his dick to hardness. "My pleasure."